UNDEFEATED

CLAUDIA BURGOA

THE UNEXPECTED SERIES BOOK FIVE

For those who fight their demons, because everyone deserves a second chance in life.

ACKNOWLEDGEMENTS

THANK YOU TO the heroes, who rescued Undefeated after a couple of incidents.

Paulina, who has been part of this family since day one. She helped me with the developmental part. There aren't enough words to explain what you did for this book. Thank you!

Melissa Taegel Parnell, thank you for helping me shape this story, for all your support and for loving Porter since the beginning.

Kristi Falteisek. Where do I start? Thank you so much for being our advocate, for spreading the word about the Deckers. And for coming to my rescue when I need you. Including shaping Undefeated into this wonderful book. #TeamILovePorter. Love you much.

Thank you to Holly, Hang, Gloria, and Christine; thanks to you ladies the manuscript became the book.

My beta readers: Suzanne, Christine, Becca, Kaila, and Pam. Thank you ladies for going through the manuscript during the different stages of the process. For your love and support to the Deckers and to me. You're part of the Decker family, and part of me. Hugs, and much love to you.

A huge thank you to my babes, who help a little with the content, and are such a lovely group. To all my readers and Decker supporters. Thank you so much for all your love.

Last, but not least. My family. The hubs who encourages, and cheers this crazy journey I decided to take. And of course my children who are the three most amazing people I've met.

DEAR READER

THE SERIES BEGAN with an idea, and became a entire series about a family. They are the beginning of my journey. Because I not only want to write love stories, I want to write contemporary romance books that deal with real love with all its forms. But with Undefeated, the fifth book, it's time to let the Deckers step away from the spotlight.

Wow, I can't believe this is the last book of the Unexpected series—for now. When I wrote the last scene I couldn't contain the tears. These characters have been with me for almost two years. They're my babies. And they'll forever be in part of me—of my heart.

Of course this isn't the last you hear from them. I plan to write a spinoff or two about Chris and Gabe's grandchildren. Can you imagine them as grandparents? Plus, you'll see the Deckers crossing over some of the upcoming series.

I hope you enjoy Porter's journey. It's not only about love, but second chances and … family ties.

After you finish the book, and if you enjoyed it. Please, do me a big favor and leave a review. Let other readers know about it and spread the word.

Thank you much,
Claudia

ONE

PORTER

Six years ago . . .

THE SOUND OF the blades cutting through the wind deafens me as my immobilized body is wheeled out of the helicopter. Voices are muffled by the thwap-thwap-thwap-thwap sound and the squeaking of the wheels are the only sound I can make out until the squealing doors opening and closing isolate the outside noise.

"Move it people, let's take him in to clean those wounds and start a series of X-rays," a male voice interrupts over the chatter. "Call the orthopedic surgeon. Looks like his wrist will require more than adjusting. I want him on standby in case we have to operate soon."

Surgery?

My eyelids are heavy. My mouth is in no great shape either. Every cell of my body hurts. I made it out of that hellhole where they tortured me, but I'm not sure if I'm going to make it. Knowing that these may be my last moments, my mind drifts back to her. *My girl.* I see those bright emerald eyes that have captivated me since the day I met her. The same eyes that have kept me going since I was kidnapped.

She became my lifeline the moment I first laid eyes on her. There wasn't a day where I wouldn't go above and beyond to be the boy, and eventually, the man she needed me to be. Except when I was weak and couldn't keep my promises. Those times when I fucked up and forgot she was my reason to exist. Fuck, I'm jolted out of my memory as someone takes my wrist and I feel a pinch. A needle slides in, followed by a cold liquid rushing through my system.

"He should be out soon," I hear a female voice drift in and then I'm gone.

I HEAR A constant beep-beep-beep in the back of my head. This time, when I fight to open my eyes, I'm able to see the light through the narrow slits. The pain is gone, but so is my mobility. A collar traps my neck; my arms are covered with plaster along with my legs. Plastic tubes snake around my arms, attached by needles on my left hand. As I move my eyes, I find him. Mason Bradley is in the corner of my room speaking with one of his men. I recognize the man's face, but can't remember his name.

Mason's hands gesture animatedly as he speaks, "The doctor explained that he has some broken bones, several bruises, burns, and cuts all over his body. He was in surgery for a few hours, something about internal bleeding and screws to set the bones back together." That explains the white plaster and the grogginess. "He'll need a few more surgeries to reconstruct part of his face. The doctor plans on keeping him for a while."

A while? This sounds fucked up, but I don't have a penny to my name to pay for any of this shit. Taking a second glance at my arms, I can forget about going back to playing music for a few months. Maybe under these circumstances, Chris will give me a hand. Let me release an album to make some money. He can hire a few musicians to play while I do the vocals. There's no fucking way that my foster parents will leave me to lick my own wounds when they see me. With some good PR, I can recover my career, and if God is good enough, the girl. *My girl.*

"I never thought I'd feel bad for the fucker. That's a lot of shit for one person." I hear Mason tell the stranger. "Even for him."

The other man scratches the back of his head and shakes it before he speaks, "Well, let me know if you need anything. I'll be at home for the next couple of days."

"Yeah, take care of yourself, Kowalski."

My eyes are heavy, but the curiosity makes me fight to keep them open. Why is Mason Bradley here?

Out of all the people I know, he's the last person I'd expect to see here.

"Kendrick?" His eyes land on me. "Are you awake?"

Though I try to say yes, my voice sounds like a mumble.

"Good, I called the Deckers. They should be arriving soon; we don't have much time to talk." He takes a few steps closer and his hateful gaze doesn't change. "This is your last warning—stay away from Ainsley Janine. She's off limits. Next time you get close to her, I'll be the one pulling the trigger. You put her and the entire Decker family in danger, Kendrick. The people you're mixed up with shoot before asking questions. I've got to be honest, I expected to find your dead body. Celebrate your miraculous recovery by keeping your distance from all of them. Because if I ever see you again, it'll be your funeral. Got it?"

He pivots and heads back to the corner not waiting for an answer. I refrain from asking him about my condition, or thanking him for saving my life. That can be said later when I'm better, or . . . my thoughts stop, as AJ rushes through the door. She comes to a halt when she spots me, her soft gasp filling the room. The moment her eyes find mine, she halts and the worry in her eyes disappears. She turns her head slightly and immediately her body relaxes, her lips stretch into a smile and her eyes brighten the way they usually do when she's happy. She *sees* him. They shine for him, as if he's the only man in the room—in the world. A burning sensation ignites in my chest and every part of me is aware of one thing.

She's no longer mine.

"You idiot." She walks toward him and they stare at each other. Mason's head tilts down and his eyes soften. The smile he gives her is unbelievable for a badass like him. The man who usually punches your face before asking questions gives her a look full of love. She throws her arms around him and their conversation becomes private—intimate.

Bradley clears his throat and his voice interrupts the exchange they had, which just fucking killed my soul. "Bruised, broken, but he'll live. You guys planning on caring for him?"

"Not sure. I heard my parents talking about sending him to some hospital to help him with his rehabilitation." There's no anger in her voice, no resentment. "After everything he has put us through, we can't do much for him. There's no way for us to put all that shit aside and try to deal with who he's become."

Mason's words come back and this might be the last chance I have to talk to her. Unless I can convince her that I've changed, that I'm a different person.

You can do it; she's always had a soft spot for you. Make her listen to you. You can't lose her, fucker.

"AJ?" I call her.

She rises on her tiptoes, kisses him, and walks to me. "How are you, Porter? I hope much better than you look." As her eyes travel over my body, she flinches a couple of times.

"All hurts," I struggle to breathe, but I won't let that stop me from trying to talk her into taking me back. "This time, I thought I wouldn't make it."

"The doctors will make it better." She pats my hand with that nurturing care she's shown me since the first time we met. Fuck, I need that to recover. Her love. Her care. All of her, but that soft-loving look she used to give me is all gone. Her eyes are neutral. There's no hate, no love, no nothing left inside her for me. "By the time you're out, there won't be any pain."

A loud laugh goes off inside my head. There's an unbearable pain inside my heart, my chest. Every inch of my body hurts because not only has she stopped loving me—somebody else took my place.

"There's one that will remain deep in my chest," I confess. "The excruciating ache of knowing that I not only lost the love of my life, but that the love of my life is now in love with someone else will never fade away. Baby, I lost you. You were the only person in this world who ever loved me, AJ."

Her gaze drops as she bites her lip. For a few seconds we connect at the level we used to. The brief connection is a final goodbye. What happened to being soul mates? I want to ask her, remind her that we were supposed to have an endless love. Something that no one will touch.

Soul mates are forever. Aren't they?

"Goodbye, Port," AJ whispers. "I wish you the best."

No, no. Don't leave me I want to scream, but my lips remain closed tight.

She turns around, walking to him. Mason Bradley. The man who has always been there for her through thick and thin. One call and the fucker would appear. They've always had that fucking connection that I could never break. No matter what I did, no matter how many times I tried to keep them apart or forbid her to talk to him, she ignored me. Understanding dawns—*he's* her soulmate. Maybe she never belonged to me the way I thought.

Fuck, this can't be happening. I need her. *Don't take her away from me*; I want to beg Mason.

Instead, I call out to him as they leave, "Mason. Thank you for rescuing me. I guess the best man won. Be smart and don't throw away the best thing that can ever happen in your life: being loved by Ainse."

He doesn't acknowledge me, his jaw tightening as they leave. My lungs burn. I'm about to close my eyes to avoid shedding any tears when MJ and JC Decker enter the room.

Two cold stares are directed at me. "We're fucking done with you," Jacob growls. "No matter what the parental units say, you stay away from us. In fact, we've decided that Porter Kendrick has retired."

My gaze switches to MJ, who is easier to talk to. The guy always looks after others. Hell, he saved my life once. Maybe he can change Jacob's mind. Music is the only shit I know how to do. I never finished college because . . . why would I? I had my career and I made it big. I'm Porter Fucking Kendrick. The public loves me. As long as there's a studio willing to take me, I should be fine.

"Retired." Matthew, the mellow one of the three, repeats. "Our connections know that you're out of the business. Sorry, dude, but after what you did to AJ and the shit you put our parents through, well, it's time to take care of you our way."

"Matthew!" Chris' severe voice comes from the door. "He's family."

"Dude, he's the kid that you picked up from the streets and repaid you by fucking the entire family all over," Matthew responds.

"Matthew, I'm your father!"

"Pops, sorry but it's done," Jacob's voice is neutral. No disrespect to his father but he's not backing down. "We Deckers protect each other, not destroy each other. He's not a Decker."

His words stab through my heart.

I'm not a Decker.

Both brothers leave the room. Gabe and Chris remain in the room, staring down at me and then at each other. "Gabe, talk to him. Jacob listens to you better than he does me."

"That's a lie, babe. And no, I won't talk to him."

My breath hitches; they can't abandon me. Can't they see how I look? I'm in the freaking hole. If they do this, I'm fucking done forever.

"Porter, you have to help yourself, son." Chris pats my hand just the same way AJ did earlier. "Pull yourself together."

"We're taking care of the hospital bills and paying for the rehabilitation center, Porter," Gabe informs me with his cool, business-like voice. "The place we chose will help you physically and mentally."

"My music, Gabe. Please, talk to them," I beg because MJ and JC have a lot of connections. They're not only great musicians, but they're the sons of Chris Decker, a rock legend. If they say shit about me, I'm fucked for life. "That's the only way I know how to survive."

"Twelve years ago, when I found you, I saw possibilities," Gabe says, running a hand through his hair. "A child that had escaped and tried to survive. This was my chance to save someone like my husband. Back then I thought, if only he had a chance to find a family that loved him . . . That's why we opened our house and our family to you. I won't talk to anyone, Porter. But do you know why?" His eyes soften and he gives me a sad smile. "Because we love you like a son, Porter. You can't handle fame. It's your downfall. College, kid. Finish school and find another way."

"We love you, but the doors to our home are closed to you, Porter," Chris tells me holding his husband's hand. "Take care of yourself, kid."

The last time I shed tears was when I woke up in the hospital and a nurse told me that my mommy had gone to heaven and she wouldn't come back for me. I had no idea where that heaven was, but I understood that I was alone. Mom never returned and today I lost the only people who had cared about me.

TWO

PORTER

Five years ago . . .

It's in your smile,
Your eyes,
The way they see me
With you I'm invincible
[Chorus]
Because it's only me and you
Me and you, no matter where you are
I own your heart and you own mine
You gave me the strength to be who I am

I ABRUPTLY TAP the guitar strings, stopping the music. My fingers can't move from one string to the next fast enough. The strength is almost back. But the only songs I come up with are the first ones I composed to my girl. Fuck. This shit isn't helping. My counselor insists that I have to move on. I need to forget AJ Colthurst-Decker. It is so fucking hard because my physical therapist encourages me to play the guitar to strengthen my fingers. These days, I listen to the PT guy, because music keeps *her* alive. Her memory is what keeps me going. I remember everything about her, including the first day I saw her, as if it was yesterday.

Standing close to the corner of the kitchen, I watched the two men that found me the previous night. They promised to feed me, give me a bed and that they wouldn't call the police. The sandwich that Gabriel handed me sealed the deal; I hadn't eaten in so long. At least, that's how I remember it. My past is mostly a shadow, but I fight daily to keep two things present: her and my music.

The two blond boys watched me but neither one spoke to me. JC and MJ. Both glanced at each other and nodded, reading each other's mind. As one of them began to mumble under his breath, she skipped into the kitchen with her long brown curls, bright green eyes and a bright smile.

"Morning, JC, morning, MJ," she greeted her brothers, then turned around to look at the two men. "Morning, parental units. How can I help?" Her nose wiggled as she stared at the table. "Do we have a guest?"

"No," answered one of the twins, angling his head toward me. "More like a new resident."

She pivoted and scanned me from head to toe. Everyone's attention turned to me then diverted back to her. The parents watched her closely and neither one breathed as she spoke, "Hi." Her voice was the sweetest melody to my ears. "My name is AJ," she introduced herself closing the distance between us. "Well, Ainsley but AJ is what everyone calls me. Who are you?"

Dumbfounded by her, I spit out my name, sounding like an idiot, "Porter Kendrick."

Unlike the boys, she asked why I was there.

"Your dad found him yesterday night, during my concert, baby girl," the man named Chris explained. "Hiding in the bathroom of the bar." I dropped my head, ashamed to hear the story.

The man with green eyes similar to hers continued the explanation about how they found me. Cold, hungry, and holding onto my old guitar. Pathetic. My heart pulsated rapidly, waiting for her rejection.

"Where are you from?" she questioned.

"Alabama." To this day, I've no idea why I shared my story with her. Why I told her about the accident that killed my mother and two siblings when I was four. "My father was driving the car," I continued, pulling my shirt up revealing the scar that begins on my left clavicle and goes down to my ribs. I then pointed out the scar on the back of my ear. "A piece of glass cut through. If it had come closer to my jugular, I'd . . . He's in jail—my dad, for killing my family."

AJ extended her hand, grabbing mine. Squeezing it gently, the warmth that she sent through my body was different from any touch I've ever felt. Tender, *loving. I had no previous memory of feeling safe, at peace. In that moment, I knew that I'd love her for the rest of my life. But loving didn't mean I'd be able to keep her with me forever.*

No.

I lost her and now I'm paying for not treating her like she deserved, for losing myself instead of being the man she believed I was.

"Mr. Kendrick." One of the nurses approaches me. "Dr. Arnett is ready for you."

I set my old guitar inside its case and let the nurse push my wheelchair toward the building. Three weeks ago, I had my last surgery to reconstruct my femur. I have screws, plates, and artificial bone in different parts of my body. This is what my foster parents meant when they said: "Drugs destroy you." I should've listened to them. There are some lessons we should learn from others' experiences, but I learned my lesson the hard way. I got mixed up with who I thought was a dealer, but no, I got myself mixed up with an entire cartel.

"Porter," Dr. Arnett greets me as I enter his office. "How are you feeling today?" I shrug, because I don't feel like talking. "Anything in particular you want to talk about?" I shake my head. "Maybe about your family? A friend who isn't AJ?"

AJ is the only person I've spoken about. There's no family, friends, or acquaintances I'd like to mention. My first family died in a car accident when I was four. I don't remember my mother's face, her voice, or her scent. It's hard to picture my older brother, or my baby sister. They've been gone for so long. Closing my eyes I concentrate on my childhood, but the earliest memories I can grasp are from when I went to live with the Decker family. When I tell Dr. Arnett that I lost my memories, I'm not lying.

I recall the basics; that my father was the one who drove the car when our family died. That I was left behind and went to live with my grandparents. But then everything is a black hole, nothing else is clear until they found me. His blue eyes found me cowering inside one of the stalls in the restroom.

"Are you lost?" he asked and I didn't move. "Don't be afraid." My stomach tightened and I hugged my guitar close to me, afraid that he'd take it away. "You like to play music?" I nodded. "My house is full of musicians. I'm the only one who doesn't know how to play an instrument."

"Gabe are you here?" A deep voice asked and I made myself into a small ball, hoping that they'd go away. The other man approached me; he was almost as tall but with brown hair and green eyes. His eyebrow crooked as he spotted me. "What do we have here?"

"Not sure, babe, I think he's afraid and maybe hungry." He squatted and lowered his voice, "Why don't you come with us? There's enough food in the dressing room for everyone. Maybe later we can take you home for the night while we find your parents."

"No, I . . . no, you're going to try to send me back to him," I responded, my gut tightening—fearing the worst. "I don't want to go back."

Something bad happened at my grandparent's house, but I don't recall what I did or why I feared going back again. They didn't force me to tell them my story, but convinced me to walk with them to an office where I was given a sandwich. The two men introduced themselves as Gabe and Chris Colthurst-Decker. They were husbands and had three children at home—triplets. Chris was a musician. Gabe was an actor. Their unconventional family was loving, caring and I became a part of them. Until I fucked up so badly it almost got them killed and lost them forever.

"Porter, these sessions only help when you participate," Dr. Arnett says after a long silence. "If you want to talk about AJ, I guess we can revisit her."

I shake my head, talking about AJ will take more than two hours. She's special. Different from anyone I had met. She saw something inside me that no one had seen before. She made me believe that I wasn't stupid. It's because of her that they found I had dyslexia and, because of her, I learned how to read. Fuck, I swore to always kiss the ground she walked on, to care for her. But I didn't. I bang my head a couple of times with the heel of my hand.

"Porter, are you okay?"

"No," I finally speak. "My purpose in life was to protect her, to make her happy, to be her best friend. She loved me and, instead of keeping that love safe, I took it for granted. I pushed her away. I lost her."

My heart aches with the reminder that it's been almost a year since I saw her last. I laid in bed battered with several broken bones and a shit-load of issues. The moment she entered my room, her worried eyes set on me. As her lips quivered, hope filled my heart, until her bright eyes connected with mine and in a second, they moved toward him. That's when my world collided and I knew that I'd lost her forever. Her eyes radiated love, her voice spoke sweetly to him, and they embraced as if they hadn't seen each other for centuries. She had found someone else and I had no one else to blame but me.

The buzzer announces that my time is over; a nurse enters the room to wheel me away. "Porter, only you can help yourself. We're here to guide you, but we can't take you to the next level if you refuse to work."

I shrug, because there's nothing they can do for me. No matter what I tell them, what I do or whom I talk to, my woman is gone, my kid is dead, my career is over and the only family that loved me now hates me.

THREE

MACKENZIE

Two years ago . . .

LOVE IS A four-letter word more powerful than the energy of the sun. Love can move mountains. Love can conquer all. Those phrases have been around since . . . Forever? Are they even true? The fact is, we all want to believe them. But there's also the other side of the story, the sad truth. Love can destroy. Once, there was this boy I met with a set of amber eyes and a bright smile who took my breath away. It wasn't love at first sight. No, we fell in love slowly, through the day-to-day contact. Between AP Calc and art class, it was innocent, pure. And as we grew, our love did too.

He promised to be my prince charming as long as I could save him when he needed me. No other man could make me feel strong, safe, loved, and cherished. Leonard Brooke and I experienced so many milestones together. We celebrated the small successes and our biggest achievements. From waiting for me at the DMV during my driving test, to holding my hair while I puked my guts out on my twenty-first birthday. Anywhere one went, the other followed. We fought together during the small battles and those big wars. He taught me how to live; I taught him how to laugh. We were partners, each other's teachers in life. In front of God and our families, we swore to love each other in sickness and in health until death do us part.

Pressing his portrait to my chest, I let the tears that I held in during the funeral service fall. He's gone. Left me without a warning, a good-bye . . . Leonard Brooke broke his promise. He swore to grow old with me. Among everything he taught me, he forgot to teach me how to live without him. My heart can't beat any longer, my lungs forgot what to do with the air around me. Five days ago my husband was snatched from this world, leaving his wife and adoring children to learn how to live without his smile, his blueberry waffles, and his love.

The words of Detective Murray, from the homicide division of the Arapahoe County Sheriff's office, resonate inside my head, "Mrs. Brooke, we're here to take you to the coroner's office to identify the body of Leonard Brooke." He said much more but I can't recall the words. The moment he mentioned body my world crumbled. Of course, I accompanied them, praying that they had the wrong person—maybe Leonard lost his license.

But there he was, sleeping like an angel on top of a metal table pale and lifeless. I lost my husband.

I lost my life.

A year ago . . .

EACH MORNING I reach to my left side hoping that the past months have been nothing but a long, bad dream. The longest nightmare in the history of the world, but no. Leonard's side of the bed remains emp-ty—like my heart. The inside of my wrist misses his feathery kisses that would travel all the way up to my mouth. He took a piece of me with him. No, he took all of me.

"Keep on going, Mac, don't stop breathing," I mumble, squeezing my eyes shut. I'm working hard to keep the burning tears at bay, but I fail.

"I can't. Please, come back to me," I plea. "Help me because I'm drowning, Leo, this isn't worth it without you."

His loss is still a sharp knife that cuts deeper and deeper into my heart. My heart has holes. I might look alive, but I'm dead inside. Wiping the tears with the edge of my sheet, I sober up, because even death has responsibilities. Two beautiful responsibilities that became my life support. Harper and Finn. It is because of them that I drag myself out of bed every morning and pretend to function like any other mother. But inside I'm incomplete.

Losing my mind.

Living in hell.

Broken.

"Mommy, you forgot to open the blinds again," Harper, my five-year-old daughter says, as she storms into the room. I wish I could stop her, but I don't have the energy to argue with her. With two swift movements, the morning illuminates the cold walls of the bedroom. "Good morning, Mom it's time to head to school."

"It's Saturday," I remind her. Her small shoulder slump and her face falls. These days school is more fun than staying at home with her mom and brother. "We'll find something fun to do."

"Like what?" She narrows her gaze, with the same "I-don't-believe-you" look Leonard had, yet she waits because maybe today she'll have her mother back.

Grocery shopping trips aren't fun with me. Not like when she went with Daddy. They'd organize a treasure hunt and if they found everything, they'd get ice cream afterwards. Sounds easy, but I don't have the energy to enter into Leonard's office and search for the maps he created. No. That room will remain closed for as long as I need it to while I pretend that he's in there. Leo is working on a secret project for the United Nations and can't come out until he finishes it. Whatever he's building will stop global warming, bring world peace, and eliminate world hunger. That's why he's there, because the entire human race depends on him.

I tilt my chin up, looking at the ceiling. Expecting a miracle, begging for a sign, or anything that'll take me out of this hellhole. Waiting for the wave of sadness to drift away, working overtime to be the mother she deserves. *Why did you leave me?* I ask one more time.

What would Leo say to make her smile? "For ice cream, then how about we—"

"We haven't had breakfast yet, Mom." My gaze shifts to the clock on top of the nightstand. Seven in the morning, another twelve hours before I can crawl back in bed. "How about if you make Mickey Mouse waffles."

That was Leonard's favorite breakfast, another thing I refuse to make. My heart squeezes as I realize that everything was his favorite. He was full of life, love. A happy man that found greatness among everyone and everything. Living for the moment, every minute counted. *"In a blink of an eye something can happen"* was his motto. In fact, it happened in the blink of an eye. A junkie mugged and shot him, leaving him on the side of the road bleeding out to die.

Grief, the pain that you feel when you lose a loved one, never goes away, but you learn to handle it. I thought we had, that it had diminished in some sort of way, but it hasn't. Not one bit. Each holiday, each milestone, each anniversary or birthday, we're all reminded of who we lost. His absence is bigger. It fills the house with a certain void that asphyxiates me. I'm not sure how we'll survive without him. Every time we're supposed to celebrate, we mourn more and more.

A sob escapes from my gut and I can't stop myself. My body crumbles and Harper's little body is suddenly next to me. She's sobbing with me. Fuck. I need to find the strength for them.

A month ago . . .

LYING IN BED next to my son, I wait for him to fall asleep. I wonder when he'll come back to me. Finn Michael Brooke was once a happy boy filled with life. A curious kid who, at twenty-six months, spoke in full sentences and asked more questions than I could answer. His light brown eyes crinkled when he grinned or as his full-blown laugh filled a room. All of that disappeared when he realized that daddy wasn't coming back. The therapist says it's a phase. Phase or not, I'm desperate. It's been almost two years and he's half-alive.

"You need a change," Mom said during our weekly call. *"Get out of Colorado, find a new place. You're not even from there, sweetheart."*

"Where would I go, Mom?" I asked without disclosing that my financial

situation wouldn't allow me for much. We both knew there was no way I'd move with her and Dad to Florida. They lived in a retirement community.

"Aunt Molly has space; she's offered it before."

Aunt Molly lives in Portland, alone with a cat and two extra rooms. I love her dearly; she's a little eccentric woman with a kind heart and a wonderful sense of humor.

"Mom, I have to go, let's talk later."

At the end of the call, Mom suggested I move away from what makes me sad. My aunt has a free place that would give me the new beginning I urgently need. "Think about it, honey."

What's there to think about? If for some miraculous reason Leonard came back, he wouldn't find us. For just a second I close my eyes, finding Leo's amber ones staring at me. The brightness coming from them illuminates the dark room. His presence warms my heart, making it beat fast and hard. That fresh aftershave scent of his softens the thick atmosphere. Finn's room is filled with my husband's presence, but is he real or am I losing my mind?

The panic is back. My eyes sweep the room, then look back to the bed's footrest. He's still wearing a pair of khaki pants, a button-down shirt, and his wool sweater. His brown hair swooped to the left, not one hair out of place.

Thank God.

It was all a dream.

"You're back," I murmur, not wanting to wake up my little boy. "I knew you wouldn't leave me—leave us."

"Kenzie, you're never alone," he says, his unmoving lips giving me a tender smile. "I'm with you, inside your heart—always. But it's time to let me go, baby. Find a way out, for them. For our little ones."

"Leo, I can't," I choke with my tears. "Take me with you, please."

"You're my strong girl; be their hero, pull through this. I promise you that better days are yet to come and even when you don't see me, I'll be next to you."

"I don't know where to start." He tilts his head giving me his typical, "Kenzie, who are you fooling" glare. "Leo, please just come back."

"Portland, start there. I can't stay long, but remember—I'll never leave you."

"No, Leo, don't go," I beg when the phone rings and he's gone.

My eyes flutter open, I'm still in Finn's room, but on top of his Mickey Mouse bedding is Leo's wool sweater. I snatch it, hugging it tight. Absorbing his essence and believing, for a second, he was here. The sweater has his fresh scent. The ringing of my phone, pounding my head like an electric hammer, wouldn't stop. With each ring, the automated voice repeats: "Call from Mom."

There's no way I'll answer her call, not while the shattered pieces of my heart become atoms. My mind remains trapped inside that dream, or whatever had happened just now. After several attempts, Mom finally gives up, but leaves a message. I carry myself closer to my room, to listen to her voicemail.

"Mackenzie, sweetheart, call me," she sounds neutral. "Your dad and I want to offer to pay for the moving truck and the plane tickets so you can move to Portland. Please, sweetie, think about the kids."

Leaning against the doorframe of my bedroom, I stare at the nightstand where I placed my husband's ashes earlier today. I want to believe that he'll come back, that this is a bad joke, or that as a special favor from God, he'll come back to us.

His words come back to me: *"I promise you that better days are yet to come and even when you don't see me, I'll be next to you."*

Better days, that sounds right. My babies needed a breather, a new light.

FOUR

MACKENZIE

Present

IF ANYONE ASKED which author would write my life's story, I'd answer Charles Dickens, without hesitation. For the past month, I've been dreaming of Leo's ghost. Sometimes, he's in the background, while I sob for his loss.

"Move on, Kenzie," he repeats over and over again.

An easy phrase to say. He's asking me to perform a miracle. Forget our future, our promises. The vows we told each other. He left me without a word, a goodbye, a hug. One last kiss. Am I supposed to accept that I was cheated out of our happiness? Why me? I was a good person, wasn't I? There's nothing left for me to bargain, to get angry at, or to give in exchange.

I peer between the blinds, toward the foothills where everything is still. Nothing changes, only the seasons. Couldn't that be us? Leo and I staying together in one place, forever. Our only time together is in dreams.

"How can you ask me to move on?" I whisper, gripping the hem of my sweater, holding myself tightly so I don't fall down.

"Would you?" I release the blinds, looking around the dark room. "Would you move on if I had been the one to leave you behind?"

It happens in an instant, like a stroke of lightning hitting me on the head, a surge of electricity travels through my entire body. The answer. A sob escapes me and the tears begin to stream. The only way out of this cycle hurts almost as much as it hurt to lose Leo.

Moving out.

For my kids' emotional health, my own, and our financial future—we have to go. Maybe far away so I can begin to heal. Look beyond what happened inside the walls of my home. I don't have much money to continue the lifestyle we've had for so many years. The house expenses are costly while my income is zero.

Whether there's a life beyond what I planned, I know that my children have the right to a better life. The one Leo and I had imagined for them, with some adjustments. In order to do so, I have to pump some life into my heart and my soul. Maybe I can't continue waiting for him to come home.

I have to accept it, he's not coming home.

GRIEVING IS A process, a set of phases that one follows until we learn to live with the pain, the loss. Until we remember how to breathe. There are no rules on how to get to the point where the hurt is bearable. No timelines. My lips draw up in a small smile as I place one of Leo's physics books inside the *for Finn* box. Maybe Leo knows the mathematical equation that will provide me with an accurate answer on how long the pain of losing him will last. It's been more than two years and breathing is as hard as leaving my bed. I'm years away from reaching a place where I can imagine a world where Leo and Kenzie aren't one. But I made the promise to my children, to him, and to myself that I'll find a way to speed up the process.

Shit, I clear the tear I feel slipping the moment I find one of the love letters I wrote to him inside of another one of his college books. One of the thousands I wrote while we were apart. He went to CU Boulder; I was at Colorado State University in Fort Collins. Separated by an hour drive didn't sound bad when we received our acceptance letters, but damn, it was a long distance when neither one of us owned a car. It was a small obstacle that didn't matter, our relationship survived the four years, and after, we swore never to be apart for more than a day. Until now. Seven hundred plus days without the man who made my heart skip every time he entered a room.

My first love, my only love.

This week has been as painful as the first few nights without him. Each time I set an item that he owns—that he owned—away, I lose him all over again. Deciding to pack at night or while Harper is at school and Finn is next door was the best. They shouldn't see me break down over and over while trying to gain . . . what is it that I'm trying to find? Myself, my courage, a new way to live? All of the above, or whatever might happen during this new phase. Opening my barely alive heart to the unknown frightens me, but I have to do the right thing.

Goodwill's truck is coming tomorrow to pick the items I'm not planning on keeping. I'm keeping a few things for myself and some of Leo's most meaningful possessions for the kids to remember him by. Things that their father cherished while he was alive. Shit. I don't realize that I'm crying until I notice the droplets hitting the books I'm packing.

Everything of his reminds me of who we were, who we became, and what we lost that tragic night. The little pieces leftover from my shattered heart are trying to rebuild the mess inside me, but it's impossible. There's nothing but an empty body and I'm tired of fixing the pain with pieces of Band-Aids that fall off with a small gush of air.

"Two more days, Mackenzie," I tell myself while taping yet another box of books closed. "Portland should change everything. A different life where your kids can see you smile again."

FIVE

MACKENZIE

SPLITTING THE EIGHTEEN-HOUR drive from Colorado to Oregon was either the best idea, or the worst. Day one is over. We stopped in Ogden, Utah, for the night. Luckily, the hotel I booked had a pool, affordable rates, and a McD's next door. By nine o'clock, the two kids were fast asleep, neither one protesting about us three sharing a bed.

To beat the traffic, I woke up at five. Shoving Harper and Finn inside the car, I drove along I-84 until Boise. We had breakfast at Denny's. After, I drove to a small park where the kids ran a few laps and played on the swings. An hour later we continued our way to Portland, we had six hours to go before we arrived at my aunt's home.

"I'm hungry," Harper reminds me for the millionth time that we hadn't stopped for lunch. "Mom, you're killing me."

My drama queen makes an appearance. Taking the next exit, I drive to the first gas station, parking next to the pump. After a couple of calming breaths, I shut down the car engine and take the keys out of the ignition. Turning around I give her what I hope looks like a pleading face and not an annoyed one. "Let me fill up the tank and then we'll have lunch."

"You said that millions of miles ago," she protests.

I press my lips, avoiding any further discussion with my little hungry girl. Walking around the car toward the pump, with my debit card in hand, I hear a bell ding. I halt, my eyes lift, and I spot him opening the glass door of the convenience store. A tall man, with broad shoulders, dark blond hair, wearing a leather jacket, and a devilish smile directed at me comes out.

"Howdy," he grins as he approaches the bike parked on the other side of the pump I'm using.

The man owns the place, the streets. Maybe the entire city. The smile never leaves his lips, not even as he takes his helmet from the seat and adjusts it over his head. He mounts the bike and pulls his aviator sunglasses off his collared shirt. They look like they were made just for him as he slides them onto his face.

"Have a safe trip." His full lips move, his deep voice sounds, and I realize that I hadn't moved since the moment he open that damn door. He's handsome, in a Charlie Hunnam way.

As his bike pulls over and leaves the premises, I feel normal. Not the widow that mourns for her husband. More like the old Mackenzie who would enjoy when a guy gifted her a smile even when she was married. Because there's nothing wrong with receiving a smile from a stranger. It's, in fact, uplifting to share those around. Maybe moving on won't be as hard. It doesn't mean that I'll forget, or that I'll find someone else. It only means that I can let myself live again.

I'M STANDING IN front of a gorgeous Victorian style home, along with a gorgeous guy who is staring back at me. The house isn't as big as my aunt described it, but we'll make it work, at least for now. We're only staying temporarily until I find a job and a place for us to live in. I double-check that the number is right, three forty-eight, and my eyes land on him again. He might be in his early thirties, with short dark hair, perfectly sharp cheekbones, firm angular jaw, and a perfectly straight nose. A pretty face that maybe one of those plastic surgeons could've designed for a Hollywood actor. His deep melted-chocolate-brown eyes, framed with long, thick lashes, stare down at me. He's about eight inches taller than my five-three, and under the gray t-shirt he wears, there are some lean well-defined muscles.

Not bad, but instead of ogling the Portland-welcome-committee, I ask the obvious, "Um, I'm looking for 348 North East Holman?" I show him the printable version of Google maps I have.

He narrows his gaze at the paper and points at the letter A I overlooked, then shows me the letter B right below the big numbers on the wall. "Next door," he says with a low voice, turning around and leaving me standing in the cold.

What the hell, and what door?

I glance over to the driveway where I parked my car to make sure that the kids are still asleep and push the keyless remote to lock it and set the alarm. I then pull out my phone to verify with my aunt that she gave me the right address and find out where the heck the entrance to her house is. But Mr. Few-words comes out of the house wearing a jacket and a cap before I can call her. He tilts his head, signaling me to follow and walks across the driveway.

Chasing behind him I stare at the fine ass wrapped up by a pair of loose jeans. My head tilts from side to side appreciating the male form in front of me. Oh, shit, wait. I halt in my tracks. Why am I eyeing this man? I'm a married woman and Leo wouldn't appreciate it if . . . I lift my left hand looking at my bare fingers. Right, moving on from Leo and Kenzie. It doesn't mean that I'll jump into bed with the first hot body I notice. Only that I have to push away the guilt from looking.

Crossing the driveway, there's a tree hiding a small porch and right in the corner there it is, the second door. Before I knock on it, it opens wide. Aunt Molly rushes out with her arms wide open. She hasn't changed much—same curvaceous body, short, blonde hair and happy, blue eyes. She looks just like Mom.

"Mackenzie?" I hear her voice. "You made it sweetie. It's so good to see you."

"Aunt Molly," I greet, hugging her back.

"Where are the kids?" She asks releasing me and looking behind me.

"In the car." I take a step back to make sure both kiddos haven't woken up. "I thought it'd be best to swing by to let you know I'm here, but I want to bring them by when their stuff is delivered. For now, we can pretend we're still traveling and we'll stay at a hotel."

"Nonsense, I have the bed ready for you." She walks around me and toward the car. "The two of them can fit on that bed and you can sleep on the couch. Maybe tomorrow we can break down that bed and set up the kids beds in that extra room."

"How many rooms do you have available?" I ask trying to understand the setting. Shit, no one told me she owned a duplex—and that one of them was leased to somebody else.

"Two. My room and the guest room," she explains, standing right by the minivan. "We'll make it work, sweetie."

Pivoting toward the door I knocked on earlier, she calls out, "Porter, dear, are you working tomorrow?" The guy leans against his door, his gaze focused on me for several beats. He gives his head a shake. "Good, you can help us move stuff around my house." He salutes her, enters his house, and closes the door.

"Who is he?" I point my chin toward the duplex.

"Porter. I lease the other side to him," she answers. "He works at the gas station down the block and helps me around the house."

Shit, this isn't what I expected. Mom said she had two extra rooms. When I spoke to my aunt, she confirmed that she had two rooms. She insisted that I stay with her for as long as I need, that she'd help me with my kids while I worked. It all sounded nice, but maybe I should call a real estate agent and search for a place of my own. Mr. Serious-Neighbor doesn't look like the kind of man that will enjoy having children around.

"That's nice, having someone to help you around the house," I tell her, fidgeting with the keys. "If you don't mind, I'm heading to the hotel. The room is paid for and I don't want to lose that money. Tomorrow morning I'll come by and we can talk about my next step."

Though, the biggest step has been taken—leaving Colorado. Putting the house on the market, packing Leo's belongings and starting to move on with my life. Searching for a place to live is easy in comparison to the process I went through since Leo died. Maybe Molly's offer was the excuse I was looking for to leave everything behind. Yes, she's my only close family, my favorite aunt, but do I really need to stay in this tiny house close to . . . yes, that's why I'm second guessing this arrangement. Him. Porter made me feel uneasy from the moment he opened the door. Something about him unsettles every nerve in my body.

Aunt Molly places a hand on top of mine and gives me a sad smile. "You're going to be fine, Mackenzie. The hardest step is over. The rest will come easily. I'll see you tomorrow morning, rest well."

SIX

MACKENZIE

WHAT'S GOING ON? The little bit of furniture I brought with me, along with my boxes are in my aunt's driveway. I turn off the ignition, staring at my belongings and wondering what in the world is happening. A shirtless male figure with broad shoulders and sun-kissed skin decorated with several tattoos walks toward my aunt's door carrying a twin mattress. Behind him, a couple other men carry the rest of the bed.

"Is this where we're going to live, Mommy?" Harper asks as I nod, trying to figure out what's going on. "This is too small, where am I going to put my dollies?"

"We'll figure it out, honey." I sigh because I have no answer for her. Earlier I tried to contact the movers to find out if they could store my belongings for a week or so, but the cost of doing so was outrageous and the hotels in the area are booked up because of some convention. The real estate agent I contacted is on vacation and my laptop died before I could find a new one. That should teach me not to pack all the cables in one box. "For the next couple of days, we're having a sleepover."

"Like when I stay with my friend Hannah?"

"Yes, baby, just like that."

"But Hannah is far away, in Colorado," she murmurs, her head drops and my energetic girl is gone. "This is unfair." My almost seven-year-old crosses her arms and I can feel it coming. Some nonsense speech about violating her human rights. "Dad won't find us anymore. He's never going to visit me again."

Her tears quickly turn to sobs and Finn joins in. I drop my head on the steering wheel, squeezing my eyes tight and wishing myself somewhere else. Maybe to the time when I had a husband and a two-year-old girl who wouldn't talk back. A knock on my window startles me; I straighten my back as my aunt's neighbor-handy-man is rolling his finger, as if signaling me to lower my window.

"Can you give us two more hours?" His words lack something . . . humanity?

"Why, what's wrong?"

His shoulders slump, his eyes look at the sky for a second and he lets out a loud breath. "Your aunt can explain. I hate talking." With that, he turns around and heads to her home.

Peachy. What is he, four?

I flinch when I spot Finn's reflection through the rear view mirror. It's been two years since I've heard my son speak. Some days I'm angry with Leo because of it. If he hadn't died, Finn wouldn't be this quiet boy who sits next to the door waiting for his father to come back. "Harper, stay where you're at sweetie, I'm going to find out what's going on."

I leave the car, locking it behind me, and charge toward my aunt, but first I stop right in front of Porter. "Can you please keep an eye on my children?" I ask, and continue my way toward my aunt's house.

The doors are wide-open, one of the men I saw earlier is heading my way empty handed. My aunt trailing right behind him.

"What's going on?" I question, signaling toward the chaos.

"Well the movers arrived an hour ago," she answers, walking me outside her house. "Porter explained how you guys won't fit in my house, and he offered his place."

"What does that mean?" I frown, watching the surly man standing right next to my car watching my children. "Where is he going to live?"

She wiggles her eyebrows and smiles widely. "With me, of course." She raises her hands and shrugs, as if she's going to sacrifice for the greater good. "He promised to keep his distance, but I won't complain if something happens between us . . . after all, I am a woman—with a heart and needs, you know."

Is she serious? Really, my aunt and her tenant? Instead of listening to my aunt's disturbing comments, I walk back toward him.

"Thank you, but this won't be necessary," I say, pointing at his house. "We can find a place next week, there's no point of moving all the furniture around."

He rolls his eyes and huffs. "Lady, it's done. You can use my living room and dining room furniture since you don't have any." He taps the car window. "They can't live with your aunt in that tiny room." He shakes his head.

"One more thing, never leave your children inside the car unattended, the next time I'm breaking the windows."

"But you're here and I'm here . . . I never . . ." but there's no point of telling him anything else, as he already left me standing in the middle of the driveway, alone.

AS PROMISED, TWO hours later the movers are gone and my stuff is inside Porter's house. Surprisingly it's comfortable, though, I wonder why he owns expensive furniture and lots of books. He's a single man. The expected rundown couch, one table and two chairs, and a wall-to-wall television screen are nowhere to be found. I don't want to sound ungrateful, but he not only left some bits and pieces of his stuff behind, but also his sandalwood smell. A scent that is starting to make me feel uneasy. There's something about him that bothers me or intrigues me. I can't even pinpoint the emotion that he evokes. What is it about him that has me on the edge?

"I'm not sleeping with Finn," Harper sneers, rushing down the stairs. "Mom, you took me away from my house, my friends, and Daddy. Then you brought me into a place where I can't have my own room. Why are you doing this to me?"

Placing a hand on my mouth, I count to ten before I raise my voice. Lately, her attitude and bratty tone are wearing me down. The sassy girl she once was crossed the thin line and has become a brat. I barely recognize her and I fear that if I don't find a way to change that attitude, I might lose her inside this new person she's creating.

"Harper, this is hard for the three of us," I use the gentlest tone I can find inside my raging body. "But we have to find a new way to exist. There's nothing left in Colorado for us and before you mention Daddy." I gently touch the left side of her chest. "He's inside you, baby, wherever you go he'll follow. No matter if we're on the moon or travel to Pluto, he's right with you. This is what he wanted, for us to find a new happy place."

"This isn't a happy place." She stomps her foot. "Everything is gone, you threw away Daddy's stuff, and he's never going to come back again." Harper's eyes fill with tears. She crumbles to the floor, as she begins to cry. "I miss my dad, I want him. You're not the same since he left. You don't love me anymore."

A hand squeezes my heart tightly, my lungs can't take in any air, but I drop next to her and I hold her. Cradling her back and forth, murmuring, "I love you, Harp. I love you so much. We're going to get through this mess, I promise." As I hold my baby while she cries in my arms, I'm reminded that for the past months—years—I've abandoned my duties as a mother. They lost both parents in one day. Shit. I've been fucking up really badly. "Mom's going to take care of you, baby. Maybe for a few months you'll share a room with Finn, but it's just for a little while. This isn't permanent. The sadness, the pain, the tiny house . . . we're going to find a new way to be a family. I'll find my way back to normal—my new normal. And then, we'll conquer each one of the emotions that we've let overtake our lives, one step at a time. I'll do it for you, I promise, baby."

Finn sits right next to me, leaning his small head on my arm. I reach out for him and set him on my lap, next to Harper. He presses his lips together while watching his sister cry. After shaking his head, he rests his head on my chest just like Harper. Fuck, what did I do for the past two years? Nothing, that's the answer I come up with. I barely breathed, I hardly functioned, and I abandoned my precious babies.

As the main door screeches open, I lift my gaze. Porter enters the room. He stares at us, then his gaze connects with mine for a few breaths. For a second I see the hard shell around him cracking and, as it happens, he moves his attention away from me.

"Sorry to barge in, but I forgot to take some of my shit," he mutters.

"Stuff, things, could you try not to use that other word around my children?" I correct him and regret my tone, clearing my voice. "You know, *cussing*, I'd really appreciate if you can keep everything PG, please."

He nods, then heads upstairs, rushing back within minutes holding two guitar cases and a frame.

"Are you a musician?" I ask him. His jaw tightens and he slams the door behind him without an answer.

Touchy.

SEVEN

PORTER

Eighteen years ago

I LEAN AGAINST the wall watching AJ play the piano. The melody she plays is different from anything I've heard before—a new composition? It's soft and peaceful. What I'd give to play the way she does. Her long fingers travel from one side of the keyboard to the other. So far, this is my favorite time of the day, when I get to listen to her play. It's been a few weeks since I arrived at this house. The adults are nice to me, but they are pushing me to start doing some schoolwork and to help them with some of the household chores, too. The chores don't bother me, but the school work . . . I can't do any of it. Everything is too hard to understand and if they learn that I'm stupid, they're going to kick me out of here.

If only they were as understanding as AJ, everything would be okay. She explains what I don't understand and makes sure that I'm not left behind. One day I'll do the same for her; take care of her. That's why I have to learn to play all the instruments that they have in this house, because I'm going to be a musician, like her father Chris. I'll play in big places and make a lot of money.

"Porter." AJ stops playing and turns slightly to watch me from her seat. "I didn't know you were here. Why don't you bring your guitar? Maybe the two of us can play something fun."

I nod at her and she flashes that smile that I like so much. Rushing to the room where I'm staying, I grab my guitar and head back to the piano room.

Unfortunately, I'm intercepted by Gabe who gives me a stern look. "Porter, have you finished your assignments for the day?"

I shrug at him, because I refuse to tell him that I can't read.

"Porter?" AJ calls out as she approaches us. "What's taking you so long?" Then her attention moves to her father. "Hi, Daddy. We're going to be in the music room."

Gabe frowns, leaning his head closer to me. "When you're done with her, go back to your room and finish your school work. It's important. I understand that you have to adjust," he says, lowering his voice. "It's a process for everyone, but you have to be willing to become part of the family. Work with us, Porter, I have faith in you."

AJ's smile makes me want to do it, become part of the family, work hard, adjust. No one has ever had faith in me before she did.

EIGHT

MACKENZIE

SINCE I COULD walk, I've been fascinated by nature. Plants, animals, and the weather. Curiosity, love, and passion pushed me into choosing a career that I love, instead of studying something practical. Botany fit like a crystal slipper, the future I envisioned for myself. Because at eighteen I believed that after I graduated, I'd work for some big company and help them create the ultimate crop to feed the entire world.

Instead, at twenty-two and only weeks after my graduation ceremony, I became Mrs. Leonard Brooke. Six months later, Harper Ann Brooke came into the world. Leo landed a job at one of the most prestigious global aerospace, defense, security, and advanced technology companies. To this day, I don't know what he did within the company, only that he had a classified position and was one of the head engineer physicists in his department. He earned a generous salary, and that's how I became a stay-at-home mom dedicating her life to her children and garden.

If only I'd have known that my life would take such an abrupt turn, I'd have . . . . I let out an audible breath, because I really have no idea how going to the past will fix my present. For the past week, I've been applying for different jobs. There hasn't been a call back from any of them. My half-page résumé has my qualifications, but I have zero job experience.

"Open yourself to the possibilities," Aunt Molly said earlier during dinner. "Something will come along. Have you considered changing careers? It's never too late to find a new passion."

Passion?

It's not about Passion; it's about training. For the past seven years, I've mastered the art of cooking, laundry, ironing, scrubbing, reading, and whatever else my children might require. I'm passionate about it, but I don't see myself offering my services as a childcare provider. Looking at my checking account, I ponder my next move. Without the outrageous mortgage payment, I have more time to find the right job. Not sure about finding a home. Moving out would be the smart thing to do, Harper begs for her own room every day. Daughter's begging aside, staying is the best for the three of us, as my aunt isn't charging me any rent. She said that her tenant is paying for that until I can find something that will let me be independent.

I sigh, thinking about the tenant. Mr. I-Hate-Talking puzzles me. He works a block from here at the convenience store next to the gas station. The high-end furniture he left in this house is classy and brand new. How could he afford it when his job only pays minimum wage? At night, I hear his music as his fingers gently lick the strings of his guitar. There are no lyrics to the heart-wrenching melodies he plays, but I feel like every word must be about someone he loved and lost.

I'm curious about him and I want to study him, discover what's behind those coffee color eyes. And that's exactly why, instead of being tucked in bed and reading a book or watching some old movie on Netflix, I'm outside waiting for him to appear. That's the beauty of the famous scientific method. You observe your subject, ask questions, and then research before establishing a hypothesis. I just want answers and this little research should be solved with only the first steps.

The creak of the back door startles me, but I remain sitting on the steps, waiting. "So how long are you planning to stay outside?" His rough voice cuts through the silence of the night. I shrug because I didn't think about time and it isn't wise to disclose my motive. "Look, I need some time to unwind before I try to sleep. Can you do me a solid and head back to your house?"

I take that as an invitation, because so far I haven't thanked him for letting me live in his place.

"Thank you, for . . . you didn't have to give up your house for us." I fight the stutter. Shit. What happened to my voice? It's his eyes; they create a strange discomfort inside me.

"How's the job hunting going?"

"Huh?" I perk up, how does he know? "Molly told you?" He presses his lips and nods. "No one wants to hire a botanist with zero experience." I let out a loud breath. "To think that I left Colorado searching for a new life. Escaping the memories."

His eyes close for a few moments and as they open, he takes a seat right next to me. "Were you escaping memories or someone?" A soothing voice takes over.

"Both." I pull my legs to my chest holding them tight. "My husband died two years ago. My high school sweetheart. The man I thought I'd spend my entire life with . . ." I squeeze my eyes tightly holding back the tears. It's been a long time since I've talked about this, how we planned to spend an eternity together. From everything I've read, there's not one piece of advice that has worked yet. "How do you teach your heart to beat again, your lungs to breathe and find a new way to live?"

He shakes his head. "You just do," he responds. "With one foot in front of the other, one exhale after the last inhale. It's hard and takes time, but you learn to be with yourself and the memories. The good ones that will drag a smile out of you during those moments when you can't breathe. They become your oxygen, the energy that carries you to the next day."

"You lost someone?" As I turn my neck lightly, our gazes meet. "Did you lose your first love too?"

Porter remains stoic, his eyes fixated on the moon. I wonder who he lost and how long he has been grieving for her. A girlfriend, a fiancée, his wife? Maybe she died in some terrible accident, or worse, he cared for her while she slowly died from some terminal illness.

Communication might help him open up. With that in mind, I tell him what happened to Leo. "My husband had a meeting in LoDo—that's downtown Denver." I look at the sky, to gather enough courage to continue. "A homicide detective arrived at my front door around four in the morning. I didn't get the chance to say goodbye. Did you say goodbye to her?"

His hand fidgets with a dark guitar pick and his eyes finally leave the sight of the moon. Yet, there's no answer. Nothing breaks the silence of the night.

"How did you lose her?"

He rises from his seat, takes a half-turn, and leaves me without another word.

NINE

PORTER

Sixteen years ago . . .

IT'S BEEN A week, an entire week since AJ started hating me. If only I had listened to her and left the pool when she asked. But I wanted to spend some time with her and waiting by the back door felt like the right thing to do. Except, when I saw her. Fuck she has a sweet little body that I wanted to stare at all day. Before last week I thought she was pretty, now I know she's the prettiest girl I've ever seen in my life. However, for some reason, she freaked out when she saw me and ran away to her room. Since then, I haven't seen her. She holed herself up in her room and only her parents are allowed to go in and out.

"What happened, Porter?" Gabe asks for the fourth time during dinner. "We just have to find out so we can help her. The last time I went in, she said that maybe she'll come out by Christmas. That's more than six months away."

"Nothing, I swear, Gabe." I rub my eyes with the heel of my hands. "She was swimming for a long time. As she came out and saw me, she ran to the house and that was that. I'd never do anything to her. She's my friend."

"Hormones?" Chris stares at Gabe, who only tilts his head to the side with some kind of 'I guess so,' gesture. "We'll just have to let her ride this one out, like all the others. Shit, handling her is worse than the boys. They might destroy the house, but I get them. Ainse . . . I've no idea what to say or do sometimes. Maybe her brothers will work their magic when they come back."

"We just have to love her, babe," Gabe responds. As if love is the solution to whatever I did to AJ. "If all else fails, as you said, JC and MJ will drag her out . . . as long as they don't set her room on fire."

Love.

From the first time I saw her, my life was dedicated to her, but during dinner when they said that we should love her, it all clicks. I have to show her that I'd do anything for her.

Early in the morning, armed with my guitar and a bottle of water, I knock at the door and begin to sing.

Come out

Or I'll never stop singing.

I sing it over and over again, annoying the hell out of her in hopes that she'd come out to talk to me. If I could just find out what I did, apologize to her and show her just how much she means to me, everything will go back to normal.

But AJ doesn't budge; it takes hours for her to finally react to my singing. "Shut up," she screams.

I sigh with relief, leaning my head against the wall, hopeful that she'll come out soon, and continue. "Not until you come out . . ."

My plan is working perfectly until Gabe rushes through the hallway and bangs on her door. "Come out before we kill him, AJ." I gulp, but he gives me a smirk and leaves me when the door handle wiggles.

"What do you want?" her eyebrows form a V and her eyes have that red rim around the iris that scares me. Usually, it appears when her brothers upset her.

But I don't let that bother me, I have to convince her that we're friends and she should keep talking to me. "Duh, for you to come out. You promised to hang out with me and that was a week ago. I'm waiting. My patience is running low."

"I'd rather not." She slams the door on my face. Fuck. I strum the guitar again because I have to talk to her. Convince her that I'd do anything to fix whatever I had done wrong. "Ugh, shut up."

"You went back in," I sing.

"You saw me, I'm a freak," her annoying tone is making me rethink what I'm doing. Maybe I should back off and come back tomorrow. "I won't come out of my room for the rest of my life."

Shit, she went from Christmas to forever. "That's a long time." I lighten up the conversation with a forced laugh.

"Well, I'll wait until you head for college. Whatever happens first."

College? That's a long time from now. "Why are you a freak, exactly?"

"Because I'm hideous," she mumbles through the door.

"No, you're beautiful and you have the prettiest green eyes I've ever seen and you have to come out before I die of boredom," I strum the guitar singing those lines.

Nothing I say brings her out. I set my guitar down and decide to show her the freaky scar that I have. Knocking on her door, I call her. "Check this out." As I pull my shirt off, I point to the scar I got when I was four. I draw a line from my clavicle to my stomach. The pink scar doesn't look as threatening as it did when I was younger, but it still freaked people out. Except AJ who accepts me no matter what. "This doesn't make me a freak; it makes me, well, me."

She opens the door and approaches me, we're so close that I could hug her, but I refrain from doing that. She's too young and her parents might kick me out if I act out of impulse. But I want to hug her so badly.

"You were my last friend," she murmurs, her eyes settling on my clavicle.

"I'm not anymore?" My stomach drops and fear begins to eat my heart. "Is it because of my scar?"

"No, of course not."

Relief washes over me and I come even closer to her. "Then we're friends forever, to me, you'll always be the most beautiful girl in the world."

Her gaze lifts and the biggest, most amazing smile is shining just for me. A voice inside my head whispers: *This girl is mine. She'll always be mine.*

TEN

PORTER

Sixteen years ago . . .

T HERE'S A LOT of ground that I have to cover before I turn eighteen. As of today, and after two years of applying myself on a daily basis, I'm at a ninth grade reading level. A freshman in high school. According to my tutors and my foster parents, that's a great accomplishment. When they tested me two years ago, I had a reading level of a first grader. Today I'm capable of reading any book, and of course, I have audiobooks and a laptop to help me with my assignments.

All the tools they gave me are part of a bigger plan to help me become a productive member of society. The Deckers want me to have a college degree before I have a music career. A backup plan, in case things don't turn out the way I want. It'll be complicated to explain to them that backups aren't necessary when it comes to my future. In no way will I let myself fail. Once I reach for the stars, I'll stay up there in the sky. That's the only way I can be close to AJ. She's the sun. The one who illuminates my days. In order to care for her the way she deserves, I have to work hard. At least be as famous as her parents are.

"Hey, it's midnight," I hear her raspy voice before I see her enter the music room. "Why are you up so late?" AJ's long hair is tied up into a messy bun and she's only wearing a t-shirt and a pair of shorts.

"Why are you up so late?" I ask straightening the music sheets I'm trying to read. Reading music is the hardest part of being a musician. Two years ago I didn't see the point of their existence, now I understand that to make my compositions permanent, I have to write them down. Also, to play a classic piece, I have to memorize the sheets. According to Chris Decker, playing by ear is a great ability, but an accomplished musician can do both. "Your parents hate when you go to sleep so late."

She shrugs.

"What happened?"

"Gabe." She scrunches her nose. Uh-oh. "He's leaving for a couple of weeks. I heard them . . . his publicist found a new girlfriend for him."

"Do you want to talk about it?" She shakes her head, turning around and walking away. That's my cue to follow. "AJ, you know that's how they have to do things, don't you?"

"What if one day he falls in love with the girl and leaves us?" She sniffs, walking toward the back door. When she arrives at the swings, she sits on the tire swing and stares at the stars. "Aren't we enough for him?"

I can't answer her question, because I don't understand much about who my foster parents are or why they behave the way they do. They're a gay couple with three children who live in a secluded area. No one knows about their marriage to each other, or that AJ, MJ, and JC exist—other than family and friends. They hide from the public and, according to AJ, they hide a lot of shit from their children too. All these fucked up shit hurts AJ, but her parents don't give a damn about it.

"You're enough for me," I say, sitting on the swing next to her. "They are your parents, I get it, but you have to grow immune to what they do. Celebrities never have long-steady relationships. I wouldn't be surprised if they split one day."

The sound of her crying intensifies with the stupid shit I just told her. I'm fucking bad at this shit. For a moment, I think about heading back to the music room. A girl is crying next to me because I said the wrong thing. How do I fix it? With a lie? I mean, how many Hollywood couples marry and stay together? Not many. My foster parents have been together for maybe eighteen or twenty years. If AJ hadn't been sheltered for so long, she'd understand the dynamic and the shit her parents do wouldn't hurt her as much.

"Maybe I'm wrong," I say, regretting everything I blurted out without thinking. "You know I'm not very smart."

She faces me with a grief-filled face that makes me want to punch myself for being such a fucking idiot. A slight frown starts forming on that sad face, her lips twitching a couple of times and she shakes her head.

"I hate when you say that, Port, you're smart," she whispers while wiping her tears and shaking her head in disappointment. This is one of the many reasons why I love her so much. After fucking up really badly, this pretty girl is trying to make me feel good about myself. "I'm crying because maybe you're right. Why would anyone keep hiding the love of his life?"

That's an answer I don't have and I don't dare to think about, one wrong move and she might head back inside the house to pick a fight with her parents.

"When you're famous, you're not going to do this, are you?" I shake my head at her question, because when I'm famous, I'll be dating her. AJ being mine would be an honor. In a few years, I'll ask her to be mine and we'll be different from her parents. "Good, I trust that you'll do the right thing with . . . whoever."

"Ainsley Janine," I hear one of her parents calling her. "It's past your bed time, young lady."

"Is it wrong to hate them a little?" she asks and I tilt my head to the side not wanting to answer that question. "Have you ever heard them calling my brothers because it's past their bed time?"

"You have to sleep eight hours," I remind her.

"If I were Gabe's daughter, he wouldn't hide me and Chris would love me as much as he loves my brothers," she whispers, tears rolling down her cheeks. "If I were Gabe's, I wouldn't be sick . . . fuck, I hate when I get emotional."

As she clears the new tears with the hem of her shirt, I rise from the swing and pull her to my body, holding her for a while and letting her cry. Tonight this is all I can do; my words are worthless. Maybe my arms will be able to scare the sadness away, but I want to do so much more with her. Kiss her; feel her, as I fill her body with something else to replace the sorrow that her parents evoke.

"Some days I think you're the only person who understands me, Port." Her words fill my heart with love. After releasing a long breath, she pushes herself lightly from my chest and gives me a fucking smile that weakens my knees. "Thank you, for listening. I don't know what I'd do without you."

"I don't know what I'd do without you either," I respond, offering her my hand and walking side by side toward the house. "No matter what, I'll always be by your side, AJ."

"Good night, Port," she says, entering her house. As her green eyes meet mine, my world makes sense again.

ELEVEN

PORTER

Fourteen years ago

"WHAT DO YOU mean you're not going to college?" AJ exclaims, as she takes a seat next to me. "My parents wouldn't allow us to do that. Before you can have a music career, you need to have a degree."

Yes, that's the rule. Except, I'm not their kid. Last night my foster parents and I had a long conversation about my future. Chris had sent a demo to a few of his friends to see what they thought about my music. The feedback we received helped me change their minds as to what I should do after I finish high school. A couple of his friends wanted me to sign with their label, but of course, Chris told them that I'm taken. He agreed to be my agent and produce my records. In a week I'll be recording my first EP, the four songs we picked are from some of the music AJ and I have been composing.

My foster parents have their reservations about the no college thing, but if I show them that I'm capable of handling myself in the music business, they'll get off my case. If everything that Chris told me comes to fruition, I'm going to live on a tour bus for almost a year, and if I do everything right, in about four years, AJ and I will have our own home just the way she wants. A big house for a big family—our family. We haven't taken any steps yet, but soon we will. I can only be away

UNDEFEATED 45

from her for so long.

"AJ, next week I'm recording an EP," I explain. "This is my start to becoming a famous musician. Our music will be heard in places we haven't visited yet."

"College is important, Port," she retorts. "I believe in you. You're so talented; it won't matter if you start now or wait for a couple of years."

Her eyes dim, and I don't want to disappoint her because she's the reason why I work hard every day. The reason why I wake up at five in the morning to practice. The reason I go to bed long after I finish all my homework. But as much as I love her, I can't wait any longer. College isn't for everyone, and it's definitely not for me. I don't belong in some classroom, and whatever they can teach me there, I can learn in life. Chris Decker was inducted into The Rock and Roll Hall of Fame a couple of years ago and he didn't go to college. Well, he eventually went back years later. Still, he's a prime example that college isn't necessary to succeed. Except, I won't bring that up to AJ, she always finds a way to prove me wrong.

"Can you be happy for me?" I take her hand. "Please, your approval and support mean everything to me."

"Online classes?" I growl at her suggestion. "That's what Jacob, Matthew and I are doing, taking some general-ed college classes from home so when we turn eighteen, we can head to a real school and graduate early. Dad doesn't want us to miss the *college experience*. Why not do it? You can work, attend classes from wherever you're at, and graduate in four years."

AJ is the last person I want to disappoint. There are plenty of reasons, but the biggest one is because I love her. Since the first day we met she's tried to protect me, to nurture me and make sure I'm happy. Just as I do with her. I'd give anything to see her smile all the time; I'd give my life for hers and would cross the entire universe if that's what she needed from me. The only thing I don't do is kiss her or touch her more than a friend would. We're not ready to take that step, and I fear that if I do before she's old enough, her parents might kick me out or hate me. Gabe and Chris Decker are important to me, even if they are only my foster parents; I love them as if they were my real parents. Fuck, this entire thing with AJ sounds fucked up, but it's so real. A few more years

I tell myself. Once she turns eighteen we can be together. They'll understand, and I'll always be the man that she deserves. That's why I work hard, to deserve her.

I brush a strand of hair from her face, watching her irises grow wide. Fuck, if only I could kiss her. "You're the smartest person I know, AJ. If you think that's what I should do, I'll do it. For you."

She shakes her head. "No, do it for yourself, Port." She places her delicate hand on top of my chest. "You're also smart, I believe in you."

THERE'S A FAMOUS saying claiming that what happens in Vegas stays in Vegas. As I look around the dressing room, I consider this. The other two bands I'm playing with have been fucking around with the fans. A couple of them have girlfriends and the vocalist for Paranoia is married. The groupie who is riding him doesn't seem to give a shit about it. Hell, Archer Doherty isn't giving a shit about his marital status either. I pledged my love, my heart, and my soul to one woman four years ago—when I met her. Correction, a girl. She's only sixteen. A beautiful, girl who doesn't know I love her. She's miles away from me and we're not a couple.

Then why is it that I feel guilty by only looking at the groupies with barely any clothing on who are trying to score a man tonight?

Searching for some wise words of advice from my foster parents, I only remember one phrase: Always use condoms, boy. Yes, Chris told me that I was old enough to have sex, but not to drink or experiment with drugs. If I am to stay a part of his record label, I have to accept and follow his rules. No alcohol, drugs, or disturbing behavior. Not sure what the latter meant, but I am staying away from alcohol and drugs.

"Hey, Kendrick, relax," Archer shouts at me, as the woman who rode him only seconds ago gets off his lap. "Get laid! Estella here knows how to treat the newbies, right, babe?" He spanks her bare ass.

Estella flips her dark hair to the side giving me a tempting smile with those full lips that I want to bite. Fuck. I swallow hard. Rubbing my face, I search around for something to distract me. I need an excuse to push away the hot, fucking, little number that is right in front of me.

"Here," Archer says, handing me a joint. "Have a little something;

it's mixed with some other shit to wake you up."

"No man, Decker will have my balls if I do."

"What happens on the road, stays on the road." Archer winks at me, pinching Estella's tits. "Decker won't know that his prodigy is having fucking fun like the rest of us."

I close my eyes for a moment, thinking about AJ. We're not serious, and no one would ever tell her the shit I do. When the time comes when I can be with her, I'll stop whatever I'm doing. For now, I can have fun and learn a thing or two before I make her mine. It's only two years, how bad could it be?

TWELVE

MACKENZIE

FROM THE KITCHEN window, I watch Harper and Finn playing outside with their new toys. Three days ago, a tricycle appeared in the backyard along with some other fun things that my kids can play with including a big, pink plastic dollhouse. All slightly used, but clean. My kids think they're brand new and their daddy sent them over from heaven. I don't have the heart to burst their bubble yet, but I might have to tell them the truth. That maybe Porter is the one who bought them.

"They look happier than they were three weeks ago," Aunt Molly mentions, as she chops the carrots. "How's the job search going?"

I chew on my lip, thinking about the stupid job I need and laugh as I'm washing the spinach. That's as much hands-on experience I have with plants. "The Department of Agriculture called, they have an entry level offer. I'd love to accept, but twenty-five thousand dollars a year with no benefits is not going to cover much."

"That's all?" she replies and I nod.

Then I voice what I've been thinking, "The holiday season is approaching. Chances are they're going to be hiring at all of the department stores."

As I'm about to hand over the spinach to my aunt, I spot him, Porter. He's sitting by the tree, strumming his guitar. Finn stops pouring sand and his attention goes to the man who, from what it looks like from here, is singing too. Harper's head shows through the dollhouse window.

"He's the whole package," my aunt says, standing next to me. "Handsome, thoughtful and he can sing."

"How long has he been living next door?"

"Two years, and no, I have no idea what happened to him." She moves toward the counter and continues chopping. "All I know is that there's loss in his heart."

Diverting my eyes from the sink back to the yard, our gazes collide. I feel as if there's a part of him that wants to tell me his secret, let some of the weight he harbors inside go. Free himself from whatever loss he carries. And the scary part is that I want to know it all and be the one he trusts—and takes away his pain.

"Finn likes him," my aunt continues. "Which reminds me, have you thought about taking him to another specialist? It's not normal that he won't talk."

I shake my head. "They tested him in Denver and the psychologist didn't find anything wrong with him. She called it a phase."

She sighs and the words she's not saying linger inside the room. *Two years is no longer a phase.* Something more must be going on with him.

"Well, everything is ready." She dries her hands. "Go and set the table while I call them."

I do as she asks, thankful that unlike my mother, she restrained herself from saying something more about my little boy. It already frustrates me that I spend a couple of hours a day working with him and he refuses to speak. With the lack of insurance, I'm just trying to do what I've learned on the Internet and the books I got from the library.

"Don't forget to wash your hands," my aunt yells. "You too, Porter, that guitar must be filthy."

As I turn toward the backyard door, our eyes connect again and he gives me a boyish smile. "Yes, ma'am."

My gut clenches and the uneasiness is back. It's not fear, or distrust. Whatever his presence provokes is better to ignore. When my aunt enters the dining room I have to ask, "He's eating with us?"

"Of course, we share a kitchen." My aunt winks. "And the best way to a man's heart is through his stomach. That's why I'm cooking him three meals a day." She fixes her hair and sets the side dishes down before heading for the meatloaf.

I don't know if she's serious, but I release a loud laugh. She's about thirty-some years older than Porter is. Would that make her a cougar or a saber-tooth?

Finn approaches the table, looking at each place. Then his gaze goes to Porter who starts placing the silverware I haven't set yet. Once he finishes, he slides on one of the chairs and Finn follows suit—on the seat right next to Porter. The man smiles down at Finn before we start serving the food. I'd love to think further about their connection; instead, I enjoy the meal and forget about the serious man who has conquered my little boy's heart.

"SHOULD WE WRITE down a schedule? Because you're cutting into my alone time every night."

I shake my head when I hear Porter's voice. "No, I just wanted to thank you."

"For?"

"The toys that you brought. For the way you treat Finn—my son. You're easygoing, patient with him. He likes you."

"He doesn't speak at all . . ." Porter trails his sentence and doesn't finish it; instead, he takes a seat next to me placing his guitar on his lap. "Does he have some kind of disability?"

"God I hope not," my words stumble one after the other without even putting any thought into them. Placing the tips of my fingers on top of my lips, I think about rephrasing. I sounded cold and insensitive. The real answer should've been that I've prayed every day that whatever my son has disappears one of these nights. Because if there's something else going on with him, I doubt that I'm strong, or capable enough to help him. I'm emotionally and financially drained. But I can't explain how fucked up Mackenzie Brooke's life is. And how much I've failed as a mother.

Depressed for the first few months after my husband died—eighteen, or maybe twenty-four of them. I neglected my duties as a mother.

I went from president of the PTCO to the mother that always dropped off her children in pajamas and who never waved back at the rest of the perfectly dressed and pristine mothers. Harper can mention at least a hundred ways how I've made her life miserable. While Finn hasn't said a word in so long I can't remember his sweet, beautiful voice.

"She'll be alright—Harper." Porter's voice sounds like a promise, and I can't help but frown at him. How does he know that she'll be alright? "She looks like a smart little girl and kids are resilient." He scratches his chin and his coffee-colored eyes give me their full attention. "Change is hard and sometimes we show anger when we're scared. Love her, as a parent that's all you can do. Finn . . . maybe you can look into some kind of government insurance and have him tested again." He lets out a big breath and looks at his guitar. "If all fails, I know someone who can help you. She has some fancy degrees in childhood education and special education for kids with disabilities."

His eyes go vacant for a few seconds and I wonder who he's talking about. His sister? A friend? "How's the job hunting going?" I give him a one-shoulder shrug and look into the dark night, wondering if Leo is watching me. Afraid that he's disappointed with my parenting skills. He was the one who helped me with this ship and right now I'm trying my best to keep it afloat. "Have you checked the flower shop on Broadway St.? They have a help wanted sign posted in one of the windows." There's a ghostly smile on his lips. "You'd be using your botanist skills."

Some boyish smirk appears on his face and his eyes shine. I like that and I wish he did it more often. Feeling bold, I decide to ask him about himself. I've shared so much about myself that I figure it's time for him to at least give me more than a grunt or a few sentences that give zero information. "Why do you work at the gas station, Porter?"

His attention sinks to the floor. "I haven't found my passion yet." I laugh, but he doesn't. "Well, I did but I lost everything."

"Why not rekindle that old passion?" I dare to ask, intrigued about this passion he had and lost.

"Because I fucked with the wrong people." His low voice almost lost in the humid air. "Figuratively and literally. Lost it all while pursuing the wrong dreams." He pulls the sleeve of his hoodie up slightly and stares at a tattoo. Three letters. JGK. Who is that? "It's late and I have to work early tomorrow."

Who did he fuck with?

I follow him with my eyes, thinking about my next question. I want to know more about him. The subject I'm studying grants zero information. Next time I should ask better question—the right ones.

Who is Porter? What happened to him?

THIRTEEN

PORTER

Twelve years ago . . .

LIFE IS MADE of dreams of all shapes and colors. Each dream takes you to the next step. My dreams are a reality. Most of them. My records sell like hotcakes or shaved ice on a hot summer day. Plus, I'm dating the girl of my dreams. AJ and I have been going steady for more than a year. I had promised to wait until she was eighteen, but as I began to tour and her seventeenth birthday got closer, I put myself out there. It's nothing intense yet. She wants to wait for the right moment and I respect that.

For now, only her brothers know that we're dating. Gabe and Chris wouldn't understand and both will get on my case. She's too young; I'm just starting and shit. None of that matters. In the end, we'll always be together—forever. She makes life perfect; closing my eyes, I picture my girl. Those enticing, deep green eyes that always give me the one thing I crave the most from her. Love. As I stroke each key, the music AJ and I composed together comes alive, like our love. Our songs bring together the best parts of the two of us. Except, shit, one of the songs we came up with sucked. I hate the lyrics she came up with; they're direct and to the point.

Sleepless night
Missing you every day
You told me it's just for some time
But I can't help think that this is it
[Chorus]
It's time to let our love bloom
Let everyone know
Stop living between the lines
Days go by that I only have a photograph of you
Babe, let our love shine

Each time you leave I think I lost something
In a day or two you'll call
But nothing will feel the same
When's the last time we spoke
Your tobacco scent will be gone and my heart will hurt again . . .

The shit is good and it'll sell like candy during Halloween, but I know what she means and what she wants. As much as I adore her, things can't be out in the open. She might not believe me, but what I feel for her is real and not being with her hurts me, too. While I lie awake, I crave having her in my arms. Leaving her side kills me, but we're both pursuing our dreams and we can't jeopardize our futures because we want to be together. My heart hurts after yesterday, yet I have so much energy inside me. Visiting AJ in Austin always revives me, gives me some new perspective and after this visit, I have four new songs. The last ones I needed to record my next album.

Right after I dropped her off I called Chris and he agreed to meet me at his studio in Seattle so we can start working. He said that he'd drive. Hopefully, he will be late, because I have to head back to the hotel and change. Paranoia is in the studio recording their next album. Archer, the lead singer, and I shared a joint in the upstairs patio. I fucked up. One of those fucking rules that Chris has for Decker Records is that no musician can step inside the building under the influence of alcohol or drugs; or ingest them on the property.

"You smell like pot," I hear a voice say and slam my hands on the keys. Fuck. I forgot that MJ and JC now live in Seattle. "Dad's going to kick you out of the studio. The rules apply to you too."

I choose to ignore him; maybe he'll get the fuck out of this room.

No such luck, as he walks closer to the piano. "That's AJ's."

"More like ours. We compose together sometimes," I say, wondering why he's here and why he talked about Chris. My gut hurts, holy shit, is he here already? "Is he here?"

He gives me that typical "he's going to fuck you up" look, and I know that he will if he sees me. Time to play nice with Jacob.

"Fuck, do me a solid and stall him," I try to sound friendly, but I'm not sure if I'm hitting the spot. "I have to go back to the hotel, take a shower and change. I hate when he gets touchy about my personal choices."

"Whatever. You know my sister wouldn't like it either."

Well, now he's fucking with me. AJ is off limits and he has no idea what happens in our relationship. "I never do this shit when my girl's around." I give him a warning look. "Now go and entertain him while I leave. See you later, dude."

Rushing, I grab my guitar case and leave. If either one of his fathers hears that AJ and I have something going on, I fear things will get ugly and I'm not ready for ugly.

As I reach the stairs, though, I hear his loud voice, "Kendrick, are you high?"

"Not exactly," I respond.

"You've got to be fucking kidding me," Christian screams. "Do you think I'm a fucking idiot? That I was born yesterday?" I open my mouth to defend myself but he raises one arm, showing me his palm. "There's no fucking way I'm going to work with you under these conditions. Head to wherever it is that you're staying, take a nap, shower, and come back when you're sober."

"It was a one-time thing," I say, thinking of a way to get out of this shit without being a snitch.

"One time?" He laughs. "Your behavior on the road is almost the same. Porter, I have no fucking idea what you think you're doing, but you have to stop. Alcohol and drugs aren't your friends. They're poison. Take it from someone who knows."

Great, here it comes. The lecture about how he almost died and he lost years of his life because of the shit he messed with. Time and again I tell him that we're different people. He doesn't get it, he thinks that one day I'll end up at the bottom of the pool at a party like him and I won't be lucky.

His eyes, so much like his daughter's, stare at me for a few moments and he shakes his head. "You might be my foster child, but this behavior won't fly at the label." Hurray, there's no lecture coming up, only a brief warning. "As I said, go sober up and come back with a better disposition."

It's on the tip of my tongue to tell him that I can go somewhere else with my music, but I don't because he's like my father, after all. One of the only two adults who have given a shit about me. Without a word, I salute him and leave the studio. Later today I'll come back in better shape.

Nine years ago . . .

WHEN AJ WAS looking for a college, I suggested she look south. The weather was a factor; I hate cold temperatures. But her parents were my main reason to stay away from the northern states. If I could keep her away from Gabe and Chris, they wouldn't know that I was dating their daughter. And no one that they knew would ever connect the dots between our relationship and her relationship with the celebrities.

In a few years, I'll come clean, tell them that I love her and plan to spend the rest of my life with her. Without her I'm nobody, she's the person that keeps me afloat when I can barely swim in the sea I live in. Coming home is what I cherish the most. At least, I used to. Lately, it's been a fucking nightmare. She complains about our relationship. The thrill of not telling anyone is being replaced by something else. The constant nagging keeps me away from my own house and my woman.

"I talked to Dad last week," AJ says. "He wants us to go on vacation and wanted my address to send me my ticket. I think it's time."

"AJ, don't start," I advise her before this becomes a freaking fight.

Today I'm not in the fucking mood and if she continues, I'm leaving for the closest hotel. "They can use your email. They know what an electronic ticket is, darling."

Fuck, I didn't just call her the same thing I call the groupies. I massage my forehead with the heel of my hand hoping that the drugs wear off soon. One misstep and my life can crumble down because of one moment of stupidity. This is why I hate when she starts her shit with me, I can't straighten myself up, and I do stupid shit.

"We've been together for so many years," she pauses; her shoulders slump and I want to know why she's not sticking to the fucking program. As she says, it's been many years. She should be used to it by now. "They deserve to know. I hate to lie to them, and I'm harboring a huge secret."

"This is not the right time," I claim, coming up with a shitty diversion. "They lie too, don't they? For all we know, they have never been honest with you."

That should hit her right where it hurts and distract her from the agenda she wants to push. But instead of flinching or reacting like she usually does, she continues speaking. Damn, what the fuck is wrong with her?

"I know things are . . . strange. We have an unconventional life."

"You want us to come out of the closet?" I chuckle, as I circle back to her parents fucked up relationship and the fact that they keep it in the closet. Everyone knows that Gabe Colt and Chris Decker are best friends, but if you're a close friend of the family, you know the truth. They're a married couple. AJ can't understand why they keep the façade when same-sex marriage and relationships are common these days.

But when I see her flinch and the sadness in her eyes increases, I apologize. I'm going too fucking far. "Sorry, I didn't mean to hit so close to home, baby. I don't know if we're ready for that kind of pressure. That might open up questions about your origins and then drag your parents where they aren't ready to go."

"This is about us, not my parents, Porter."

Damn, that strong armor is back and I have to fight her again. If we talk she'll create chaos where there's calm. Her parents love me, but I doubt they'll approve of me if they realize I'm doing their daughter.

There's also the question of my close relationships with my fans, I'd have to avoid them during tours. AJ wouldn't understand that sex with groupies on tour doesn't count; they're . . . groupies. "Can you stop being selfish for once and think about others, AJ?"

"You should stop being selfish, prick."

That does it, she goes in for the kill, and I don't have the strength to stay and fight. Instead, I head out. A few weeks of ignoring her will teach her that if she's not careful she can lose me. Not that she will, but I have to show her that I have the upper hand. To make sure I stick to my guns, I turn off my phone and shove it in my luggage, taking out the other phone. The one I use for everyone else.

"SIR, MISS AJ is not well," the maid left a voicemail. "The doctor did some testing, but not to worry, she's at home resting."

I smoke an entire joint laced with coke before I turn on the phone and call AJ to find out what the fuck happened. If she's not careful with her health and keeps those glucose levels in check, her parents are going to fly down to Austin. One slip and she's going to damage my fucking career.

"Hi," she whispers over the phone.

"I checked my messages; the maid said you were in the hospital?" No, fuck that wasn't what I wanted to say, it was . . . I couldn't remember. "You okay?"

"I didn't go to the hospital, but the doctor came by. My sugar levels were out of whack," she says, and I sigh with relief because she can fix that easily. "When will you be back?"

Not for a long time, sweetheart, I think but don't say. Like fuck I'll go back right now. "Two, three weeks." I hear a loud huff on the other side and I can feel there's something that she has to get off of her chest. "I don't know, why?"

"Nothing . . ." There's a long pause and I want to hang up, my mind is running wild with this fucking call. What does she really want from me? Break up? No, fuck not that. "I guess . . . I'm pregnant."

What the fuck? I want to scream at her, this isn't part of the plan. No fucking way am I going to be a father. Hasn't she noticed that I'm a fucked up idiot? Of course not, she still thinks I'm an amazing guy. Smart. I can conquer the world according to her. A kid? Her parents are going to castrate me. Fucking hell, I can't think.

"I can't do this. Not now." I slam the phone against the wall, thanking God for unbreakable cases or that piece of shit would be history.

Hanging up doesn't fix shit; I know that I have to face this soon. Maybe tomorrow, just after I escape from reality. A day, maybe two. A few weeks?

FOURTEEN

MACKENZIE

THE FIRST STEP has been taken. I have a job. That should give me some work experience, a place to start and build from. Green Blooms Boutique hired me with some odd hours to fill. From two to eight in the morning during the week and eight to two every other Saturday. The hours sound like a killer, but I don't sleep more than five hours at night. If I switch my habits and go to bed at the same time as my children, it'll all work out.

As I park the car outside of my aunt's house, I spot her cleaning her flowerbeds while Finn sits next to her. I search around for Harper and spot her with Porter tagging along next to her as she rides a bike. A bike? We gave hers away because it was a childish bike. The one she rides is a little bigger, but also bubble gum pink with a basket in the middle of the handlebars. Where did she find it?

Leaving the car, I realize that the bicycle doesn't have training wheels. Wait, she doesn't know how to ride without them. What's going on? Staring at them, I wait until they turn around and head back my way. Harper's eyes grow wide and her smile grows along with them. She loses her balance, but before the bike and my pretty girl take a bad hit, Porter's hands reach for her, catching her almost in the air.

"Are you okay?" I run toward them, but Harper hasn't lost her smile while Porter is helping her find a steady foot. "When, how?" I look at my daughter and the bike, then at the man who might have had something to do with this whole thing.

"Porter bought it, for me." Harper gives me another round of smiles. "He taught me how to ride like a big girl."

I check my watch. I've been gone for about two hours. During this time, he managed to buy a bicycle, teach my daughter how to ride it, and the best of all, make her smile. He's like a dream.

"Okay kids, it's time to get a snack, come with me," My aunt yells, standing up and gathering my children. Then her attention goes back to me. "You can tell me later about your new job." How does she know that I got it?

"So did you get it?" Porter's low voice asks.

I nod, telling him about my crazy schedule. Then tilt my head toward the bike he holds. "Thank you, for telling me about the position . . . and the bike. How much do I owe you?"

"Nothing." He shakes his head. "I thought this might help her out of her funk, you know." He gives me his typical shrug, as if saying, "I do this for everyone." I find his actions endearing. "When I learned to ride a bike, it gave me a sense of accomplishment and pushed me to find my way for a little while."

Wow, he's giving me some background information and I take the chance to ask questions. "Your dad taught you?" He shakes his head. "Mom?"

"No, my mom died when I was four." His shoulders slump and my heart hurts for him. "My big brother and my baby sister died along with her." Oh, God, he lost his entire family. I want to open my arms for him, hug him, and tell him . . . I don't know what, but make it better. Well, that explains why he avoids connecting with others, doesn't it? "Nothing was easy, but everything changed when I found my foster parents. One of the things they taught me was to ride a bike—I was fourteen, but it felt good. They . . ." He goes silent, his head dropping.

Did something happen to them, too? I take a few steps closer to him. We're so close that his deodorant is all I can smell. It's a masculine combination that I can't name but it makes me dizzy. "What else happened to you, Porter?" My voice comes out all breathy and wrong. What happened to the confident Mackenzie? I have no fucking idea, but whatever is going on inside me isn't something I want to analyze.

"Me. I happened to myself," he says and I don't understand. He brushes a strand of hair off my face and curls it around my ear, making my entire body shiver. "Once upon a time I had everything. I was on top of the world. Lost what mattered most because of the material shit and then some more." Some more what? He's making zero sense. His eyes fixate on me as they start to warm up and I lose myself in them. Embraced by him I feel safe and protected, yet there's an edge hiding inside. "I have to go to work." He breaks the spell, turns around, and leaves toward the gas station.

I wrap my arms around myself, rubbing them to warm up from the coldness that overtook my body as he ran away. *What the hell just happened?*

I want to promise you a blue sky
Promise you that nothing will touch you
I want to take the pain away
Promise you that I'll never hurt you
But I won't since this time I don't want to fail
[Chorus]
Baby, nothing is perfect
Nothing is painless
But after the rain, the flowers will bloom
The pain rooted in your heart will dissipate
And only love will remain

I wish I could promise that I'll be here for you
To hold your hand, to listen to you
But I can only promise that I'll see you through
The storm of rain and blood
Ready to catch you, or to hold your hand
[Chorus]
Baby, nothing is perfect
Nothing is painless
But after the rain, the flowers will bloom
The pain rooted in your heart will dissipate

And only love will remain

I promise to collect each teardrop you shed
Every story you say
Every smile you gift me
Each and every memory you share
I promise to safeguard all of them next to my wounded heart
[Chorus]
Baby, nothing is perfect
Nothing is painless
But after the rain, the flowers will bloom
The pain rooted in your heart will dissipate
And only love will remain

I watch Porter from the window, as he finally finishes the song. Now I believe that he's also a songwriter. This is the fourth day he's been working on that song. Instead of heading to bed to be ready for work, I stay awake until he gives up and heads back inside the house. Yesterday when it was raining, he did it from his room, which happens to share a wall with mine. Whoever inspires his lyrics is a lucky person. The more time passes, the more I want to know about him. The less he speaks, the more my curiosity piques.

Harper, who doesn't take well to strangers, is starting to warm up to him. Finn follows him around everywhere. They communicate through music and head nods and I want to kiss him for trying so hard to spark something inside my son. There's just something about Porter that . . . I can't find the words yet, but something about him calls to me.

There's so much more I have to learn about him. He intrigues me. In only a few weeks, I've developed this inexplicable need to be close to him. Am I attracted to him? I don't know if I can think that far ahead. His deep, smoldering eyes could melt anyone into a puddle of goo. He's handsome and he has a heavenly voice I could always listen to.

Porter could be a heartthrob anyone could watch serenading thousands of fans from afar while he's playing on stage. The question remains, though, who is Porter?

FIFTEEN

MACKENZIE

AS I WATCH Harper ride her bike and Finn his scooter, I spot a black sedan approaching my aunt's driveway. A lady with silver hair and a pair of trendy sunglasses honks twice and waves the moment my aunt comes outside her house.

"See you guys tomorrow," Aunt Molly calls out, waving at us. "Rhonda, you look fabulous."

See you tomorrow? Who the hell is Rhonda? I don't get to ask where she is going and why didn't she tell me before because *Rhonda* takes off the moment my aunt shuts the door of the car. Those crazy ladies look like they're ready to raise havoc and I'm happy for my aunt. She spends too much time in her house.

"Mommy, I'm hungry," Harper says, and Finn nods, I assume seconding her. I check the time and it's five thirty. Where did the time go? Feeding them sounds like the motherly thing to do.

I help them bring their toys inside the house and send them to clean themselves up while I start dinner. After washing my hands, I open the refrigerator and the damn thing doesn't have anything that I want. Shit. There are multiple perks to living next door to my aunt. For one, she cooks for me.

Every Sunday, we head to the grocery store where we buy whatever she writes down on her magical list. A list she prepares based on what she plans to cook for the week. I have a list too. My list usually contains a few items like milk, cereal, fresh fruit, and snacks. Of course, I pay for everything that we purchase, but she keeps most of the food because she does the cooking. The only items I keep are mainly for breakfast and snacks. It never occurred to me that my aunt has a social life. Said life includes getting together with her friends to share a meal outside of her house.

"We're doomed," I groan, shutting the door close and leaning my head against the door of the refrigerator.

"Are we going to die?" Harper is in a gloom-doom stage, everything dies and we're all doomed.

I sigh and shake my head. Me and my big mouth. "No, but we're going to have to head next door to cook some dinner."

Without another word, we head to my aunts. As I open the door I spot Porter walking toward the kitchen.

"Did she leave you without food too?" I ask, closing the door behind me.

He turns around and nods his head. "Yes, she said, and I quote. *"Feed yourself, and if Mackenzie comes over, feed her too."* So I guess tonight we're ordering Chinese food or you'll have to eat what I prepare."

"With fortune cookies?" Harper bounces excitedly all over the kitchen when Porter nods. "Mom, pretty please. We haven't had Chinese in *forever*."

That's true, it's been a few months since I shook the slump and went back to cooking healthy meals. Since Leo died, the only lists I relied on to feed my children were the takeout menus. First it was comfort food, because Leo and I ordered takeout to celebrate, or when it was too cold outside to kick the blankets off and get out of bed. Then it became easier to let others cook for me, since I had a hard time getting out of bed. Planning an entire meal felt like a task I couldn't accomplish in less than an hour. It wasn't until my checking account informed me that I was spending too much money on meals that I could prepare at home while bringing back my cooking skills.

Porter pulls his out phone staring at me, when I nod he taps his phone, and then frowns. "What do you guys usually get?"

"Chicken fried rice, beef and broccoli, and sweet and sour shrimp."

"That's my favorite," he says, keeping his eyes on the phone while he finishes tapping it. Then lifts his gaze. "I should be back in twenty minutes."

"Aren't they delivering it?"

"No, that'll take about an hour, it's best if I go and pick it up."

LEO WAS ALLERGIC to shrimp. The countless times I ordered sweet and sour shrimp, I had to wash my hands, brush my teeth, and make sure I sanitized the area where I ate. Today I don't worry about anything but savoring my meal and sharing it with my neighbor. It's strange that he's somehow becoming part of our family. We share at least one meal together every day—dinner. He interacts with Finn and Harper daily, playing the guitar for them while they play outside, or helping them while they ride their bike and scooter.

Porter waves at my kids who are placing their plates in the sink. "If it's okay with you, we could take them to the park," he whispers so close to my ear that his warm breath raises the hairs on the back of my neck. I shake slightly as the sensation ripples through my entire body. It's a strange sensation that I brush away. "We can take Harper's bike along with us."

I respond with a light, snarky remark. "For a guy that hates to talk, you're being too social today." I smirk at him.

Between the permanent frown and serious lips, a smile appears. "Is that a 'yes, let's head to the park?'"

I agree, because for once I don't want the day to end. Today I don't miss my old life. This is one of those strange perfect days, which I haven't had in a long time. Once we finish cleaning the kitchen, we ready the kids and ourselves and head to the park. It takes a while for us to arrive, since Finn is set on riding his scooter all the way there. Once we reach the park, I stay with my little boy on the playground while Porter jogs behind Harper as she rides around the bike trails. If I had met him today, I'd assume he's a father, or that he's close to his nieces and nephews. But he doesn't have a family. Another puzzle piece appears and, as all the others, I don't know where to place it.

When it comes time to leave, Finn extends his arms to me so I can carry him. But Porter intercepts him, picking him up as if he's used to having a little boy in his arms, and then scoops up his scooter too.

Porter helps me with their bedtime and stays while I read a book to them. Once I shut the door, I can't help but ask where he learned to be so good with children.

He shrugs. "One of my foster fathers has a huge family back in New York. The times I visited, I had to pitch in—everybody helps one another. Babysitting, cooking, or something alike."

I add that information to the tapestry of stories and memories he shares. There aren't many pieces yet, but it builds on who he is. Maybe someday I'll know him well enough to consider him a friend.

"Thank you for today," he says, taking a step with each word. "For the company." Another three steps. "It was nice . . ."

He's in front of me when his voice trails and his eyes lock with mine.

Shit, shit.

His head tilts down. And yes, his mouth is soft when it touches my forehead. Warm as it trails down the bridge of my nose, caressing the tip and finally moving away before reaching my lips. Damn.

"Sorry, I don't know what I was thinking." He turns around and leaves, closing the door behind him. I touch my tingling mouth with the tip of my fingers.

What happened?

SIXTEEN

MACKENZIE

AUNT MOLLY HELPS me with the kids in the morning. By the time I come home from work Harper is ready to go to school, I walk with her to the bus stop and then head back home. The schedule we set up has been working well for the past three weeks. Every day I'm thankful that I have her. Today is no exception. Unless I count the shirtless guy coming down the stairs with messy hair that screams, I just rolled out of bed. He's lean, yet each muscle of his is perfectly delineated under his tattooed skin. Is this the way his hair looks after fucking?

My eyes widen after the question pops into my head. What is wrong with me? That kiss. The one that didn't happen. It left me . . . wondering.

"Good morning, Mac." He grins and my heart skips several beats. My skin tingles. Wait, is he flirting with me?

Fuck, what the hell is going on?

As he steps closer, I spot a thin line of scar tissue on top of his clavicle. It travels down his chest, but the welt is masked by a dragon-snake tattoo. I can't help it and I raise my hand, touching the fading mark with the tip of my fingers. "What happened?"

He shrugs. "A car accident when I was four. I can't recall the details, but I recall the doctors saying that if the glass had gone closer to the jugular . . . well, I wouldn't be here."

"You were there when they died?" He nods. My hand moves to his square chin, peppered with a light stubble. His hands move on top of mine and the touch makes my stomach flutter. Fear of what's going on between the two of us makes me snatch my hand and take a step back.

He clears his throat, checking his wrist where the initials AJ are, and smiles.

"Today is my day off," Porter says. "Do you want me to come with you to Finn's testing?"

My eyes open wide, I pull my phone to check my calendar and realize that yes, today is the day. I found a place where they can test him and where they'll only charge according to my financial abilities.

"Let me eat a bowl of cereal and then I'll go and get dressed," he says, without waiting for me to agree to have him with me. Porter walks toward the entrance door and grabs a set of keys. "In the meantime, why don't you put his booster seat in my truck."

"I can drive," I tell him, staring at the keys.

Wait, he has a truck?

"I don't doubt your capabilities, but let me help you today." His words are firm and they reach every cell of my body. He sounds like a man who wants to take charge, be in control. With a relaxed smile and a sweet caress of his thumb along my jawline, he leaves me staring at him. Yep. I think he's flirting indeed.

I REST MY head on the seat while Porter drives back home. They can't diagnose my boy with anything specific. Other than recommending a place that costs a lot of money, where they can give him other tests that can give an accurate diagnosis, they helped with nothing. The fact that he lost his speech when he lost his father threw them out of their element. Maybe the first counselor I saw in Colorado was right about Finn and it's his own way of grieving.

"I wish I could lend you the money," Porter's voice draws me out of the funk, as my eyes flutter open, he pulls his sunglasses down the bridge of his nose and his brown eyes stare at me full of concern. "We can start by using those booklets they gave you. Maybe it will drag out a word or two. He might not have anything interesting to say yet" He chews on his lip. "Sorry, I'm just saying stupid things to try to cheer you up."

"And I appreciate it," I tell him. "Thank you for coming with me, this was easier because I had you next to me."

I blink a couple of times absorbing what I just said. Fuck. I am grateful, but confused about feeling safe with him. The entire situation is creating pandemonium inside my head. When I made the appointment, I was upset at Leo for leaving me to deal with everything all alone. Then grieving because I wouldn't have anyone coming along and would face whatever they tell me alone. Finally, resigned to deal with it alone, I just casually made the comment during dinner and . . . he's there by my side. Porter, the unlikely support that my son and I needed today.

"Thank you for letting me ride along," he responds, opening the garage and pulling his truck inside.

Why would he do that, thank me for doing me a favor? Because we're becoming friends? A few benefits should come from that title. Sharing information should be one of them.

Yes, Mackenzie, do it.

"If I ask you something . . . would you answer this time?" I bite my lip, fearing that he won't answer.

"It depends," he responds with a smooth, yet reserved voice.

"What happened to you?" Four words that carry so much force. Porter's face hardens, as his jaw clenches.

His eyes darken; he pinches the bridge of his nose as his chest rises and lowers a couple of times. "We shouldn't stay in the car for so long."

That's it? Where is my answer?

I want to ask him but he jumps out of the truck. Carrying Finn's sleeping body, he heads to my house. Rushing behind them, I open the front door and follow him to the kids' room where he places him on top of the bed, covers him with a blanket, and kisses the top of his head. As I'm about to ask him a question, he steps closer to me, looking down at me with a serious gaze. His mouth drops to the top of my head giving me a gentle kiss, and hugging me tight.

"He's going to be okay. We'll help him. I'll . . ." He walks away as he releases me. "You're going to be okay."

His words confuse me, but I want to believe them. Trust that my son will come back to me. That we're going to be fine. But how?

SEVENTEEN

MACKENZIE

LISTENING TO THE giggles coming from the swings fills my heart with happiness. It's been a long time since they've been enjoying themselves this much. These evenings at the park, after dinner, are becoming part of our routine. Harper finishes her homework before setting the table just to ensure that we won't cancel our trip to her favorite spot. Finn helps Porter dry the dishes after I'm done washing them. They both look forward to spending some time at the park climbing the slide and traversing the monkey bars. Finn has a new bike and he's trying to keep up with his sister. Maybe soon he'll be riding without the training wheels.

"Mom!" Harper calls out, getting off the swing and running toward me. "Can we play hide and seek? We can all take turns. You and I hide while Porter and Finn look for us, then we switch."

It's been years since we've played hide and seek. Usually, Harper would hide and I'd look for her around the house. Some days Leo would join us and I'd be looking all over for both. Finn was a baby. I don't think we played much when he was old enough to hide with us. I look around the park, smiling, as I think back at the fun we had searching for the oddest places to hide.

"Maybe that's something we should do at home," I say, saving my reservations about the plan. Is it safe to hide in the park?

"Teaming up will help find one another," Porter says with a playful grin. "Girls versus boys," he says, helping Finn out of the swing. "You can start, because when it's our turn, you won't be able to find us. Right, sport?" He looks at Finn, who nods once.

"We'll find you," Harper says, tilting her chin up, indignation pouring with those words. "You can go first."

Finn jumps happily, holding Porter's hand. Porter smiles at Harper, and extends his hand. "You're on, Harp. If you can't find us, you get to dry the dishes tomorrow."

"If I find you?" she narrows her gaze.

"We'll set the table for you," Porter responds, and with that, he jogs away, Finn right behind him. "Count to hundred before you search for us."

"I FOUND YOU," Harper shouts, as she opens the door of the tree house. I'm sure the entire neighborhood is aware of her discovery. Finn plugs his ears, burying his head against Porter's shoulder, who hugs him tight.

It took us a long time to find them. We walked around the entire park, searching behind the trees, trashcans and every place someone could use as a hiding spot. Harper almost gave up, but they were at the toddler playground inside the "treehouse" that's not on top of the tree.

"Your giggle gave us away, sport." Porter tickles Finn when they come out.

Harper opens her arms and walks to him. "I don't want to play this game ever again." Harper says, and Porter presses her toward his body with his free arm, giving me a lost stare. "I worried that I wouldn't find Finn—or you."

"Time to go back home, maybe buy ice cream on our way," I offer, trying to cheer her up. She shakes her head.

"Slushies," Porter counterparts. "You love them."

She does. When we go to the gas station and head down to the convenience store to visit him, Harper begs for a small size slushy. She promises to behave for the rest of the day, but they're empty promises that fall through as she's on a sugar high after only taking a few sips of it.

"I like slushies," she confirms, releasing her tight hold and giving me a smile.

My happy girl doesn't return for the rest of the evening. She remains glued to Porter, who stays with us until they go to sleep.

"Thank you," I tell him, as we walk down the stairs.

"Some days I miss my mother, too," he says. "After losing a parent, the fear of losing someone else stays with you for a long time. I learned that during therapy—I was twenty-eight."

"Patience and love," I add, as if I guess he's about to say that. He nods. "So where are you originally from?"

"Here and there," he answers, his dark eyes looking sad. It's nagging me to push him for more details; I just have to find the right question. "What part of Colorado are you from?"

I shake my head, huffing with frustration because he's doing it again. Turning the conversation around and making it all about me. This time, I can do the same, switch it so it is all about him. "No, I'm from Charlotte."

"North Carolina, right?" I nod. "I've been there once, boring city. Two days and I found nothing to do in town."

"Impossible," I retort. "There's plenty, it's all about looking for the right place."

"No, the two nights I searched for a good night club, I couldn't find any."

"Hmm, I wouldn't know about the night life," I slump my shoulders. "After graduating from high school, I moved to Colorado for college. My parents bought a condo in a retirement community in Florida and the only times we went back to Charlotte were to visit my mother-in-law."

"Your parents retired early." He cocks an eyebrow, crossing his arms. "Were you the baby of the house?"

"No, I'm an only child. My parents met when Mom was thirty-five and Dad was in his early fifties. At forty-two, my mother thought she was having signs of early menopause. Instead, she was having me." I laugh remembering that my father always joked about being his early retirement present. He took a sabbatical to care for me when I was a baby, while Mom continued working. "Of course, they made sure I was their only 'oops baby'. Not because they didn't love me, but they were too old to have little ones."

"I don't blame them, you look like you were trouble back in the day," he says, laughing. His guard is down and I enjoy this Porter. I'd give anything if he could stay like this all the time. "Imagine having more like you."

"I did. When I was a child, I begged them to give me a little brother, or a sister." Remembering those days are fun now, but back then, I wanted to scream at them for not giving me the only thing I wanted, someone to play with. They both had their careers and couldn't imagine taking more time off from their schedule to tend to more than one child. "It was hard growing up alone with them. Most of the time they treated me like an adult instead of their child. But they're loving, and at some point we understood each other."

I abstain from telling him about the times I snuck out of the house to go to parties or went to my friend's house to drink, because they wouldn't let me have my own fun. They were afraid that I'd drink like the other kids my age. Which I did, and sometimes I smoked. I also smoked weed a couple of times. They held a tight grasp when it came to my social life. Thinking back, maybe my parents were the reason I looked into moving out of Charlotte for college. My dad wanted me to go to the same place he taught for decades. I couldn't fathom the idea of being Dr. Grant Oliver's daughter for four years. The same way I couldn't imagine working while my children grew up under the care of some stranger.

"Sounds like a boring childhood, doesn't it?" He nods. "We had our hobbies. Other than watching the Discovery channel and the History channel—hiking at Crowder's Mountain Park was my favorite. They fed my love for nature; bought me a nice camera and I shot pictures of everything that I saw during our weekend hikes."

"You miss them." It's not a question but a statement.

"Yeah, even though we talk often over the phone, I miss them," I confess, looking down at the carpet.

The nostalgia for my parents isn't the only thing that's making me wonder about the past. Thinking about those years makes me wonder where I lost Mackenzie the woman with plans, goals, and dreams.

"Are you going to be okay?" I lift my gaze and he's checking the time. "My shift starts in ten minutes. I'll be back before you have to go to work."

"Thank you," I say, wanting to say much more, but not knowing the words that'll express my gratitude. Instead, I touch his hand and squeeze it. He squeezes it back. "For everything."

"Thank you," he repeats back. "The three of you have brought some light into my life. Get some rest." He lifts his hand, almost touching my face, but he hesitates and leaves without saying another word.

EIGHTEEN

MACKENZIE

THE DOORBELL RINGS right at eight thirty in the morning. I know who it is before I open the door. Porter. He's wearing a leather jacket, a white button down shirt under it, and a pair of jeans. His friendly smile, as usual, is the first thing that greets me. After a few months, Porter and I have become friends. But there's also some kind of attraction swirling between us. Often I find him watching me, winking at me, or just giving me a sexy smirk. I can't help but smile back at him. At times, I find myself thinking about him. His coffee-colored eyes, that manly smell of his.

Every time I see him, something inside me stirs. It's not only the outside. He's just as beautiful on the inside. To say he's wonderful doesn't begin to describe him. He's patient with my children, my aunt, and at times, even with me. Before I head to work at the godforsaken hours of the night, he comes to my house to keep an eye on Harper and Finn, so my aunt doesn't have to wake up late at night. In the morning, he prepares them breakfast and walks with Harper to the bus stop.

Finn isn't talking yet, but he can follow along Old McDonald animals. I want to think that imitating them is a promise that someday something will change. That he'll come back to me. Then there's my little Harper who is now a social butterfly. Not sure if it was the change in scenery, Aunt Molly, Porter or a combination but as Mom and Aunt Molly said, "things would get better in Portland." Of course, I still miss

Leo. They say it gets easier with time. But no, it doesn't. He's all I've known and loved since I was a teenager. It's hard to look beyond our relationship and our old life. My heart might get a glimpse ahead, but my mind stops it with the reminder of what it could've been. Like when I look at Porter.

"Hey," Porter says, as his fingers tilt my chin and our gazes lock. "What's with the long face?"

"Hi," I respond, with a small voice. "My mind got trapped where it shouldn't, not today anyway."

"Damn right." He bends down kissing my nose. My breath hitches with the gesture. Damn it, what's been happening between us? It's nothing deep or serious but the stolen caresses and gentle kisses . . . they confuse the hell out of me. "Where's the birthday girl?"

"Porter!" Harper yells, racing outside the house, leaping into his open arms. He sings happy birthday to her with that beautiful voice of his that makes me swoon like a teenager in heat.

"Are we ready to go?" He asks, setting her back on her feet.

"Yes, yes!" She jumps up and down and runs back inside the house.

We both enter the house. Porter shuts the door and Finn comes running toward him, jumping into his arms. "Good morning, sport. Are you ready to have fun today?" Finn nods, hugging his neck.

I turn to the couch to finish getting ready. I grab my infinity scarf and my jacket, hoping that I won't need anything heavier for the day. "What's the plan?" For the past week, we've been planning to do something special for my sweet girl that will keep her mind occupied. Porter said yesterday night, "Leave it to me." I am, but I have to know.

"Seaside. It's a small town an hour and a half from here. Close to the northern coast," he explains, lowering Finn to the ground. "There's an aquarium where the kids can feed fish to the seals and so many more activities that by the time we finish, they should be ready for bed." The last word emphasized just when he reaches for the bottom corners of my jacket and helps me zip it as if I couldn't do it myself. The slow movement of his hands gliding all the way up my torso makes me tingle all over. As it reaches the top, he lifts his hand, tucking a loose strand from my ponytail behind my ear. My mouth parts and I can't remember how to breathe. Fuck, it's just a freaking zipper, what is wrong with you today, Mackenzie? "What do you think?"

I bob my head in agreement, as there's not one word I can come up with to answer his question. I can't think. Confusion. That's the only word that pops inside my head. To settle back down and act as the grown woman that I am, I walk to Finn who is now kneeling down while drawing on his new coloring book. "Time to go, baby, we're going to celebrate Harper's birthday."

"Yes, my birthday." She's running down the stairs holding her jacket and Finn's too. "Can you tell me now what the surprise is?"

Porter shakes his head, takes Finn's jacket away from her and helps him put it on. "Time to go. If you have a lot of fun, I might give you your birthday present."

Present, the best magic word there is to make a seven-year-old do whatever we want her to do.

PORTER CARRIES HARPER'S sleepy body. Finn's head hangs on my shoulder, his eyes half-asleep. After feeding the fishes, riding the bumper cars, the carousel, and walking along the arcade playing all the games they had, we were exhausted. We had dinner at the Astoria and rode the trolley. We missed the Maritime museum, roller-skating and ice cream time, but they were too fatigued to continue walking. The promise to go back there soon made the kids happy. At least Harper, who jumped up and down when we told her that would be our next outing.

Our next outing . . . when did we become this little family that shares so much together? Should I look more into what is going on between Porter and me?

"Babe, I'm settling Harp on her bed. Get them ready for the night while I head to the garage for her present. Did you change her bed with the new sheets?" Babe? It takes a minute for what Porter called me to register. He said it so naturally I don't think he realized what he said. He's left me stunned, so I just nod as he leaves the room.

In the mean time I hurry before he's back with the presents. Harper has been asking for her own room and, of course, that's close to impossible. My job only covers the daily expenses, but I hope that next year I can find a position that pays better. I sold the house in Colorado, but I don't want to use the little money that I made for a down payment to buy another house. At least not until I'm working at a place that gives me better benefits and of course, an increase in salary.

She wants a pink room with a dollhouse bed and flowersu. Porter came up with a few ideas that included a dollhouse headboard that he made. We bought decal flowers that will go on her side of the room and some farm animals that will go on Finn's side to make it fair. For his birthday next year, Porter wants to build a farmhouse headboard. Unless his interest for animals is gone and we'll have to rethink the theme.

"Thank you for my birthday, Mom," my sleepy Harper murmurs as I tuck her in bed after putting on her pajamas.

"I love you, baby," I whisper and her eyes close again.

And while Porter moves her bed to set the headboard, she remains asleep. When he's done, I set the new soft pink comforter down and we put the decals on top of her night stand so she can decorate with them tomorrow morning. Maybe Porter was right; we should have done this last night. Waking up to a new room on her birthday would've been a bigger surprise.

"Thank you, for everything you did today," I whisper, as I make sure both of my kiddos are properly tucked inside their beds. "The room, the trip, everything. You know the area well. Do you go out often?"

He gives me his signature shrug and I'm hoping this is one of those rare occasions when he'll confide in me.

"No. My foster parents' home is in Washington State. Not far from here," he says. The nostalgia he carries when he talks about them is infiltrating the air we breathe. "Their parents took us—me and their triplets—there a couple of times. James and Janine were cool with me."

"Sounds like the family is lovely."

"Let's go, you need to sleep." Porter takes my hand and guides me outside the room. The conversation is over before it began. So much for him opening up to me. At this rate, I'll die before I get to know him better.

"Don't worry about me, I took a day off today," I respond. "I'm rested."

He lifts my hand and kisses the inside of my wrist. "I wish I could stay, but I have to go to work."

I don't want him to go, but I don't tell him that. There's no reason why he should stay with me tonight—or ever. Unless I count the fact I feel alone and cold today—more than usual. That being with him makes everything less . . . Everything is easier to cope with when he's around. The loneliness dissipates.

"You okay?" I nod. "Are you sure? Because the last thing I want to do is leave you alone when you need me."

"Yeah, I'm just tired," I lie, because I do want him to stay longer. "Thank you again, for everything that you did for us today. Try to rest after your shift." With a final goodbye, he leaves the house, and I regret not asking him to stay a little longer.

NINETEEN

PORTER

"YOU'RE NOT STAYING for dinner?" Molly, my landlady asks as I put on my leather jacket. "Did something happen between you and Mackenzie?"

I roll my eyes. She's been trying to fish for information since Harper's birthday. I tilt my head watching her as she guesses why I'm leaving early, or if something is going on between Mac and me.

"You have a date," she states without hesitation.

"Did you find a woman? Or is it a guy? I'm okay if you're gay, but that takes away the chances of *us* having a relationship." She winks at me.

I laugh, because this flirty woman will never take any conversation seriously.

"I have to work, Molly," I say wiggling the door handle. "Have a good one."

There's more to the story. Tomorrow is Halloween and I'm going trick-or-treating with Mackenzie and the kids. Harper invited me and since it's the first time they're celebrating since Leo—Mac's husband—died. I accepted without hesitation. It doesn't hurt that I adore Finn and Harper, or that Mac is great to be around.

Yes, keep saying that, Porter. She's a good friend, great to be around . . . maybe soon I'll accept that I'm attracted to her. Hell, I think I'm falling in love with her, just as I'm falling for her children. Stepping outside, as I turn towards their home, I spot them. Mackenzie and Finn are walking toward me. Her hazel eyes find mine. Her smile appears naturally the moment I wave at her. The beautiful creature never fails to take my breath away. It's the tenderness in her face. Petite perfection that looks great wearing a pair of sweats or a sundress.

"Leaving so soon?" She comes to a halt right in front of me. "Thought it was your turn to cook dinner?"

"Left it in the crock-pot." I bend to pick up Finn, who extends his little arms toward me. "Hey, sport, are you ready for tomorrow?" He nods. "Where's Harper?"

"A playdate," Mac informs me, her smile widens. "She's finally making new friends. How about you, did you have dinner?"

I shake my head as she frowns and her small hand reaches my chin. Those happy eyes are now harboring worry. "The food won't be ready for another hour."

"Tell you what, since we're not going to the park today," She takes Finn in her arms and continues, "We'll visit you and bring some food. I hate when you don't eat."

"You spoil me," I whisper, leaning in to kiss her cheek. "How about we make it seven, that's when I take my break."

Her cheeks turn a slight shade of red. She flusters easily when I compliment her, caress her, or give her a kiss. Some days I live for those stolen moments. Things between us are progressing slowly. At least I want to believe that there's something building between the two of us, something that if I protect it, and nurture it, might grow to be . . . everything for us.

"Seven it is then," she mumbles.

"It's a date." I wink, turning around and leaving her in the middle of the driveway.

Fuck, sometimes we behave like two teenagers. But how much heat can you add to a relationship when her children are always around. Plus, I want this to be significant. And the only significant relationship I've had was with AJ Decker when I was a kid. My conversations with any other women went as deep as your place or mine?

I rub my face before crossing the street. I'm wondering if I'm doing the right thing. Wondering if I'm ready to start a relationship. It's been years since I've been close to anyone that doesn't have initials after their name and charge two hundred dollars an hour to listen to the story of my life. Mackenzie Brooke made me step outside the safe area I stayed in for so long. The many questions she asks, just like Harper, her little girl, have started to chip at my defenses. Their curiosity is adorable and I can't resist either one. God knows I've tried several times.

Mac and her little ones are like a gift. They make me feel as if I belong to them, like if I work hard, they could belong to me some day. Fuck. I might dare to say that I'm starting to love them all. I want so much more from her. From them. Questions remain in front of me like a wall. We are recovering from a loss. Both different losses, but are we ready to take the next step? She doesn't talk about her husband a lot, but I just don't want to fuck up what we have.

Something about her reminds me of the Deckers. She makes me feel like I have a family. This time I don't want to fuck things up. Lose them as I lost the Deckers. Maybe I should follow what they taught me. Like love without reserves. I also remember two things that the Deckers instilled in me—always use condoms when you have sex and try to have meaningful sex. I listened to one of them. I always used condoms. The second . . . I fucked women since I turned eighteen without giving them a second thought. None of them mattered; there wasn't anything meaningful or significant. The only person who mattered was AJ. When I was with her, everything was different. Every caress, every kiss, and every I love you meant something to the both of us. AJ mattered. She meant the world to me. At least she did until I lost myself and became the opposite of who I wanted to be for her.

After losing AJ, I never thought that I'd feel the same for anyone; that I'd care for anyone the way I did for her. At least not until Mackenzie knocked on my door. She stood right in front of me. Long, wavy, dark-brown hair hanging on her shoulders framing her heart shaped face. Her light brown eyes staring at me with curiosity and fear. The yoga pants and tank top she wore emphasized her curves and there was something about her that pulled me to her.

Mackenzie illuminates and warms the dark places inside me. The past couple of months with her, Harp and Finn have been perfect. They've helped me create new memories. Having them in my life helps dull the hurt of my past. They fill a void I thought would remain vacant forever. Looking back toward the house, I decide to step up my game. Woo her. Show her that we can be great together. Trust that if I venture into a place where she's not comfortable, she'll let me know.

"NEVER?" MAC ASKS, while fixing my hay hat. "Why?"

"At least, I can't remember ever doing it," I rephrase. The period while I was with my grandparents is a black hole I choose not to investigate. Not even with hypnotherapy. "My foster family lived in the middle of nowhere, trick-or-treating was out of the question. We usually watched horror movies during Halloween."

"Ate candy?"

"No. One of their kids was diabetic," I explain without detail. Maybe someday I'll share more about Gabe and Chris. Even tell her about AJ. For now, less is more.

"Shouldn't you be a scarecrow too?" I question Harper, who finally comes downstairs dressed in a glittery dress, fairy wings, and she's holding a wand.

"No. I'm a farm-fairy." She touches me with her wand. "Now you're a living scarecrow."

"That's the best I could come up with," Mac sounds a little defensive, handing her a cowboy hat. "Compromising with her was close to impossible. All her friends are going to be princesses or fairies. You ready for this?"

I nod, pulling her cow ear slightly, then kissing her black nose. I wink at her, walking to the kitchen for the buckets that Molly bought for the kids.

"NOT BAD FOR a first timer," Mac says, handing me a glass of water. "You should head home to sleep."

"Sit." I pat the couch. "We agreed on watching movies after the kids went to bed. Something scary. Psycho, Halloween, The Shining?"

Her eyes grow wide, her head shaking. "Scary movie?" she counterparts. "I don't watch scary movies. Ever. Not even the classics. Find something mellow. A comedy."

"Romantic comedy?" I ask as she frowns. "What? I happen to know a lot about movies. You don't grow up with a movie fanatic and not learn a thing or two."

"Your foster parents?"

I nod, remembering the first time I stepped foot on a movie set. Gabe needed a background band for a scene and he took me to fill in as the guitarist. He showed me the studio, explained the process of filming and how they add in the sound. It was a lot of shit to take in when there were so many famous people around, but after that day, I tried to pay more attention to everything he explained about his work. Fuck. Not many are as lucky as I was and I threw away so many opportunities. The biggest regret is throwing away their love.

"You should look for them," she suggests one more time. "If I could be closer to my parents . . . I'd do it."

"Why don't you?"

"They live in Miami, the living cost there is higher than here," she explains. "I don't know. I've been there only a few times, but the place isn't for me. Still, I talk to them often. At least you should try something; start a conversation."

Sounds simple. It's been years since they closed the doors to their home. Time has passed. Enough to know that I truly fucked up. If I hadn't, maybe I could seek AJ's help. She'd be able to help Finn. For him, I'd do it, break my promise to Mason and look for them.

"I know a teacher who specializes in learning disabilities. She's a therapist too." I change the conversation slightly from Gabe and Chris, trying to find out if Mac would be open to go with AJ. "If I can get in touch—"

"Do you think she can help Finn?" I nod. Her face brightens and I pull her into my arms, soaking up that beautiful energy she's radiating. "I . . . I'd try anything."

I kiss her temple. "Okay, if we can't come up with the payment for the test, I'll get in touch with her. I promise. Now, back to our movie night, if you're not willing to watch a scary movie, what do you want to watch?"

"Anything but Never End," she says, laughing. "My father loves those movies. He has the entire collection, including the last one. Mom only watches them with him because of Gabe Colt but they are bad."

Gabe's movies provided the background noise to our long conversation where I learned more about Mac's childhood. What it was like being an only child, her summer road trips, and her love of science and living things. She wanted to have a farm and land where she could have a garden. After a couple of hours, we decided to watch Say Anything, but after the first ten minutes, she's fast asleep. Carrying her to her room is the obvious thing to do, but I choose to keep her in my arms for as long as she remains asleep.

Maybe someday this won't be a stolen moment, but real life.

Yes, I'm falling hard.

TWENTY

PORTER

MY HEART THUNDERS, as fear rushes through my veins along with adrenaline.

Does life repeat itself?

I think, as I stare at the white envelope from Limestone County Jail. I try hard not to shake as I open it and unfold the white paper inside of it. Years ago, when my relationship with AJ started crumbling into shitty pieces, I received a letter from Steven Kendrick. My father. Back then, he wanted money, and today, who knows. Nothing has happened with Mackenzie, but what if my shitty luck repeats itself. The wicked get no rest and I'm a wicked son of a bitch.

Dear Porter,

It's been a while since our last letter. Life continues even as I remain sitting inside this cage. Before it takes me by surprise, I'm taking the step and writing you this letter. A letter I've been thinking about composing before it's too late. With it, I'm hoping to beg for your forgiveness, and maybe help you with the rest of your life.

During my library periods, I sometimes search for your name on the old computer. Some years ago, I read that you were in trouble. The reports included an OD and issues with the law. Son, I don't know where you're at with your recovery, but I'm sure you've heard that addiction is a disease of the brain. Those substances are capable of controlling our thoughts and actions. We believe that we need the shit to survive, to breathe. The disease fools us into thinking that without the alcohol—or drugs—we will die.

I'm an alcoholic; your grandfather was one too . . . Was this something I—we—inherited? I don't have the answer, all I know is that I wished I had a place to rewire my brain and beat the disease before it was too late. Your Mama asked me to do it several times; she worried that it'd kill me. I made promises to her, many and often. All of them broken the next day or within hours. I couldn't stop boy; I never stopped. Not until that night. My Georgina, God bless her soul, it was she who paid the price of my negligence, my weakness, the disease. Our entire family suffered, and you, poor thing. You ended up alone.

Porter, I'm sorry for the part I played in your life. Sorry for snatching you away from your mother and family, leaving you alone. It's been a long time since the jury decided that after killing my family and the family of another man, I should spend forty-five years behind bars. For these past years, I've gone through stages. Like anger, depression, mourning . . . finally, I found God. Maybe it's too late for me to find religion, maybe I found it just at the right time. The most I learned is that it's never too late to find peace, son.

There are many things I have to seek before I reach the end. One of them is your forgiveness. For everything that I did wrong during those days, I'm sorry, Porter. There are not enough words to apologize for everything that I did to you. Only prayers that your life has turned around, and that maybe you'll find in your heart to forgive your old man. If possible, can you visit me? Give me a chance to say in person what I should've said years ago.

Love,

Steven Kendrick

My instincts tell me to shred the letter and go on with my life. There's no point of visiting a man I've only seen a handful of times during my adult years. That same person didn't give a shit about his family and killed them. He took my mother away from me; why not send me with them? I bet shit wouldn't have been as bad if my mother had been with me.

I think of Harper and Finn losing their father at a young age. At least, they have a wonderful mother next to them, fighting to make a better life for them. Yes, she had a rough start but Mac's making things happen. If only I could be the rock she can lean on when she's tired. The shoulder she can cry on when she feels like the world is closing in on her. But we make our choices and mine had consequences that I'll never be able to shake.

Looking down at the letter, I decide that perhaps, I should give my father a chance to speak his peace. The same chance I'd like to have but no one is giving me. But will history repeat itself?

Nine years ago . . .

Dear Porter:

It's been years since I've heard from my family . . . what I have left of my family. My father, my mother, and well, you. A couple of months ago, my father came to visit. My first visitor since they sentenced me to spend the next forty-five years in a cage. A couple of times, I heard from my mother. The last time she sent me a picture you were twelve. You have your mother's eyes and her brown hair.

After that letter, I never heard from her again. When my father visited, he gave me the news that my mother died years ago and you ran away. Also, he thought you were a singer. I laughed at him. A singer? You? My mother said you couldn't read a full sentence at twelve, and she feared you were retarded. A side effect from the accident we had years ago. How can a retarded child be a famous singer? I disregarded his comment and told him never to visit me again. I have lived without my family for more than twenty years: I can handle the rest of my sentence the same way.

Yesterday I received the news that your grandfather died. I wished I could feel sad about his passing, but he was a hard person to live with. He wrote a letter, apologizing to me, to my mother, and to you. He told me to look for you, that you're real and you're famous. During my library time, I went to the computer and found you on the Internet. It's you, living large with those beautiful models and all-you-can-eat buffets. You're lucky.

In the back of this letter, I'm sending you the details to make a monetary deposit to my commissary account. You know boy, they sentenced me to forty-five years in jail.

That's a damn long time, don't you think? After twenty years in jail and having spent a third of my life thinking about what I did wrong, it occurred to me that maybe it is time for me to get out. However, it isn't as easy as it sounds. Waiting until my eighty-seventh birthday to get out of this place doesn't seem fair. It occurred to me that you could pay a lawyer to help your father. I don't think having a father in jail is good publicity.

Waiting to hear from you,
Steven Kendrick

I stare at the letter, or maybe it's the letter that stares at me. Fucking hell. What the hell does he want? Money? The letter makes little sense. I take a swig of whiskey. My second bottle. Being away from AJ is fucking killing me. But she has to learn. She has to know that she can't fuck with me. First, she's pregnant, then she's saying there's no baby. I stare at the tattoo healing on my wrist with my son's initials. Fucking hell. I lost everything.

I rub my face, reading the letter from the man that killed my family. He killed my future. If . . . I have no idea what to think. AJ would know. She does. But now that she fought with her parents I have no idea where to find her. Hell, I might have to visit Steven, figure out what the fuck he wants. Later, maybe later when I get her back again.

Present

THE BLAZING SUN of the morning beats down on me. The one fucking day I decide to hit the asphalt early to burn the tension, anger, and adrenaline that my father's letter created. The sun is out and I'm sweating like a pig. For fucks sake, it's November. My shirt is damp and I wipe my forehead with the sleeve of my sweatshirt. It's been four long days and I haven't come up with a decision yet. My supervisor said he'd take me off the schedule for next week.

Do I want to visit him?

He deserves to be heard, but I fear that this encounter is going to fuck up all the good I have going on with Mac. Approaching the house, I spot her minivan arriving at the house. I check the time. Eight thirty. Fuck. I forgot Harper. Coming to a stop, I try to catch my breath.

"I'm sorry," I say, as Mac approaches. "Lost. Track. Of–"

"Are you okay?" She hands me a Starbucks cup, stands on her tip-toes, and kisses my cheek. "Something is going on with you. You're quiet again—sad."

I massage my forehead with my free hand to fight the headache building up. Drinking the caffeine might help me. Despite the run, I couldn't shed any of the feelings I've been harboring. My body needs something to control the plethora of emotions that Steven created. The memories of my past are threatening to come back and I refuse to let them take the front seat again. Should I call my therapist?

"What happened?" Mac cups my chin, our eyes connect, and her soft gaze calms me. "Porter, I'm here for you."

My arms encircle her petite body and I press her against me. I catch the floral scent on her hair. Home. That's the word that comes to mind when I have her in my arms. Today more than any other day, I wish I could tell her what I feel for her. Take this relationship to the next level. Impossible, as I'm in a bad place. One mistake and I could fuck up more than my life. The last time I almost killed the woman I loved.

"The past," I finally speak. Experience taught me one thing, to communicate. Today I won't tell her everything, but the least I could do is tell her that I'm going through a hard time. I push her away lightly, holding her shoulders. "Promise to tell you about it soon, I have to work it out before I can talk it out."

"I understand, Porter, I'm here to help you anytime. Always remember, I'm your friend."

The knowledge that she's with me, settles some of the uncertainty that has me tied into knots. Facing the past might be the best way to build the future. A future with her.

TWENTY-ONE

PORTER

FOLLOWING THE GUARD through the hallways of Limestone County Jail, I stare at the gray walls illuminated by the artificial lights. Purgatory is the word I'd use to describe this place. A place to repent from your sins before you head to whatever is next. My purgatory is much more different from this one, and I have yet to find a way to compensate and apologize for each one of my offenses.

"Take a seat, the inmate will be with you soon," the officer says, opening the door to a small room occupied by a metal table and two chairs.

I stare at the walls, the furniture, and wonder why they changed the regular visitors place with the phone booths and zero privacy. I scratch the nape of my neck, wondering if I made the right choice. There are so many thoughts inside my head, they sound like a gushing river, and I'm unable to concentrate on just one. The questions that prevail are the ones about my decision. Is he playing me?

"*. . . give me a chance to say in person . . .*" he wrote.

Shredding the damn letter had been my first impulse. But instead, I use the old saying 'treat others the way you want to be treated.' For years, I've lived in my own prison. It doesn't have walls, but it's as suffocating as any other place. Unlike my father, I'll never get a chance to say anything in person to my son. There's no way to send a letter, but every night I ask him to forgive me for what I did to him. And for the way I treated the best person in the world—his mother. Before I fall asleep for a few hours and, while the guilt pounds my chest, I think about the numerous ways to change my past and have my son and my girl right next to me. If I had been who she thought I was, if I hadn't abandoned her, cheated or . . .

I trace the tattoo inside my wrist: *JGK 02/03*. My little boy, James, was supposed to be born on February third. James would've had his mother's green eyes and he'd be as smart as her. He'd be a gifted musician with many brothers and sisters because AJ always wanted to have a big family. From everything that I've done, my biggest regrets are killing my son, almost killing my girlfriend, and killing our dreams.

"Porter, you made it." Those four trembling words snatch me out of my personal hell and I'm back inside the small room. Craning my neck toward the door, I find him with thin winter-white hair, his thin timeworn face making his brown eyes look bulgy. He's not the sixty-three-year-old man I expected to find. The man in front of me looks more like a ninety-year-old guy taking a step closer to God. Meeting his fate.

"Father," I say, moving the chair closer to him so he can sit down.

"We'll be outside," the officer that walked him to the room announces, closing the door behind him.

"Thank you for coming." His sad, way-worn eyes stare at me. "How are you doing, Porter? I haven't heard any new music from you."

"I stopped, at least for a while." I lightly tap the metal table, trying to find a rhythm, searching for some internal music to take over the deafening void settling inside my chest. This probably wasn't a good idea. That hatred I harbored for him is gone; there's nothing for him. Not a feeling. Is this how James feels about me? Nothing? My lungs collapse and I want to run away from this enclosed space, search for an outlet to calm myself.

"Everything okay, son?" I nod. "You look troubled. I hope it isn't the visit; it was never my intention to open old wounds. But I wanted to . . ." he shrugs. "Leave in peace."

"Leave?"

"Cancer," he says, dropping his gaze toward the table. My hands curl and uncurl unable to stay in one position with the news. His words are like a bullet hitting me straight in my gut. "Stage four colon cancer; make sure you get tested often. They found it late, and it metastasized, it's just a matter of time before I . . . go."

Until today, I haven't given him a lot of thought. Not with all the fucked up shit I did for the past ten years. I barely remember my old life before the accident. At the tender age of four, I lost everything, and now, I have no memories from those years. The images of my mother and siblings are gone forever, I can't remember what she looked like, but I do remember her love. That part is forever ingrained in my heart.

On instinct, I grab his clenched hand, squeezing it lightly. "I'm sorry to hear that."

"No, don't feel sorry for me, boy. I'm ready to leave. There's another life, a better life after this one." He touches his chest. "In my heart, I know God forgives me. Leaving is easy, but leaving without your forgiveness is hard. And I want to make sure you found your way." His lips fight a smile, but they don't stretch far enough.

"I found a way, don't worry about me," I tell him, because there's no place in the world of happiness for people like us. Family is out of reach and second chances are for those who deserve them. Not me. Mac's face appears for a few seconds, but the image vanishes the same way she did.

"Life is good," I assure him.

"Your eyes look lonely." He sets his bony fingers on top of mine. "If you're not happy, it's never too late. Make it a good life, Porter. Live as if every day is the last. Be grateful every morning for the chance to reinvent yourself and every night for what you received—never go to bed with any regrets."

Old memories flash as he speaks. AJ's mesmerizing eyes appear behind my eyelids. The girl gave meaning to my life. My love songs, the meaning of every note and word I'd written. Then her parents and her brothers followed. Regrets . . . I regret losing the only family that I've known. When I open my eyes, the only one I see is my father. Because of him, I lost so much. Yes, people like us, we don't deserve to escape the hell.

"Some don't deserve forgiveness," I say. He flinches. "Though I wish that you find peace."

"Sorry."

"There's nothing to forgive," I say, because he's dying and he doesn't deserve any cruel words. "We're good."

"No. I'm sorry that you live in the same darkness I lived in once." He touches my hand again. "Change, son. As long as there's life, there's hope." My mouth doesn't have a response to what he said. "Try to visit before . . ." I nod, as his strained voice disappears. "Thank you."

He exits the same way he came. Opening old wounds, bad memories splatter all over the floor. I need a fucking smoke. Pushing myself out of the chair, I leave. I'm not sure when I'll be strong enough to come back again. I hope my visit brought him some peace.

TWENTY-TWO

PORTER

MY TRIP TO Alabama left me with a hole in my pocket and my heart. The thirty-six-hour drive cost five hundred dollars for the two stops and meals. Not counting the money, I didn't earn a dime while on the road. The visit with Steve didn't feel like a successful one. Did I fuck up? Should I have said more than I did?

Poor man, he's dying and the last thing he wanted was peace. I could've given him more than I did, yet I refused. Like a total asshole. Maybe it's true; people can't change. As I turn onto North East Holman, I click the remote to open the garage, but slam on the breaks as I spot Harper on her bike. My heart races as I witness the action in front of me and I can't do anything but watch. Everything happens in slow motion; she loses control of the bike and is toppling over Finn who is close by. Fuck. I finally react, throwing the truck into park running toward them.

As I reach them, I hear the screams, the cries laced with pain. Pulling Harper up, I check that she's not hurt, but Finn isn't as lucky. His face is pressed against the concrete, his body under the bike. I hold Harp with one arm while trying to move the metal away from him so I can take him into my arms.

"Finn," I hear Mackenzie's voice before I see her arms reaching for him, pressing him against her.

While she tends to Finn, I check Harper again. "Are you okay?" I ask as she nods. Her lip is quivering and her eyes are filling with tears.

Her small arms reach for my neck and I hold her tight. "Everything is okay, you're safe now." She rests her head on my shoulder and continues crying.

My attention then goes to Mackenzie and Finn; she's looking at his arm, which looks crooked. Her eyes close for a moment while tears fall down her cheeks.

"Is Molly in the house?" I ask her, as she shakes her head. "Give me a few minutes; I have to grab a few things from my room before we leave."

I don't wait for a response, with Harper in my arms, I go to Molly's place, grab some snacks, my iPad, and two pairs of headphones. Then grab the first aid kit from the bathroom, so Mac can clean his face scrapes while I drive. Finally taking Mackenzie's emergency keys from the key holder, I head to the minivan where I settle Harper into her booster seat. Once she's secure, I go back to where Mackenzie is holding Finn.

"Babe, we have to take him to the hospital," I whisper, taking him from her arms and holding him tight to my chest. He's whimpering too, and I wish I could do something to take the pain away. "Sport, don't worry. I'm here and I'm going to take you to the doctor. They're going to set your arm and you'll be good as new in no time."

Holding my hand out to Mackenzie, I help her stand up. "Let's get going, Harp is waiting for us in the car."

A few hours later, after some x-rays, and a cast, we're on our way home. The ride was short and silent. When we arrived, Mac took them to bed. It was time for me to go home, but I wanted to stay the night to make sure they were okay. I didn't know how much I missed them until I turned onto the street and felt anxious to see them. Find out how their week was. I just wanted to see them. But shit, what met me was a nightmare. The fact that I couldn't reach them in time to prevent their accident flipped my stomach and squeezed my heart.

Mackenzie

Not having insurance affected the speed of the emergency room. They didn't deny us, but they certainly weren't in a hurry to help us either. Once our turn came, the doctor sent us to the x-ray department where they confirmed that my little boy had broken his wrist. A clean cut, they only needed to set it and cast it. As I held him during the ordeal, Harper remained glued to Porter.

Porter, the man I missed for an entire week. I worried that I wouldn't see him again because he left without a word, without a goodbye. Six and a half days with this crushing pain of the unknown. Fearing the worst because he hadn't been himself for several days before leaving. After he asked me to give him some time to work through his issues, he disappeared. Seeing him in one piece alleviates the fear, but not the anger. A phone call, a text. Some kind of sign to let me know that he was fine would've been enough.

Shit. I want to slip into his arms and feel them around me. Thank him for standing next to me during an emergency—supporting me. His presence, his steady voice, and occasional caresses anchored me during these past few hours. I have no idea what I'd have done without him.

It's been two long, strenuous years without support, trying to keep my head above water when everything was pulling me to the bottom of the sea. Today, I took refuge under someone's shelter. I borrowed a place to safeguard myself from the storm. A place where I'd like to stay for a few more minutes, days . . . but can I?

"You know, sometimes even the strongest person is allowed to lean on something—or someone," Porter says, opening his arms. Without giving it a thought, my feet move, one in front of the other until I'm nestled into his chest. As his warm, strong arms close the cocoon, I let go of everything that I carry on my back. Tears prickle my eyes, but I hold them together until he speaks again, "I got you, Mac, let it go. Give yourself one night to fall apart, I promise to help you put the pieces back together. For a few moments let me care for you. Allow me to be your rock, if only for one night."

My determination fades and the tears flow freely. He bends his head, his hot breath warming my face as his lips seek mine. The moment they touch; I give into him. It's a slow, gentle, heartwarming kiss that touches each curve of my body, my heart, and my soul. For tonight, the broken-defeated woman is standing in one piece, letting her worries disappear and seeing herself in another dimension with someone that will be there by her side.

TWENTY-THREE

MACKENZIE

"I THOUGHT YOU left us like daddy," Harper's syrupy voice makes my eyes flutter open.

The sunlight slipping through the windows makes me squint as I sit up. Shit, it's the morning already. Pushing myself up from the couch, I walk to where the noise is coming from. My kids sit at the kitchen table eating scrambled eggs with pancakes on the side. Porter faces the stove. By the looks of the stack of pancakes on the counter, I guess he's flipping a few more before he sits to share breakfast with the kids.

"Morning," I say, kissing Harper's little head, then walk to Finn who is holding a piece of bacon in his hand. "How's your arm, baby?" Finn lets out a loud breath and continues eating his bacon.

Porter turns around, holding a plate similar to Harper's; he sets it on the table and pulls the chair out. "Breakfast?"

The short brown strands of his wet hair, combined with those cocoa color eyes remind me of last night. His arms around me, his soft gaze holding mine, and his body cradling me as I let him care for me. All innocent, yet my body heated. I must confess there wasn't anything PG about the places my mind traveled as his scent became one of my favorite aromas.

Pushing away those thoughts, I blurt, "You cook?"

"I can't believe you still doubt me. You're in for a treat. Breakfast is my strongest suit," he confides. "My foster parents believe that's the most important meal of the day. They made sure we always spent the first minutes of the day together while preparing the meal or setting the table."

"You miss them." It's a statement, not a question. Each time he speaks of them, I feel the sadness in his heart.

He shrugs. "Eat."

"I should be at work," I counter, looking down at Finn. Worried that he isn't able to tell me if something hurts or where it hurts.

"I called the flower shop earlier to let them know about Finn," Porter says, taking my hand and guiding me to my seat, pushing the chair in after I sit down. "You went to sleep late and he needs you by his side for a few days." He scratches the back of his head. "A couple of days won't affect you, he needs you."

I look toward Finn, and the moment I'm about to apologize for being such a bitch, I hear Porter's voice. "Yes. Speaking." My eyes move to where he's standing, he's holding his phone over his ear and his brows furrow, his jaw tightening along with his back. "I . . ." He closes his eyes, his shoulders slump and he presses his lips forcefully. "Yes, if that's what he wished. That's the address. Thank you for letting me know."

He shoves the phone back in his pocket, opening his eyes. Regret and sorrow reflect through them.

"Bad news?"

"Later," he answers abruptly. It's not mean, but the warmth of his voice is gone. Harper springs out of her seat and her thin, delicate arms grab on to his waist. Porter hugs her back, looking down at her for a few seconds before he picks her up and holds her against him. "Thank you." The words sound like more than gratitude and appreciation, but I bite back any other questions for later.

"HOW IS HE?" Porter asks as I walk down the stairs. He's sprawled on the couch, holding his guitar.

"Asleep," I answer. "Thank you for staying with him all day."

After breakfast, Finn and Harper remained close to Porter. Finn wouldn't leave Porter's arms. I don't blame him; they're made out of steel and heavenly clouds.

"No worries, he wasn't feeling well." He answers, trying to sound normal but the edge to his voice doesn't change. He's been like that since the phone call he received during breakfast.

"What happened?" I ask, sitting next to him.

"My father. He died yesterday night." Oh, no. I bring the tips of my fingers to my lips, wondering what to say. He's never talked about his father. In fact, I thought he was dead like the rest of his family. His eyes close as his head leans against the couch. My hand reaches for his arm and I squeeze it gently. "This just shows that everyone is right. Once an asshole, always an asshole."

I don't get why he says that, who is the asshole here, him, or his father? "You?" I question, before assuming any further.

"Yes, me." He hands me a wrinkled paper. "I went to visit him three days ago. He needed something from me and I refused to give it to him. You think that after all the shit I've lived through, I'd know that life changes in a blink of an eye."

I hold in the gasp as I read the letter. His father caused the accident where his mother died? My heart bleeds for the poor little boy. "That's where you went, to visit him?"

He nods lightly. "One more regret added to the list," he says with a heavy voice. "He needed one thing before he died. Only one and I was a fucking asshole and denied it to him."

"What else is on your list?"

"The Deckers," he responds. I've no idea who the Deckers are and, instead of asking, I hold his hand and caress it hoping that he'd give me more information. "My foster family loved me unconditionally. They picked me up when I was homeless. Gave me the tools to become a better man and I was an ungrateful son of a bitch that hurt them with what they love the most—their daughter, AJ. Then there's AJ." He rubs his face with both hands, then pulls up his sleeves slightly and stares at his wrists.

"If I could go back and . . ." His head drops.

"Leo and I fought the morning he died," I confess that one thing that no one knows. "Instead of giving him a kiss goodbye, I glared at him for not taking out the fucking trash. It sounds stupid and because of that, I regret not giving him one last kiss because I was stubborn. If I could, I'd go back but I can't."

"Sorry, about that. It must be hard to get over it, when the last time you were with him you were upset at him." He shakes his head, takes a deep breath, and speaks. "No, when I say go back, I meant back to see them. I was warned to stay away from them."

"By them?" He shakes his head. "Then who? By the sounds of it, they're nice people and you always love your children no matter what they do. Take the chance, don't waste time and live with that regret for whatever time you have left."

"It doesn't matter. Plus, I would need money to take the time off," he explains. "The bills for the hospital will arrive soon."

I frown and wonder if he means his father's bills. But before I ask, he pulls me into his arms and I don't fight him. Tonight he needs me just as much as I need him. Using a broken man to hold my shattered pieces isn't smart, but using my brain is the last thing I want to do. Giving myself another hall pass, I snuggle myself in his arms, enjoying the safe haven they provide.

TWENTY-FOUR

PORTER

"I HAVE TO go to bed," Mackenzie says, snuggling closer to my body. "You need to leave." My arms tighten their hold, as if trying to keep her from leaving me.

Yes, going to my room next door is the right thing to do. But tonight, I need her soft curves against my body to wash away my past and patch together my shattered heart. Steven died and what punched me in the chest were the memories of the Deckers. Some years ago, Gabe had an episode and the rumors of his death spread like wildfire during a drought. I flew to Santa Barbara fearing that I lost him. Which I did, that's when the truth of what a fucking asshole I had been came to light.

Facing the consequences included losing the only family I've ever known. Today, Mac and her amazing children are the ones making me stay in one piece. Sober. Because the idea of not being able to say I'm sorry to the Deckers or saying goodbye before my life is over is killing me. What if today was my last day?

I'd want a repeat of Harper's birthday, ending it with Mackenzie tangled with me. Holding her, talking to her, and being close to her makes me whole. Happy. For some fucking reason I want to tell her that if I only have a day left, I'd prefer to spend it with her—Harper and Finn, too. Fantasizing that they're mine to protect and love. In this make believe world we'd make love after a tiring day like today. But I don't know if she's ready for a new relationship. Or if she feels something for me.

Pretending that she belongs to me, is reaching a new level of crazy. I want to offer her everything while I beg her to pretend that she cares for me as much as I do for her. This small beautiful woman crashed into my life reminding me of the good things that have happened to me. She's one of the best things happening now. Real or not, I have her to-night. And like yesterday, I take advantage of our vulnerability and hold her, pretending she's mine. She's the lifeline I have for now, because I refuse to end like Steven. Alone and loveless.

Should we talk about the possibility of something else between us? What should I say? Should I explain the feelings that are bottled up inside me? My heart beats, full of need and desire, for her. She's the only one who can take away everything that's wrong inside me and replace it with goodness. The goodness she radiates to the world.

Lowering my face towards hers, I capture her lips. Slow, gentle as if asking her for permission to allow my mouth to make love to hers. Searching for her soul within her body, that same soul that has crumbled a few times in front of me. The same soul I want to protect for the rest of my life. I try to talk myself into understanding that maybe this might only be for tonight, because tomorrow isn't promised.

"Everything is going to be alright," I blurt out, as I break the kiss. Her eyes shine, her hands hold my face, and she nods her head. Because I need to feel closer to her, I decide to leave. "It's time for me to leave. I'll see you tomorrow."

"Is everything alright?" She asks, confusion written all over her face.

"Yes, it is," I kiss her forehead and leave the place.

EVER SINCE MY father died, things have changed between Mac and me. We live in a different place where we seek each other out. Break-fast, lunch, and dinner are with the kids. At night, we spend time in her living room while I play my guitar. For the first time in years, I celebrated Thanksgiving. Finn is like a little duckling following behind me when I'm around and he loves it when I play for him. He responds to music. Old McDonald is our favorite song. Mac's too, as she can hear Finn mooing and quacking away. I can feel it; the words will come soon.

Pretending that I belong with them is easy. Harper's sassiness has me wrapped around her pinky finger. Finn is my companion and Mac . . . she's the sun fighting the dense clouds and illuminating my days and nights. But is it okay that she has that much power in my life? Does she even have that kind power over my heart? I fear slipping into the cracks, and if it happens, my heart will take a beating. Will I lose myself the same way I did when AJ was no longer mine?

I should stop whatever is going on with us. But instead, I stop analyzing it and head out to work. As predicted, the medical bills arrived. Two thousand dollars for a visit to the ER slashed my savings. It's going to take me a few months to pay the entire amount and then start saving again. Some days, I want to ignore the figurative restraining order imposed by Mason Bradley and head into off-limit territory, or at least make the call. I wouldn't care if he fucks up my face again if it means that AJ would help Finn. But for now, I work hard in the hope that what I make is enough. Christmas is coming up soon and Harper has her eye on a guitar. Finn . . . I'll find something for him, and for Mac, too.

When I cross the driveway from Molly's house to Mac's, I come to a halt. There's a short man holding a box with one arm and knocking on the door with the other.

"May I help you?" I ask, walking closer to him.

"I'm looking for Porter Kendrick," he says, reading the label on top of the box.

"That'll be me," I respond.

He hands me the box and turns his attention to the messenger bag he carries over his shoulder. Pulling out a manila folder, he takes out a few papers then clears his throat. "My name is Ernest Johnson, a lawyer for Butler, Kepler, and Associates. Our offices in Alabama worked a pro-bono case for Steven Kendrick. We're carrying out his last wishes. Those are his ashes."

As he points to the box I hold, my eyes widen. Shit, why is he giving me ashes? "Why me?"

"Mr. Kendrick left his estate to you."

"Estate?" My father was broke. Just like I am.

"Well, it is a technical word. It isn't much money, only his life insurance." He hands me the papers and a pen. "Sign the top paper, the bottom one and the check is yours. Here is my business card if you have any questions for the next step. There's a letter that he left too."

I sign the papers, hand it to him, and look through the other documents that explain what my father left and the check for seventeen thousand dollars.

"Where is the letter?"

"If you read at the bottom, it says that you can't claim it until you do what he asked for." I read through it and there's only one word. Change. With a slight nod, Ernest Johnson leaves me standing in the cold and not knowing what to do with what I'm holding.

AS THE LAWYER walked toward his black sedan, I knocked on Mackenzie's door and unloaded what just happened. She took the shipping box away from my hands and opened it. It's a black urn; thankfully, she didn't open it to verify if there was something inside. "I have no idea what to do with it," I finally say after walking back and forth from the entrance to the dining room several times.

Hell, this is the last thing I expected. Sounds like the beginning of a bad joke. A letter, an insurance policy, and his ashes. I only want the letter. What is it that he has to say?

"I can set the ashes next to Leo's," Mac says, and I don't know what's more disturbing: her serenity regarding the box she now holds, or that her husband's ashes are in my house. Well technically it's her place, but I used to live here.

"Don't they have to be at a cemetery?"

She shrugs, shakes her head, and sets the box on top of the coffee table. "You should use that money to look for your foster parents." She walks toward me, her expression filled with worry. "Sometimes we get an opportunity to write a new story. This might be your chance to find peace with your family."

Mac is right; today should mean something. Tomorrow is another day, but nothing guarantees me that it'll be here. Some of the questions I ask myself every night include what would happen if I looked for them, if I found them. Would Chris let me speak? Gabe might not forgive me. That's my biggest fear, that when I decide to take the step, they'll turn me away and show me to the door.

"This is enough money for you to take time off." She hands me the check.

"I have plans for that already," I confess. "Pay a few bills and for Finn's test."

Mac takes a step back, her eyes stretched wide, and her head shakes. "No, that's my responsibility."

Pulling the sleeve of her blouse, she covers her hand and then lifts it, reaching her mouth. This is the second time I see her chewing on her sleeve. The first was while we waited in the ER. Her shoulders rise and fall, her deep breathing alarming me but I remain quiet. Not waiting for the typhoon inside her head to settle, I lift my hands to cup her beautiful face. Even the simplest contact with her affects me. Every cell of my body vibrates with the surge of electricity that her skin provokes. Mackenzie Brooke is some sort of magician who makes everything fade away. I bend my head to take what I really need before I lose the courage. This time I'm not gentle, I press my lips hard to hers, my tongue begging for access inside her mouth, and as she lets me in, I give her a deep, meaningful kiss. Feasting on her mouth, enjoying her perfume and feeling her beautiful curves with my roaming hands. "Schedule the test; I'll be back later tonight."

"I . . . we should probably stop," she blurts out the words I never wanted to hear. The thump-thump-thump inside my chest slowed so drastically that I can't hear it. "You should look for them, for her."

"Her?" I frown.

"AJ," she whispers. "You still love her."

I laugh hard and loud, replacing the pain that her words caused with the most laughable reason to break up what . . . what we don't have. "The last time I checked, she moved on, she was in love with someone else, happy now with him. AJ was my first love, but I want to think that maybe—"

She points at herself and shakes her head. "Me?" Her shoulder slump, and as she lets out a breath, she lets out the words. "No. Porter, I don't know if I'm there yet."

"I understand, and there's no pressure from me," I tell her, then tilt my head to where the check is. "Still, I want to pay for his test. Think about Finn and his future. Schedule the appointment."

"Porter, can you tell me what happened to you," her words are soft, the demanding tone not so much. "I wish you trust me with that part of yourself."

MACKENZIE

"I LOVED HER so much, but not enough to put her before me." He tells me about his five-year relationship with a girl whom he grew up with. The love of his life. His eyes drift into the past and when he speaks about her, they fill with light, warming the cold night. Two amazing men gave him a home and a family. Suddenly birthdays, holidays and the possibilities of a better life were given to him after he had lost everything. But as the story continues, he describes himself as a low life, a cheater who manipulated his girl. "Not once did I notice what I was doing to her, I'm thankful that she was strong enough to survive my shit. I'm regretful for everything that I put her through. Fuck, she only deserves the best. That was my goal in the beginning but, that fame shit twists you."

Porter continues telling me about his girlfriend being pregnant and him not giving a shit about it. Because he was too high to understand. He pulls up the sleeve of his long sleeve shirt far enough for me to read the initials and a date.

JGK

02/03

"Instead of facing my responsibilities, I lost myself in booze, women, and drugs. Mostly drugs." His voice lowers. My heart slows down, my mind listening to every word that he says. How heartless can someone be to treat a woman that way? The love of his life nonetheless. "When I came out of the haze . . . I received a bunch of messages with pictures and . . . the day I finally went home thinking . . . Honestly, I have no fucking idea what I was thinking; I found her crying, destroyed.

She had lost him. She lost James."

I go back in time to the moment when I found out that Harper was our little-unexpected surprise. Panic rushed through my veins, because we were just about to graduate. Fear that Leo wouldn't take it well, that he'd bail on me. None of that happened.

"A baby?" he questioned. His brows shot down, his eyes narrowed and he scratched the tip of his nose. "That's . . . we're going to have to adjust our plans, won't we?" The engineer in him reacted first. Then the man I loved took over. His smile widens and arms embraced me in a delicate hug, as if I had become some fragile antique that he had to care for. He loved me more and loved Harper from that day forward.

"I was already lost when that happened, but after . . ." He traces the initials a few times before speaking again, "Something inside me snapped, I was already a jerk, but after I became an asshole who didn't give a shit about anyone. Not even her."

I want to touch him, make the pain he's going through go away, but I don't. Because I also want to slap him for being a fucking jerk. The conflicting emotions are eating me. And then there's fear that he's going to close himself off to me, which makes me ask the next question. "That's why you stopped singing?"

He shakes his head.

"No. I continued doing my thing, not caring about anyone. Not even myself. A couple of years later I found out that she was dating. I tried to kill myself fearing that I lost her." I pat him on the back as he takes another deep breath. "My family—her family sent me to rehab. I was on and off drugs for a couple of years until I found myself broke." He chuckles. "Not surprising after I spent all my money on booze and drugs. Desperate, I got myself mixed up with the wrong kind of people that ended up threatening her life, her family's life, and almost got me killed. The last words of one of my foster fathers were: You can't handle fame."

I want to sympathize with him, but how can I feel bad about a selfish man that doesn't give a shit about anyone else but himself. Even his own baby suffered because of him.

"Physically and mentally broken, I was sent to a rehab center where I stayed for two years," he says, rubbing his face with both hands. "It took me a long time to find myself. Later I went to work at a ranch to continue my rehabilitation. Plus, I wasn't ready to be part of society and my counselor agreed with that. Last year I decided it was time to find a new life, whatever that is." He shrugs. "There's no going back in time and fixing the wrongs, but I work daily to stay on track." He pulls up the sleeve of his other arm and there's another set of initials: AJ.

"She believed in me since the day we met," he continues. "I'm not pining for her, but I like to ask myself from time to time what she's doing. Now, I live like any other person figuring out what's next. From having millions, I ended up with only a monthly allowance from the sale of a house I owned. That's how I pay the rent. The rest is covered by my salary."

"That's a lot to take in," I tell him because there's not much I can add since I'm confused about how I should feel.

Rage for the woman who lost so much, or sorrow because this Porter doesn't seem like some asshole that would leave his girlfriend to suffer alone.

"I understand." His deflated voice squeezes my heart. "My shift started an hour ago. Will you give me the chance to continue with this conversation tomorrow?"

I nod, confused by everything, but wanting to continue the conversation. A part of me wants to hug him to make him feel better. The other part of me has a strange desire to punish him for everything. *Drugs destroy.* I'm a living testimony. A junkie like the one he described is to blame for the loss of Leo. Deep down I know that Porter isn't the man that he describes, he's caring, loving.

What am I supposed to do with everything he said? Should I push him out of my life?

TWENTY-FIVE

PORTER

I REST MY head on the door finding the strength inside of me to move. Tomorrow. She's confused and doesn't want to discuss anything more until tomorrow. For a few moments I believed in us, hoped that she'd understand. If she doesn't, should I give up? What if I can change the other part of my life with the Deckers? Can I afford it?

My phone buzzes. It's work, I'm running late. Do I care? I pull out the check I just received from my pocket and wonder how long it will last. It might be a check for extra money, but I have to keep my job. I have two more classes to pay for next semester to finish my degree, it'll be stupid to lose another semester and let more time and money go to waste. Then there are Finn's expenses, the list is never ending.

The money I received from Steven can close one chapter and maybe Mac will be willing to let me be a part of their new chapter. A friend, a companion. Anything. Rushing to the house, I grab my shit for work. I have so much to do—ask for vacation and catch up with classes before finals. If I'm lucky, everything will be fixed soon. Maybe I won't miss Christmas.

It took me almost a week to leave town. The old Durango didn't let me down during the three-hour drive that became a twenty-hour drive. It could drive through a hell of a winter storm, but they closed I-5 for several hours after a pileup that involved almost a hundred cars. Sheltered at one of those motels along the highway, I finished my final project while they re-opened the roads. The long drive is worth everything, each mile I drive, each minute that passes, I close the distance between my past and my present.

I want Mac to see that I *am* a different man than I once was. Making amends with the men that gave me everything matters. I'll stay as long as I need to convince them that I have changed and that maybe they can let me visit them once a year, call them during the holidays, and recover some of what I lost. With any luck, I can do the same with AJ and her brothers. Fuck, am I doing the right thing by driving to Seattle? What if they're in Albany for the holidays?

The first place I stopped by was the old house we used to live in. The compound was empty. The keys, passcodes, and everything to access the property still works, they never changed them, but the house is empty. All the furniture is covered with white sheets. The music studio is empty. I called the house in Santa Barbara and the phone is no longer in service. It took several phone calls to finally find a way to get in touch with them. From the looks of it, my foster parents have made a lot of changes in their lives. Gabe's production company moved to Seattle and is headed by MJ Decker. Chris opened a counseling practice, which is close to his old record company, the latter run by JC Decker.

The counseling office is the one that gave me access to Chris without questioning my motives. Even better, the lady over the phone promised to give me an appointment with Dr. Decker today, even though they're closed for the holidays. I hate that I lied to her by saying I was already an established patient. The beauty of calling centers is that they don't have a database with current clients. When I park in the underground garage of his office, I lean my head on the wheel. This is a mistake. Yes, vindicating myself sounded great after receiving the news that my father died. Live every day as if it was the last, leave this life with zero regrets.

I run a hand through my hair, wondering if I am doing the right thing. Yes, this is what I need to redeem myself. I climb out of the truck, making my way to the elevator. In five minutes, I'll see my foster father for the first time in years. The last time he only said two sentences, "You disappointed me, Porter. We believed in you." I had disappointed him and Gabe and betrayed the entire family. Show them that you've changed, I repeat to myself stepping out of the elevator. Once I reach the offices, I knock on the door, but no one answers. Fuck. I lean against the wall, afraid that he won't come after seeing my name. The elevator doors ding, relaxing my heart and giving me hope until I spot a tall woman stepping out of it.

Our gazes meet for only a few seconds; her violet eyes divert their attention to the phone she pulls out of her purse. For a couple of breaths she stares at it, biting her lip and then she addresses me. "Mr. Kendrick?"

Fuck, why is she here and where's Chris?

She pulls out a set of keys, opens the door and when she looks at me I nod waiting for her to tell me that Chris is on his way. Instead, she says something completely different. "Let me pull your file from the drawer and we can go into my office."

My back straightens and I can't control my voice. "We? I'm here to see Dr. Decker, the woman over the phone said that my consult will be with Dr. Decker." I repeat this a couple of times, sounding stupid, but she has to understand that I have to see Chris.

"I'm Thea Bradley-Decker," she stops me. "The other Dr. Decker."

What the fuck? Bradley-Decker . . . that's a fucked up name. This can't be happening, suddenly my hands press against my head. "No, no, no. I need Chris, not you. Chris Decker. Where is he?"

"My father-in-law is on vacation," she says matter-of-factly. Father-in-law? Who is she married to? It doesn't matter, what matter is that he's not here. No, this is fucked up, they're going to push me away, I just know it. "If you want an appointment with him, you'll have to call again next year."

Shit, of course he's on vacation. Christmas and all that shit are a family thing. Sacred shit that he never misses. Two weeks. Two fucking weeks that I'll have to wait for him. Handing her a card with my information, I ask her to tell both Gabe and Chris that I'm looking for them.

Fucking luck, I'll head back home hoping they call.

TWENTY-SIX

PORTER

JUMP OUT of my skin the moment I open the door to my bedroom and turn on the light.

Fuck. *Fuck.*

Surprise, surprise, it's Mason Bradley. How the hell did he manage to arrive before me? I stumble back.

"Kendrick." He rises from the bed; with three strides, he's towering over me. His penetrating gray eyes are holding my gaze.

My arms and legs become a couple of noodles. Six years ago, a similar situation happened. I came home and three armed men were waiting for me. They knocked me down and I ended up in another country almost dead. Rubbing my face, I take a step back. How the hell did he know where to find me? Did Molly let him in?

My gut churns when I find the determination in his eyes. He's not going to let me do this. Almost six years ago, he warned me to stay away from the Deckers. He'd be easy to ignore, except he's a force not to be taken lightly. He's capable of killing a man without a weapon and making anyone disappear. Scary son of a bitch.

"Mason—"

"Off limits," Mason says. Those gray eyes flash hatred. "We made a fucking deal, Kendrick. Hearing that my little sister shared the same space with you—alone—breaks our agreement."

"Little sister?" I gulp, trying to find a way to calm him. Six years and the fucker hasn't changed. "You have it wrong. I haven't been in contact with anyone. Unless you count that doctor. Yeah, I guess she said she's Chris's daughter-in-law."

"Yes, Thea is my baby sister." He peels his teeth.

Baby sister? Wasn't he an only child? None of that matters. My business is to find some form of forgiveness from my foster parents. The biggest obstacle is right in front of me. Mason Bradley. This is why I tried to get in touch with Chris or Gabe first. The first is the level headed of the family, but Gabe has a soft side to him. I could've talked to either or both and kept everyone away. But no. I had to stumble upon Mason's sister.

Taking another step backward, and knowing I have nothing left to lose, I speak, "My father died. Alone. He left me a small amount of money to start a new life, be a different man. I wanted to start by showing the only family that I've ever had that I'm sorry for what I did. That I've changed."

I skip Mac and the kids. He doesn't need to know about them. His eyes remain fixed on mine, his jaw tensed and his torso pushed forward as if ready to strike.

"And then what?" His clenched hands become a couple of fists.

"I come back to where I live," I answer. "You have parents, a family, and all that shit. What would you do if you made a mistake and you had to stay away from them?" I take a deep breath. "Forever. Wouldn't you at least try to find a way to apologize? Tell them that you love them and you're sorry."

"Kendrick, you can't compare me with you," he says. "Are you aware of what you did?"

"Yes, I'm fucking aware of my behavior," I answer back, frustrated, feeling like a child. But also understanding that I'm bonded by a promise I made to him. One I made after he saved my life. "My addictions ruled my entire life." I touch my temple. "Because of the need I mistreated the woman I loved, put her and my family in danger. I killed my son." Dropping my head, I look at the ink with his initials. "This time I'm not asking for a second chance, only forgiveness."

"You didn't kill him. The way you handled AJ's pregnancy and how you behaved when she told you about it was fucked up. All your actions are unforgivable, but you didn't kill him." His voice softens as my eyes meet his. "James didn't make it for different reasons. With or without you around, the miscarriage would've happened. Stop carrying the guilt."

I narrow my gaze, not understanding why he's telling me this. "Why are you saying that?"

"Because you didn't kill him. Ainse and I carried some of that blame. The two of us believed that if we had done things differently, maybe our kid would be here." His shoulders slump slightly, his eyes closing for a few minutes.

I had forgotten about it. Mason considers James his son. He made it clear years ago. *"I forbid you to ever bring up James' memory, Kendrick."* *He grabbed the flaps of my leather jacket, pulling me close to him. "I have that fucking link. Ainse called me when she found out about the pregnancy and feared the outcome, including how the jerk she lived with would react to his own child. Those days you ignored her while you were fucking other women, I talked to her daily and reassured her that she'd be fine—a kickass mom. You disappeared for weeks. It was me who was there when she met the little pea."* *Frozen, I listened as he screamed while pushing me against the wall. "His heartbeat will forever be recorded here. A beat you'll never know. Who do you think was with her after she lost him? Me, fucker." Sliding one open hand up on my throat, pinching it, pressing hard while closing my air duct. "Never speak of him again. Our pea is off limits, too."*

He said more shit, something about leaving me mute if I ever got close to her or spoke of him. Mason took care of AJ when she lost the baby, while I was getting high and fucking other women.

His eyes open, studying me as he speaks, "My wife, my children, my sister, my father, and my extended family are precious to me, Porter." My lungs deflate with the mention of children. They have kids—more than one. I'm happy that she has a family, but the memory of what I lost mingles with what I desire and will never have. "The Decker family is a big unit. Each one of us has a role. Mine is to protect them. After the shit you pulled, I can't let you get close to them."

"People can change, Mason. I did," I defend myself, taking a step forward as I clear my throat. "If it hadn't been because of you, I'd be dead somewhere in Juarez. The ordeal woke me up. Realizing that the love of my life was in love with someone else crushed me, but every day I wake up with the conviction of being better for our son and for myself." I shrug, as Mac's bright smile comes to mind. Harp, Finn. "I'm a recovering alcoholic and addict. It means that every morning I have to fight my demons. Like Chris and many others. All I ask is to be able to talk to my foster parents. My goal is to make a new life, not sure where or how, but the first step is finding peace with them."

He takes a deep breath, looking at the ceiling. "Let me think about it." He shakes his head. "I don't trust you. You can say all you want, but to get to them, you'll have to convince me first."

"I'll talk to them while you're in the same room," I blurt out without giving it a thought.

"Chris and Gabe are out of town."

I bob my head, understanding. "Albany? You aren't going?"

"No. They'll be home before Christmas. A lot has changed since you've been gone." He angles his face, crossing his arms and shaking his head. "It's time for me to leave. I'll talk to them, but for now, stay away."

He heads out of the room and I follow behind him.

"Porter, is that you?" I hear Molly's voice the moment he wiggles the handle of the front door. "With company. The nice kind of company." She scrunches her hair with both hands as she sways her round hips closing in on us. "Molly Thomas."

"Nice meeting you, ma'am," he answers, shaking her hand. "We'll be in touch."

He disappears without a word. Impressive.

"Mac is leaving soon for Pollard Farms." I frown, not understanding what she means. "That's where families go to cut their Christmas tree. Her boss gave her a coupon for a small tree. The kids are excited and hoping you'd join."

It's been so long since I celebrated Christmas. I only remember doing it when I live with the Decker family. We had plenty of evergreens in the compound and every year we decorated one. Cutting them wasn't an option, as they didn't like to chop them down. Those traditions that I followed for a few years meant so much. Checking that I have everything to head out again, I kiss Molly's cheek and leave.

TWENTY-SEVEN

MACKENZIE

EAVING THE HOUSE this afternoon was harder than usual. Finn has been parked on the couch where he usually sits with Porter to sing. Things are worse than before and I have no idea what to do with all of it. Does he have depression? At least the idea of Christmas presents—that I haven't bought because there's no money for that—made him move. I appreciate Harper for such a brilliant idea. *"If we don't have a tree, Santa won't come and bring us presents."*

Finn's new attitude frustrates me. No matter what I say or do, he refuses to interact with me, or others. After making sure that they're wearing their winter gear, we leave the house. Pushing the car key remote, the back doors slide automatically.

"I can drive." The voice shakes me. Wasn't he gone? Porter disappeared the night after he told me everything that had happened to him. The ugly stuff he had done. Without a word, not even a goodbye. The fear that he wouldn't come back lingered around the house. He had become a part of us. Looking at my two kids who are gasping at me, I realize that neither one knows how to react to him. His disappearance without a warning hurt us all. "In fact, we can move the car seats to my truck. The tree will fit better in the bed."

My eyes remain fixated on my children, waiting for an explanation of why he left without a word. Afraid that what I've been feeling for the past couple of days is bigger than I anticipated. I care for Porter. More than I want to admit. The feelings are deeper than a simple friendship with the next-door neighbor. I have my doubts, because I never thought that I'd feel anything for anyone other than my late husband.

"Mac, you need help cutting the tree," he says. "What if Finn tries to escape?"

The sensible thing to do is accept his help, but should that be before or after he explains where he's been. Does he have to? No, we're friends. Neighbors. But I've been fucking worried about him. Staying up all night wondering where he is and if he's all right. A call would've taken care of the worry. But I don't say anything, he's busy taking the seats out my van and setting them in his truck. Harper, who is holding my hand, steps closer to me and squeezes it harder when Porter finishes and walks toward us.

"Harp?" Porter's cautious question matches his steps.

"You left," she sniffs. "I saw your truck from the window the other night. You promised."

He scratches his two-day old stubble, then squats in front of her and smiles. "I went to see my parents. But I came back before Christmas to spend the holiday with you. We're baking cookies for Santa, aren't we?"

She nods, chewing on her lip. Porter opens his arms and she releases my hand walking to him and hugging him tightly.

"Next time I have to go, I promise to say goodbye," he assures her, as he rises from the floor carrying her.

He walks with her to the truck and then comes back for Finn who just mimics his sister's big hug. Nothing else needs to be said between the two of them. My children adore him.

"Mac." His voice snaps me from the internal debate about him. The moment he's in front of me, he tilts my chin slightly with his thumb. "I'm sorry I didn't tell you about my trip. It's a long explanation; we can talk about everything later tonight. After the kids are tucked in, please?"

I press my lips tight together, not knowing what to say.

"Maybe I should do this alone with them." Not the words I meant to say, but they're out.

"It's a tree, Mac. Please, don't make a big deal."

But it is a big deal. This is the first year I've decided to trim a tree since Leo's death. Evergreens remind me of so many things. We married in Vail, during Memorial Day weekend on a breezy, sunny afternoon surrounded by pines. Holding in the tears is easier these days and what upsets me is that Porter's presence makes me stronger—immune to the memories. Is that wrong? Everything is new to me, what I'm feeling, what I want . . . but . . .

"Mom, it's getting late," Harper yells from the car.

I pull up my scarf, covering my mouth and using my children to give me strength to keep my distance. Giving me the power to avoid my new weakness—Porter's touch.

HARPER, FINN, AND Porter drink hot cocoa by the Christmas tree we decorated earlier as he reads them Olive the Other Reindeer. This strange man always finds a way to wiggle himself inside the family. Yesterday he came with us to find the perfect tree. After we cut it, paid for it, and realized we didn't have any ornaments, he took us for dinner and then to buy the necessary trimmings to adorn our tree. When we arrived home, he helped me carry Harper, who was fast asleep. We didn't have much time to talk since he fell asleep on my couch while I was in the kitchen preparing some coffee. Instead of waking him up, I covered him with a blanket and let him sleep for the night.

Earlier, after I came back from work, he offered to help decorate the tree. Since tomorrow is Christmas Eve, I couldn't say no. Molly came to help, too. When I asked them if I could head to the store, Porter showed me the garage. He bought the kids several presents and he finished the headboard for Finn.

"And that's all for the night," He says closing the book.

"Are you helping mommy tuck us in?"

"Am I?" He arches an eyebrow, as he's rising from the floor with Finn nestled in his arms. "Maybe I'll just give you both a ride to your room."

Harper's head drops, her chin hitting her torso twice. "Can you help me?" I ask, not sure if it's for Harper, or for myself. Every night is harder for us to see him go, even those times we know he's heading to work. "But only if you have time? It'll be faster if you help us."

And, in record time, the two Brooke children have brushed their teeth, put on their pajamas, and said their prayers. We tuck them in and, when the door closes, I regret inviting Porter to stay. The need of him hasn't subsided and I doubt it'll go away. It might if I ignore him and stay away, but my children adore him. They come first, and apparently, the dad duties are easy for him to handle. Would he have been like that with his son if he hadn't died?

"How was your visit?" I ask him about his trip. I'm curious about his foster parent's reaction, but also about AJ—if things can be fixed. That must be something he wants, I mean the man has her initials tattooed on his wrist. My heart slows its beating with the thought of the possibility. Selfishly I'm hoping that she won't take him back. "Did it work out?"

"They weren't there," Porter says, marching down the stairs. "My foster parents are out of town. It was frustrating. The drive, the crappy hotel, everything was against this trip. I swear." I glare at him not understanding what he's trying to say.

He explains about the pile-up on I-5. Then continues with him at a hotel with poor Internet connection where he had to finish some project. There wasn't a pause to ask what the project was about because he continues with the frustration of meeting their daughter-in-law. Their family is growing and he's not a part of it.

"For the past week I've discovered that they transformed their old life into something different, something new that I have no idea about." Porter taps his chest lightly with his fingers, his eyes set on the wall. "I thought I found them and suddenly they were out of reach once again."

"Will you be able to talk to them?"

His signature shrug appears. "Mason was here yesterday," he mumbles. "That's AJ's husband. First he warned me to stay away, but then." He runs both hands through his hair. "He's going to talk to them. I'm hopeful for the chance to at least get the closure I need."

"Things with AJ?" I ask. Porter tilts his head, crooning an eyebrow. "Are you two going to fix things?"

"If her *husband* allows it, I'll get to apologize to her." He frowns and smirks. "You mean can I fix my old relationship with her? Are you jealous, Mac?"

I shrug, because it'd be stupid to deny it, but even more to accept it.

"There's nothing to fix. She was once someone important. My first love. But we grew up, things changed, and even though there's a special place for her in my heart, I moved on." He shakes his head. "You're not ready to hear more, but I hope someday we can discuss it further. Or not. I just want to ask you that you let me be part of your life in any kind of capacity. Your kids mean the world to me and I'd hate to lose them." He kisses my cheek. "Thank you for letting me spend these two days with you. It's been a long time since I've been a part of a family or celebrated . . ." He turns around, shakes his head, and spins one more time.

"You mean everything to me." With those last words he disappears behind the door leaving me flustered, wanting him to repeat it, or say more. Much more.

Does he also mean everything to me? I wish someone could come and tell me what to do next.

TWENTY-EIGHT

CHRIS

"I THINK YOU were right, College Boy," I admit, as we step inside the house and look at all the packages we've been mailing to the house for the past three weeks. "We might have overdone it this time."

"You doubted me?" He laughs, taking the bags I carry and setting them down before he takes me into his arms. "The credit card receipts never lie. I'm surprised you didn't buy the pony for Gracie."

We decided to take a few weeks off without our children, Gabe's parents, or my favorite—our grandchildren. Added to that down time was Christmas shopping for the entire family. When it came to our five little ones, we bought more than one thing for each. I even considered buying them pets. That's when the idea of the pony came, as AJ always asked for one and we never bought it for her.

"Would you have let me buy a living creature?"

"Probably not." He kisses my neck. "We'd need to move back to the compound and everyone has settled here in Seattle—where you said you'd move your entire life after you were done with Dreadful Souls."

"Told you you'd like the place and dig the music," I whisper remembering what it was like to move into a new city. Even when I liked the new scene, I missed my old routine and the only one who kept me going until I found my footing was Gabe. "We can fix this shit later, let's go to bed."

"We have to wrap some of them," he mumbles, gliding his arms up and down my back, as bodies rub against each other.

"Oh for fucks sake." I hear Matt's voice and my dick goes flat right away. "You were alone with each other for three fucking weeks and you still have to come home and . . . Fuck?"

"What do you need, Mattie?" My question sounds like a grumble. Gabe and I release each other and when I look toward the backyard door, I find my four sons standing next to it. "Does anyone know the concept of knocking on the fucking door? Using the phone, the intercom, or at least yell that you're coming in as you slide the glass door open."

Gabe rubs his face with one hand, shaking his head. "The four of you coming over with long faces and Matt trying to lighten up the mood isn't helping. What happened?"

"Porter," Mason announces, breaking the formation they have and marching toward us. He hands me one of those folders he prepares once he has run a background check on someone. "Kendrick tried to get in touch with you a couple of days ago."

"He made an appointment with Dr. Decker," Matthew takes over. "Guess which Dr. Decker went to help him, Pops." My eyes widen, remembering everything that happened to AJ, including the time that I had to run to her house when the sirens began to sound and the lights from the ambulance, fire truck and police cars came through the windows.

"Is Thea okay?" Gabe remains calm, grasping my free hand. Tristan and Matt nod.

"After Thea explained what happened, I set up a team to investigate his life since he left the ranch where he worked at. We've been running surveillance on him from that moment and we're stopping later today. I flew down to Portland—that's where he lives," Mason continues, pointing at the folder he gave me. "That's his life for the past few years in a nutshell. He wants to speak to the two of you."

Gabe covers his forehead and eyes with his left hand, squeezing my hand with his right. He's been worried about Porter. No, we both have been. Yes, he put our daughter through a fucking lot, but not knowing if he's fine is putting us though a different kind of hell. We love our children and wish the best for all of them. The moment we took him under our care, we decided that he'd be part of us, of our family. Our fourth child.

"If you want to give him a chance, it is up to you," Mason says. "AJ and I respect your decision and ask you to respect our decision that for now, we don't want anything to do with him. That's all I have to say. Only know that I won't let him hurt the family."

Jacob and Matthew look at each other, shake their heads, and shrug. They've discussed something within seconds and came to a conclusion and I wonder what it's about.

Tristan clears his throat and Matt nods at him. "The same goes for us. I haven't met him, but he doesn't sound like someone I'd like to have around my family."

"As your children, AJ, Matt, and I think that you have to talk to him," Jacob speaks and I'm fucking confused. Because Mason said something that sounded different. "He was family and deserves to be heard. Now, in regards to my little fam, I don't want him close to the wife or the twins. I know it's a shitty position we're putting you in, but we hope you understand."

Gabe removes his hand from his eyes, his blue eyes open wide and lets out a breath. "We hear you, we respect you and I'm glad you understand that this is a decision that only concerns us. Porter . . . is he clean, Mason?"

"Yes. Read the report I prepared." Mason looks around and shakes his head. "Do you need help opening the packages?"

"What do you think, babe?" Gabe asks, masking the feelings that the news of Porter's return is causing him. "Should we put them to work?"

I nod, because he needs to gather some strength and talk this out. Also, tomorrow his family arrives and we need the physical space to let everyone walk freely around the house. "Yes, find me wrapping paper, boys. We have tons to do before the Colthurst clan arrives."

"Decorating shit is Thea's department," Mason tells Matt and Tristan. "She should coordinate it. I'm going home."

"Us," Tristan corrects him. "She'll coordinate us. I doubt your sister is going to let you go without making you a part of the project.

Knowing my bossy wife, she's going to include your father too. Let's gather the troops and come back soon."

The four leave from where they came from and I'm guessing we only have a few minutes before the entire family is here to help.

"What are we going to do, babe?" Gabe asks as Matthew closes the back door. "I'm still fucking mad at him, Chris. The shit he did. But . . ."

The but is what has us both thinking. If any of our children had done the same, we'd open the door for them the moment they came back to say sorry. Should that be the same with Porter? Or not, since he isn't our biological son. No matter what we decide to do we have to set our anger and worry aside. Think of what's best for all our kids.

"We are going to do absolutely nothing, Gabe." I set the folder on the coffee table. "For tonight, we're going to set Porter and what our children think aside. We have to fix what you did, you let me buy a lot of shit, and now we have to wrap *everything*."

"My fault?" His body shakes with laughter. "Fuck, I love you, crazy old man. Text the children to come by in a half hour. I need you to take care of me."

> Pops: *Do not come by for the next thirty minutes. Make sure to bring the grandkids when you come, though. Gabe needs a lot of family love.*

"DOC, I WANT your professional opinion," I say to Thea, as we head to the kitchen to start dinner.

She shakes her head. "About?" I believe she's stalling, and assume that it's because she knows the story about Porter and AJ. My girls are like sisters and they look out for each other.

"Porter."

"From whose perspective?" She ties her loose hair up into a bun and lets out a breath. "Your daughter-in-law, Matt's wife, AJ's sister, Mason's sister, or an outsider? Because from every angle, it looks different."

"You saw him, can you tell me about your exchange, your impression about him?"

"He was agitated because you weren't there," she explains, heading to the refrigerator. "He's definitely clean. That was Mase's first question. If he was sober. The answer is yes. Anxious. Lost." She turns around holding a basket filled with veggies. Man, how does she do that? Bring over all that healthy shit from her garden. I point at the basket and she gives me that sweet smile of hers. "Brought it earlier from the greenhouse. You got to eat healthy, Pops."

"Give me your honest opinion, Thea. Not as AJ's sister, Mason's sister or Matt's wife. As a doctor." I walk towards her, grab the basket, and look her in the eyes. "The same way we consult about other patients."

She rolls her eyes. "Family aside, I've been thinking about him after AJ and Matt told me every little detail. Taking into consideration that it's been a few years since he got clean and his father dying—"

I take a step back, what the hell? "Steven died?" Thea nods. "When?" Fuck, I should've read that fucking file.

"Not long ago. According to jail records, Porter saw him only days before it happened. Colon cancer, stage four. That must have triggered a need to look for his family." She lifts her shoulders and drops them slowly. "You're the only ones he has left. Unless you don't see him as family anymore."

"He's like a son to us." She nods and continues listening. "When we found him, I wanted to protect that kid, give him a better life. Make sure he wouldn't end up like me. But he did."

My sweet daughter-in-law gives me a hug and a kiss. "As a doctor, I'd recommend that you reconnect with your kid, find out what he needs. Maybe offer him that family support so he can stay on the right track."

Before I can do that, I have to talk to Gabe. Discuss what he wants and what we are able to offer. The guys came over earlier to say that they support us, but to keep Porter away from them. I'd have to split myself in half in order to accomplish both. Support Porter while making sure he's far from my family. That's not really offering him a family, is it? The answer to my next question should come from someone that suffers the same disease that Porter and I do. A person who is always sweet and understanding.

"As my daughter-in-law?"

She looks toward the kitchen door and smiles. "I'll support you, because I've been where he is. Having the Decker bunch behind you is a blessing I wish many could have."

"Do you think they'll understand?" I tilt my head as if pointing at the rest of the family.

"I think so. They are as loving as their fathers. But take the first step, Pops. When you have a plan, I'll be here for you." She then heads to the freezer and takes out some meat. Thank God she's going to feed me meat. "Leave the cooking to me, why don't you head back and have some quality time with Piper. She misses Papa Chris."

"I can't believe you ruined my trend, Abuelo sounded better." She rolls her eyes and her attention is now focused on whatever she's planning on cooking.

Thea is right. I have to take the first steps. That includes discussing with Gabe what we want to do. That might not happen soon, but perhaps we can look into this in the coming year.

TWENTY-NINE

PORTER

MACKENZIE STARES AT the tree, her head shaking, and tears streaming. Fuck, I really thought that I was helping. Everything I planned ended up being a big fiasco. With my thumb I clear a few of those tears.

"It's . . . I, you," she finally speaks. "Why did you do it?"

I shrug, rubbing the back of my head and wondering what I'd do with all the shit I bought if she doesn't want it. Each item is from the letters that Harper wrote to Santa. One from her and the other one from Finn. I skipped the new house and bringing her father back. If I could, I'd bring him back for her and the entire family. I'd give Mac and the kids everything they wanted just to see them smile. These days, their joy is the fuel powering my life. Yes, every present I bought was a selfish act, because seeing them happy makes me happy.

So I'm honest with her. "Because I could, and I knew that if I did it, they'd be happy. I wanted to see you smile. I fucking love to hear your laughter, watch you shine when your lips stretch into a smile because it's a good day for them—and for you. I love . . ."

Her eyes shine with the moisture, revealing fear, doubt, but a sliver of more. Love. Maybe I'm not in this alone.

"Porter, I . . ."

"Mac," I whisper her name, our lips almost touching. "I think I'm in love with you." She shakes her head. "Yes. I'm pretty sure between you knocking on the wrong door months ago, and everything we've lived through."

Not letting her think any further, I do the only thing I can think of that'll stop both of us from discussing my confession. Our gaze locks, my breathing becomes labored—heated as I lean down—crashing my lips against hers. As she releases a surprised gasp, her mouth opens, letting my tongue inside. Her hands reach for the back of my head; her fingers entwining through my hair tugging me closer to her. I rest my hands tightly around her back.

Our kiss deepens; fire is traveling through my veins. Our hands release their original hold and begin to glide up and down. Exploring, searching as our bodies fit against each other. I want more; I need more. But suddenly she stops, my arms reaching for her before she vanishes.

"Porter," she whispers my name between pants. My lips travel over her the hollow of her neck, enjoying the feel of her. Enjoying her scent. "Wait a moment . . . We have to talk."

I loosen my hold; open my mouth, but my phone rings. Unknown number. Taking the call would be rude, but it's also an excuse to think about what to say to her before she sets some kind of emotional restraining order after groping her.

"Kendrick," I answer.

"Porter, it's Chris." I hear Chris Decker's voice on the other side and I shut my eyes. Fuck. He called me. The child in me wants to cry the same way he did when he realized he had lost his mother and siblings, because with the fucking shitty luck I carry, I've no doubt that Chris will tell me to go fuck myself. "Are you there, kid?"

I nod, but remain silent because that's the only way I can hold back the inevitable tears. Fuck, what I would give for a joint, a drink, something to numb every emotion that's swirling inside my head. The memories are also resurfacing. Everything I swallowed since the first time I started was to forget my actions or my emotions. Evading the consequences of what I did, or how I acted, or the past. Remembering hurts, but among those memories I find my reason to stay afloat.

"Yes, I didn't think you'd call so soon," I confess.

"There's nothing like the present, Porter," he says with that soft voice of his. "What's been going on for the past few years?"

"Not much. There was rehab," I sigh. "Sorry for the cost, I should've worked harder—faster?"

"No need to be sorry. I'm glad you worked at your own pace . . . are you still clean?"

"Yes, some days are hard, so fucking hard," I bite my tongue because sounding weak when I'm trying to show him that I'm okay is stupid.

"I can imagine," he says. "Sorry about Steven, I just learned he passed away. This must be a hard time for you."

"Maybe."

"Are you spending Christmas alone?"

"No, I think I'm going to be at a friends'," I say, hopeful that Mac won't reject me after all I said. Or even better yet, she'll want me.

"I'm glad that you have someone to be with, Porter." A loud breath comes from the other side of the line. "Okay, kid, we don't want to assume. Why don't you tell me why are you looking for us?"

"To apologize, to reconnect, to . . ." I pause, making sure that all my thoughts are in order before I continue. Opening my eyes, I see Mac right in front of me. The compassion in her eyes, along with the spark she had earlier. She comes closer and takes me in her arms. Her hold is tight, as if giving me strength when I need it most. I hold her with one hand, leaning my chin on top of her head. "Recover my family, Chris. My parents. Look, I know I fucked up badly and I can't expect you to open the doors of your house. But days like today, I'd like knowing I can call you to wish you a Merry Christmas or a happy birthday. Knowing that things with you and Gabe are okay will make it easier for me to continue."

"A lot of things happened, Porter. I'll discuss this with Gabe."

"Please, at least let me apologize in person," I plead.

"We'll see. Now I want to congratulate you. I learned that you're about to finish your degree, we're proud of you." There's an air of satisfaction in those words. That word, proud, makes my entire body zing with joy. "Tell me about your music, do you have anything new?"

"I compose, but just for me."

"That's good to know you didn't abandon it. You're talented, Porter. Keep creating the good shit." He pauses and I hear voices behind him. Loud voices. "Look, I have to hang up. It's time to play Santa and there are too many Colthurst and Deckers to deliver to."

"Thank you for calling, Chris, Merry Christmas."

"Merry Christmas, Porter. I'll call you early next year."

And as I hang up the phone, I let myself cry holding onto Mac. Thankful that he called me; that if anything happens to me tonight, I know he doesn't hate me. Hopeful, that perhaps, they'll let me be part of their lives. Not like they did before, but anything is better than all these years without them. This hope erases the need to hide myself behind drugs and stay stone cold sober.

"He called you," she whispers, her head resting on my chest. "I'm so happy for you. It's like a Christmas miracle."

"No. You're my miracle." I hug her tight.

We hold each other for several minutes and, as she starts to wiggle, I use the little courage the phone call injected to ask, "What did you want to talk about?"

"You, me."

"What a great opening." I kiss her forehead. "You and me. The possibilities are endless."

"Porter, I don't know how to feel." She starts, "Confusion is the main emotion every time I think of you—of us. Leo is the only man I've been with; the one I swore to love for the rest of my life. It doesn't . . . I shouldn't . . ." She closes her eyes.

"I can't tell you how to feel about him, or me. The only thing I can do is offer you my love and wait for you to find the answer—"

"Mommy," Harper calls out, just as I was about to take another taste of her lips. "Santa won't come if you are downstairs."

"Shit, she's going to come down," Mac says, glaring at the stairs, then back at the presents.

"Good night, Mac, go upstairs. I'll make sure to lock up on my way out."

"I wish you could stay," she mumbles, and my heart stops with those five words.

"Maybe someday, Mac," I say, once I see the door of the kids' room close.

Someday.

THIRTY

MACKENZIE

"HOW MANY DAYS before they go back to school?" Aunt Molly asks as we watch Harper, Finn, and Porter play with their guitars.

"They'll learn soon," Porter explains. Porter and Finn look adorable sitting side by side, scratching the guitar cords. Yesterday after they opened the only present Porter gave them—as Porter, they refused to put them down. A guitar for each of them. Both guitars are the perfect size for their age.

"On the second," I remind her. "You'll be gone by then."

"That's why I'm getting my fill of eye candy." She smirks ogling Porter. "There's nothing between the two of you, right? If something happens while I'm gone, text me. Because if that's the case, I'll bring myself a man home."

I groan, squeezing my eyes shut to erase the mental picture of my aunt with some Latin hottie. She leaves for Costa Rica on the thirtieth for a couple of weeks with her friend Rhonda. Mom and Dad invited me to visit them in Florida for New Year's Day. They offered to pay for the plane tickets, but I can't afford the hotel. Leo's mom, who I barely talk to, invited us to Charlotte to spend the holidays. She hasn't seen the kids since the funeral. As much as I'd love to visit her, I can't afford the trip. The plane tickets are expensive and driving is out of the question. Driving across the country with two little ones during winter would be insane.

As for things with Porter . . . there are kisses. Sweet, passionate kisses when no one is watching. Deep stares where I know he's professing his love for me, while my soul trembles, uncertain of what to answer.

It's been almost three years since Leo left, but is it too early to move on? I'm a mother, is it okay for me to do it? There's no manual on it and Google isn't helping at all. Some forums tell me that I should've started dating after a few months, while others say that I am better off alone. My heart is terrified to make a decision. Porter is handsome, smart, sweet, and caring. Any woman would be lucky to have him. He'd be better off with a single woman without the amount of baggage that I carry.

A tap snaps my train of thought. Porter's eyes meet mine and a gasp escapes my throat as he smirks. I'm fucked.

"Time for them to head to bed," he says, tilting his chin toward the wall clock.

"But it's too early," Harper complains for the third time.

"If you want to go sledding tomorrow . . . ," I remind her.

She places her guitar on its base and jumps off of the couch as if it's on fire, running up the stairs. "Finn, hurry up. We're going to get to use our new sleds."

"You are spoiling them, Porter Kendrick," I accuse, but smile at him as he helps me out of my seat.

"Are you going to punish me for that?" He wiggles his eyebrows.

"We're ready," Harper yells from the top of the stairs.

PORTER

"I HEARD MY aunt is planning on replacing you for some Costa Rican hottie." Mac snuggles closer to me. We're watching Never End Seven. The worst Never End movie made in the history of the franchise. What the hell was Gabe thinking? He plays Joe Quinton, the main character of the series. Like Gabe, Joe isn't as young as he used to be and I don't buy for one second that he can jump out a building without a scratch. "Are you okay with that?"

"Your aunt is something else," I laugh with her. "Of course, I'm going to miss her, she boosts my self-esteem on a daily basis, but I'll survive a few weeks without her. Have you talked to your boss?"

"Yes, she's thinking about it." Her voice tone lowers and so does her happiness. "I think she wants someone younger, thinner, and prettier for the position."

"Twenty-eight is young, you're beautiful, and I love your body." I bring her closer to me, fitting her curves to my body. "She'll give you the position, Mac. Maybe with that new gig you can go back to school. Find your passion."

"I love plants." Her voice deflates. "Nature. The farm is never going to happen, is it?"

"Afraid not, babe, but you'll find something better," I assure her, taking her lips.

She doesn't want to look deeper into our relationship, but she hasn't stopped me from kissing her whenever I want. As long as the kids aren't around. She doesn't want them to get the wrong idea. At least not until she can work through her internal conflict. The sweet throaty moan she makes when my hands make contact with her bare skin turns me on. As my hand trails towards her torso, the doorbell rings.

Fuck, damn it.

Kissing her one more time, I rise from the couch and fix my jeans. "I'll get it. It might be your aunt reminding me that we don't have much time left together."

On the other side of the door, there's an older woman. Light brown hair, wearing glasses, a winter jacket that covers her entire body and a scowl.

"Evening, can I help you?" I stare at the luggage she carries.

"Mackenzie Brooke," she snarls. "I'm looking for my daughter-in-law."

"Virginia?" Mac's shrilly voice scares the shit out of me. "What? Why are you here?"

Virginia pushes me aside and enters the house without giving me a second glance. She sets her luggage on the floor and looks around. I follow her eyes and make a few notes because it's time to paint the walls and maybe buy some toy boxes for the new stuff that Santa brought.

"New furniture?" She straightens her back. "I thought you said you didn't have any money."

The furniture isn't new. Fuck. AJ and I bought the shit years ago. I was what? Twenty-one? She was right, this shit was going to last. Twelve years and it's still looking classy and pristine.

"The furniture came with the house," Mac defends herself. "It's his furniture; we're just borrowing it while we find a place to stay."

"Leo worked hard to give you a home." The lady ignores Mac. "You threw everything away and came . . ." she scrunches her nose, "here."

"Sorry to interrupt, but the kids are already asleep and it's midnight." I point at the wall clock. "If you want, I can drive you to your hotel and you can visit tomorrow."

"Hotel?" She glances at me from head to toe. "Who are you?"

"Porter Kendrick," I extend a hand, which she barely shakes.

"Well, I'm staying here, not in a hotel," she huffs. "I'm family. You shouldn't be here. Are you bringing men into your house, Mackenzie?"

I take the bag, open the door, and tilt my head toward the exit. "You can stay with us, next door. Molly will be happy to show you to the guest room. Mackenzie and the children don't have space for visitors."

Gently I take her by the elbow and guide her to my room, where I change the bed sheets while she freshens herself. Taking my shit out of the room, I decide to stay on the couch. Tomorrow is going to be hell if that woman doesn't change her attitude.

What a bitch!

THIRTY-ONE

MACKENZIE

"WHAT DO YOU mean he doesn't talk?" Virginia's shriek makes me jump out of my body, while Finn runs towards Porter's arms.

Thank you, Harper, for bringing your grandmother up to date on what she's been missing.

The entire morning, this woman has been criticizing me about everything. From what I wear, to the house I live in and how I dress my children. Reminding me how great I had it while I was with Leo. How Leo would die all over again if he saw the conditions I lived under, the way I am treating my children.

"Can we go now?" Harper's pouts. "Porter promised."

"Mac, I'll go next door, get them ready, you don't have to come," he assures me. "I think it's best for everyone."

Virginia's scowl intensifies and I nod. My kids don't need to listen to their adorable grandma's rants. Maybe after they leave the house I can defend myself, because she's starting to cross the line. Where the hell is Molly when I need her snarky comments? Buying swimsuits for her trip.

"You're not coming, Mommy?" Harper pulls my arm.

"No, grandma needs some company, sweetheart," I explain, bending down and kissing her forehead. "Be nice to Porter."

Finn waves at me from the door and Harper skips toward them.

They disappear within seconds and the door shuts right behind.

"That man has tattoos," she sneers, stating the obvious. "What are you thinking, Mackenzie?"

"I'll tell you." She walks around the living room and stops in front of me. "You're not thinking at all about your children, or the consequences that being involved with a man like that will bring. What happened to the marriage vows you made to my son? A married woman doesn't behave the way you're acting. My son is dead and you're behaving like a slut in front of your children! Is that what you want to teach Harper?

"He bought you a house with his hard work and you sold it like it meant nothing to you. My son loved you since you two were children and you've already forgotten about him. I don't think you're a fit mother, Mackenzie." She pulls out her phone. "I'm going to send a message to my lawyer. You're putting the children in danger. What did you do to Finn? He used to talk. You must have done something bad to him. That's why he's like that, he's scared of you."

"Please, don't!" A sob catches in my throat. I'm trying to be strong, ignore her rant. But my kids. "I love them. How dare you tell me that I caused Finn's issues! We don't know what's wrong with him. I'm trying to do what's best for them; you can't take them away from me. They're all I have left."

There's a lump of tears in my throat and I push them down because crying won't fix anything.

"If you loved them, you would stop flirting with that man. If you loved my son, you wouldn't be considering spending his birthday with another man." She lowers her tone. "No one can replace my Leo. That man less than anyone, look at him, Mackenzie. Wake up and stop thinking with what's between your legs. Your children come first; Leo comes first. There's no place for anyone else."

"Out," I hear the door slam shut and find Aunt Molly approaching us. "Pick up your shit and get out of my house. You're not allowed to yell at my niece."

"I have this," I cut off my aunt, but she shakes her head.

"Go back to your place, I'll handle Virginia," she orders and I don't fight her, because every word that Virginia said is starting to make sense.

I need home, I need my bed. I need Porter. No. I should need Leo.

MOLLY IS A godsend, my savior and so much more. I want to kiss her feet for being such a great support system. In the morning she came over to my house making sure that I dragged my ass out of bed, that I ate some breakfast before heading to work and that I remembered the good things.

Like my first attempt at baking a cake. I learned an important lesson, when the recipe calls for baking powder, you don't replace it with baking soda. Still, Leo ate the chewy cake with droopy frosting, and said that he loved his birthday. Each year I became better at baking and a couple of years ago I even decorated it with fondant. Because every December twenty-seventh I made sure that we celebrated his day with love, and a cake baked by me.

The entire holiday season had been a family affair. The chilly weather invited us to stay at home with the kids. Movies, hot cocoa, family games and love. Always love. We went all out when it came time to decorate for the holidays. I let out a big breath, remembering the big inflatables that we set outside the house. A black cat with a witch hat and a friendly ghost for Halloween. A turkey during Thanksgiving and for Christmas we had our snow globe. Each year Leo would design a fancy twinkling light setup and synchronized it with music. The engineer had a soft side for the holidays and he planned and executed everything perfectly.

As Virginia pointed out, I settled for a sad tree and nothing outside of the ordinary like Leo would do. No, not this year, or the next or . . . Holidays will never ever be the same. There won't be a birthday cake. Worse, I dared to be with another man. I hold on tightly to the ashes and the picture close to my heart, wishing he were here tonight to celebrate his birthday. Fuck. I hid underneath a stone for a couple of years and when I came out thinking everything would be gone . . . it wasn't. The heart wrenching pain remains. The hurt appears like a tsunami without a warning. Even when I fight to push it away, it remains attached like a second skin.

"Fuck, Leo, come back," I scream at his picture on the nightstand.

"I wasn't ready for you to leave. We had so many more birthdays to celebrate together. Halloweens, Thanksgivings, Christmases . . . you gave up and left me. I'm tired of breathing, existing, and coping."

The sorrow, anger, grief, and guilt claw at my heart and soul. Not letting me go and sinking me as I fight to stay afloat. Holding my head up is freaking hard. Praying for his return hasn't worked. Not one prayer has been answered. My tear-stained pillowcase can attest to the endless pleas. Fuck, I hold my breath clutching the urn toward my stomach hoping to subdue the cries.

"Why didn't you tell me?" his low voice murmurs in my ear. His hands take away the urn and frame that I hold tight as if my life depends on it, but I let them go. My lifeless, heavy body is pulled up from the floor. "I hate to see you sad. Tell me what can I do for you?"

"He's gone," I say between gasps of air and sobs. "I keep asking him to come back, bring him back to me. No one can replace him."

"Mac," one word filled with so much power that I feel warm inside. "He's with you, walking beside you every day. Even when you can't see him, he's near."

"He's never coming back, is he?"

"Tell me how to make it better, Mac?"

"Make me forget." I finally meet his gaze. A flash of pain illuminates his eyes, disappearing as fast as it appeared. "Make everything disappear."

My plea is answered unexpectedly. He presses a kiss on my mouth. Tender. Soft. The first of many that he places on different parts of my face. At the same time, his hands pull on the hem of my t-shirt, just as slow as his kisses, he tugs it up until it goes over my head and my chest is bare. Each inch of skin he reveals tingles expectantly, waiting to be the next place where his lips will land. His hands glide up and down with grace, as if he was a sculptor and my body was a piece of clay that he molded with his masterful fingers.

Patient fingers that, like his mouth, take their time touching every inch of me. Making me feel desired—loved. Like the first time Leo touched me, loved me. We were each other's first. Everything we experienced, we experienced it together. He promised that we'd reach every milestone together—even death. And I'm here, wishing he were the one touching me, yet begging another man to take me away from the nightmare I've been living under for so long. Too many seconds to remember.

As he reaches my long skirt, his hands pull it down revealing my bare skin. "You're beautiful." He kisses my right hip, then the left, building the need inside me. "Not here. Not on the couch."

Porter sweeps me off the floor, carrying my almost naked body. His legs take long strides up the stairs and he enters the bedroom, closing it with one foot. As he rushes toward the bed, he sets me on top of it, crushing his body against mine. That luscious mouth of his takes control over mine with a feverish kiss. A greedy-hungry kiss that's trying to devour me with just one bite. But so intense that it promises to last forever. My body is igniting and coming to life. Every cell is electrified by his touch, his scent, his . . . no, no. What am I doing?

"Leo," I cry out in desperation, trying to fight what's going on. He was the only man that ever touched me. The only one I let myself go to places that. I'm his. Only his.

Porter freezes, his eyes opened wide. His arms release me and chills run through my body as he begins to retreat. Loneliness seeps through my skin. "I . . . I'm sorry . . . Do you want me to stop?"

"I don't know," I whisper, as the deluge of tears takes over. Everything is so confusing. It left for a little while and suddenly the pain came back. Porter's touch made it disappear.

"Erase it, don't let it come back," I plea again.

"Are you sure?" He murmurs, his lips tantalizing the skin behind my ear. "The last thing I want to do is to hurt you."

Closing my eyes, I decide to pretend. Play make believe. Instead of brown eyes, I see Leo's amber eyes. Loving me, celebrating his day the way we've done since he turned eighteen. "Please, don't make me ask again, take it all away."

He takes my bottom lip with his teeth, nipping at it. I lift my hands, running my fingers through his soft hair. His lips slide along my jaw, then he places lingering kisses along my neck and pulls the strap of my bra down with his teeth, tracing an invisible line with them through my skin. Shivers run through my system. Fuck, I want more. As if he can hear my thoughts, his mouth travels to my breast and a loud moan escapes me as he starts driving me to the edge.

One of his hands slides down my belly, until it reaches my pelvis. With a light push, he opens my legs slightly and slides his hand all the way to my sex, finding my clit and caressing it gently. Slowly. Building the need below my waist. As I rub myself against the heel of his hand, his long finger enters me. A loud throaty gasp resonates through the walls, as my back arches and my hips try to help me find the much-needed release. The build is intense, I can see the abyss I'm about to fall into and I want so badly to let myself fall.

"Yes," I cry out. "Please, babe, do it."

He muffles my orgasm with a kiss, absorbing everything I have to give. My insides explode as I reach the place he's taking me.

"Let everything out," he whispers, as his hand leaves me. I hear the sound of the foil and I force myself to keep my eyes shut. Live in the moment forgetting everything else. Even the man taking me to another galaxy and helping me forget my own name. Making me feel alive. "I got you, baby."

My entire body buzzes with anticipation as he begins to sink inside me. Each inch of himself filling me. Taking away the emptiness. As he presses himself inside me, something breaks; I can hear it. A shell, maybe. I don't think any further as the pleasure of having him sliding in and out numbs me and lust overtakes my actions. Each stroke of his cock has a gentle tempo that builds another orgasm. A much more powerful one that feels as if he's possessing me, making me his.

Right as my insides combust he groans my name, coming along with me. Following me to the place where there's no one else. His body shudders on top of mine.

His head drops over my shoulder. "Mac, I love you, baby," he whispers. For a few seconds I let myself go, enjoying the bliss after falling from the highest climax I've ever experienced.

My eyes open when I register his scent, his voice, and his eyes. Fuck.

What did I do? In that moment my blood freezes. Same eyes that blur with the tears I can't stop from falling. Grief crushes my throat— stops my breathing—and I push him. I push Porter away. My heart breaks all over again as the ache increases. The force of the guilt helps me to push him away from my body and jump out of the bed.

"Leo," a sob escapes me. "I'm sorry. So, sorry."

"Mac?" Porter's eyes open wide, he leaves the bed and takes a step closer to me, but I take one back.

"Leave, please," I beg him out of confusion, guilt, out of need. Because my traitorous body wants his hands, his arms, him. "I can't. Maybe I shouldn't have."

He takes his clothes with him. As he leaves I shut the door close and collapse against it. Placing a hand over my mouth, I let myself cry. How could I do this to the love of my life?

Everything inside me hurts. My stomach fills with sharp glass; my lungs deflate. I'm angry with myself. Did I break my vows? Cheat on my husband? When I see the door that Porter closed, I'm embarrassed for the way I behaved with him. My body shivers, missing the connection between us. What did I do to him? How is it possible that after everything I did, and despite the confusion, I want to be in Porter's arms?

THIRTY-TWO

PORTER

"I'M SORRY FOR freaking out," I hear Mac say. "I shouldn't have asked you to . . . Look at me, I'm such a mess. Everything you do for us is perfect. I didn't have anything to give them for Christmas and you bought them so much. God, I wish I could . . ." She takes my hand, squeezing it gently. Loving. And even when I'm giving her my best understanding face, I'm fucking dying inside. Because two nights ago I loved her with all my heart. Making love to her had new meaning; I felt a fucking connection that meant everything to me.

"You're such a great guy," she continues, her words shattering my heart. "Yes, you might've done pretty shitty things, but the man I met is strong, loving, caring, and so smart."

And I fall even more in love with her because of what she says, even when she's breaking my fucking heart. "I'll take whatever you give me, Mac, as long as you let me be by your side."

She shakes her head. "You deserve more than I can give you *now*."

"I understand, Mac." I want to fight her decision, but we both deserve more and neither one can offer that until we face our own fears and move forward on our own. "Maybe this is for the best."

Her head drops slightly, her eyes facing the floor. "Promise you'll continue being this amazing guy. You'll find someone to fall in love and have a family with."

I nod, biting down the words I really want to say to her. Staying on my two feet instead of kneeling down and begging her to let me be by her side forever. Telling her that I'm in fucking love with her, that two nights ago I meant every word I told her. "As long as you promise that you'll call me if you ever need me—or if the kids need me."

"I promise." I pull her to me, holding her tight, and absorbing her sweet energy. Hoping that it'll last me for as long as I live.

"THAT'S A LOT of money, Porter." Molly stares at the check I'm giving her. "Where are you going to go?"

"Seattle," I explain to her, taping the last box and labeling it. "The money is to cover the rent of the house and for you to help Mac with Finn's expenses. Send me her bank information when you have it, as soon as I find a job, I'll start sending more. If Virginia tries to take away the children call me. My family has money; I know in my heart that if they learn about that shit they will help."

Virginia threatened Mackenzie with lawyers, saying that she's not a fit mother. As much as I want to be angry with her for the shit that she told me, I can't. That woman came in like a typhoon and destroyed everything that Mac had worked for. Moving out of Portland is shattering my soul because I'm going to miss my family. But I have to leave for them, hoping that this might be temporary and that Mac will find herself under the mountain of grief. Yesterday, I explained to Harper that I was going to go on a trip. Left her my phone number in case she had to call me. I promised I'd come running if she ever needed me and assured her that I loved her. That I was leaving because I had to see my family. She was okay with that, knowing that she'd have me here if she needed me. I have no idea if Finn understood me, but I got a hug from him.

Yesterday morning, I searched for a place to stay in Seattle. I found a one-bedroom apartment close to down town. It's a month-to-month lease. A place where I can stay, at least, until I work things out with Chris and Gabe. After that, I'll make another plan. Mackenzie Brooke has my heart and I don't know what to do about it. I've no intention of taking it back.

"I wish she could see the amazing guy she has in you," Molly says, smiling at me. "You're a good kid, Porter. Whatever it is that happened before you came here, it's in the past. I don't want you to be that quiet, angry man again. Do you hear me?"

"Thank you for everything, Molly." I hug her. "Call me if you or Mac need me. I won't be far away." I carry the last box and head to my truck.

"Porter, don't go," I hear Harper's little voice, her arms enveloping my waist.

"Remember what you promised me?" I squat and she nods. "You keep being a good student, a loving daughter, and a caring sister. I promise to come back." I touch my heart. "You're here, in my heart, because I love you like my own. Always. It's only for a little while, but one way or another I'll find a way back here." She nods.

I walk her to her house where Mac is waiting for her by the door, holding Finn. Her eyes are filled with tears. Fuck. Someday. Someday we'll work things out. One day they'll be mine.

"Drive carefully," she says, as I nod.

"If you ever find space inside of that precious heart of yours, call me." I kiss her cheek. "I'll miss you."

With that I turn around and head to my truck, leaving behind what I love the most.

"Kendrick? Why are you calling me?"

"I thought you'd need to know that I'm moving to Seattle." I start the truck, setting the phone in the cup holder as the Bluetooth takes over the call.

"Why?"

"I had to leave my current address, and honestly, I can't be in Portland right now. Thought Seattle would be a good place to be while I recover from some shit."

"Do you have a place to stay?" I stare at the phone, making sure I'm speaking with Mason Bradley. What the fuck? If anything, I expected him to scream or threaten me. "Because my father could lease you his apartment for less."

"No offense, Mason, but why are you being nice?"

"My sister will have my balls if I treat you like shit," he responds. "That doesn't mean that I won't have an agent behind you twenty-four-seven. Another reason to lease you my father's old place. Do I trust you? Fuck no. Are you allowed to be close to my wife? Hell no. I'll text you the address, it has furniture, and all that shit in case you need it."

"Thank you."

"Don't fuck with anyone, or I swear I'll kill you."

"Now, that sounds more like the Mason I know, the world makes sense again." I kill the conversation, hoping that this is the right choice, that what I'm doing will help me to at least fix my relationship with the Deckers. As far as Mac goes, I hope one day she can care for me enough to . . . I have no fucking idea what, but I want to be by her side again.

The roads are clear and in three hours I arrive at my destination. As I park the truck in front of the address that Mason gave me, I spot Gabe and Chris walking to the main door. My heart stops and I jump out of the car to meet them and find out why they are here.

"Chris! Gabe!" I call out, as both men stop and turn around. They're wearing winter coats and hats and look almost the same as they did the night they rescued me. Except for some wrinkles around the eyes and mouth. "I didn't expect to see you."

"Mason was coming out to give you the keys and we wanted to do it instead," Gabe says, handing me a set of keys. "See how you're doing and . . ."

"That sounds better than the truth," Chris interrupts. "We need a few moments away from home; the Colthurst clan is driving us insane. I've always said it and I'll repeat it again: They need to stop reproducing, there are too many of them."

Gabe shakes his head. "Why the sudden change, Porter?"

"It's a long story, why don't you let me carry my things upstairs and I'll tell you some of it."

After a few trips, we get everything down from the truck and into the apartment that'll be my home for a couple of months. We sit and I tell them everything that I've been doing from the moment I started re-hab, until I packed my truck and left Portland. It's right after I tell them about leaving Harper crying by the porch that I realize that it's dark outside and I've been talking for longer than I've ever remembered. Never before have I done it without interruption, without much prompting. As the last words leave, my body finds some kind of release.

"You made the right choice," Gabe says, turning to Chris who nods.

"Coming to Seattle. I'd like to work on our relationship. Maybe let you into my life—into our lives."

"School?" Chris asks before I can thank Gabe for telling me that he's planning on working shit out. "The move or what happened in Portland shouldn't stall your plans."

"It's online, it doesn't matter where I live, as long as I have Internet," I assure him. "Tomorrow I'll start searching for a new job. Thank you, Gabe for giving me a chance. I swear to you that my intentions are to prove that I've changed. That I can be the man you tried to raise."

"Why look for a job if you have Steven's money?" Chris asks.

"It wasn't much, and I left almost everything to Mac. She needs it." I shrug. "Her son does. Since his dad died he hasn't spoken a word."

Chris scratches his chin and shakes his head. As he opens his mouth, Gabe speaks, "Time to go. Porter, call us after New Year, my family is here, and I doubt we'll have time to escape again."

I walk them downstairs, thanking them for the keys and for letting me unload all the shit I had inside my chest. It feels good to have someone to talk to. Not as great as it was to do it with Mac, even when she was the one who did the talking. With that in mind, I unpack my shit and decide to write to her.

Dear Mac,

Moving out of Portland was hard, but if that's what you need, I'll do it. In exchange, I want to ask for a favor. Let me write you a few lines, often, to tell you about my day, or my life. It's lonely here and you're a great listener. Exchanging letters can be a win-win situation, don't you think?

I arrived in Seattle in one piece, thought you might want to know it. Mason Bradley leased an apartment to me that's close to the record studio where I used to make magic. I miss those days, my music. Letting all the shit I had inside go through each note I played. It was better than any drug I took, but that stupid kid inside me didn't appreciate it. One day I hope to play in a venue and have you close by listening to the music I've written.

How are the kids?

Please, send me a picture of them, if you can.

Love,

Porter

THIRTY-THREE

MACKENZIE

THIS IS GOOD, Mac, I repeat while sitting in the waiting room of my new therapist. At least I'm giving therapy a try. What happened with Porter was . . . ugly. Not the making love part, that was beautiful. But the way I felt and behaved after. I kicked him out of my bed, when I wanted to lose myself inside his strong arms. The repulsion, the bad taste, and anger toward myself are unhealthy. He's a nice man. A wonderful, loving guy who goes out of his way to make me happy.

Then there's my relationship with my children. There's something missing between us, a connection we lost when we lost Leo. Or maybe it's only in my head. That's why I'm here, to find the root of my problems. No, to face my problems. I know the root and I think I'm ready to face it.

"Mackenzie Brooke?" The receptionist calls my name. Taking a deep breath, I walk toward her. "Today's session is going to be seventy-five dollars. We accept all major credit cards or cash."

"Today?" I repeat back, she nods. "How about a check?"

She points at the sign next to her computer.

We only accept major credit cards or cash. Sorry for the inconvenience, but checks are no longer allowed as a form of payment. Thank you for understanding.

Don't doctors usually send you a bill after they dealt with the insurance, which I don't have. This won't stop me. I can pay today's appointment. Then I'll figure out the budget for the upcoming ones. The step I'm taking is for everyone, not only for myself, but for my children too. They need a sane mother who won't be losing her mind every time something bad or good happens in her life.

I sign the payment receipt after she swipes my debit card and hand it over to her. "Thank you."

"Thank you, Mrs. Brooke, please take a seat. The doctor will call you in a few minutes."

Before I can sit back into the chair I sat in earlier, a tall middle-aged man, dressed in a pair of khakis and a tie enters the reception area, calling out my name.

Instead of answering, I walk closer to where he stands, "That'll be me."

His dark eyes sit behind a pair of wired framed glasses. They study me briefly. "Follow me."

We go through the narrow hallway, entering the first office. A small cozy room painted with a light gray color. A desk and a long couch sit across from a chair.

"Mackenzie Brooke," he repeats my name, smiling, as he extends his hand. "I'm Johnathan Welsh, your counselor. Nice to meet you."

"Nice to meet you too," I respond, losing some of the courage.

Taking a seat on the couch, and before I jet out of the office I blurt, "What should I talk about?"

He chuckles, shaking his head. "We can learn more about each other. For example, where I studied and my experience. You could tell me a little about yourself. But you are free to talk about what is distressing you the most."

"The most." I let out a nervous laugh. "Everything. I just don't know if coming here is the answer to my problems. Do you think it'll help?"

He tilts his head to the side, watching me, as he lowers himself into the chair right across from me. "Do you have a goal Mackenzie?"

"A goal?" I feel my eyes widen with the question, my head shakes a couple of times.

"What kind of goal? In life, my career, my children?"

He nods. "Something like that. As a therapist, I'm here to collaborate with you. Our goal is to identify what's distressing you, what you'd like to change, and help you search for a way to achieve that goal."

"My . . ." Before I can say that Leo died, my throat dries, my chest compresses, and I want to leave the room. Is this normal? The first time I tried a counselor I couldn't talk, I was crying from the moment I stepped into the office until I left. I stayed inside the car for about an hour before I could drive.

The long silence stretches out as I regulate my breathing, try to organize my thoughts. All of them are scattered throughout my mind. Images of my past. Leo. My present. Harper and Finn. My future. My kids along with Porter. Is he my future? That's a question I can't imagine answering, but how I wish I could say yes.

A simple *yes* without second-guessing myself.

"Do you have pets, Mackenzie?" I shake my head. "I do, a parrot."

"A parrot?" I question puzzled. "Does he talk back to you?"

"He can only say cracker," he says laughing. "Such a cliché, my children are allergic to animal dander. My now ex-wife and I thought that a parrot would make a great pet."

"Was it?"

"No, and I got the parrot during the divorce settlement," he complains.

"Leo didn't want to own a pet," I confess. "At least not until the kids were old enough to help with the chores. I'm glad because after he died I could barely take care of our kids. A pet wouldn't have survived my depression."

"Leo is your husband?" I nod. "How long ago did he die?"

"Almost three years," I say, drying my sweaty palms with my jeans. "It's hard to look at the big picture. Guilt engulfs me each time I try to think outside the lives we . . . We had so many plans and he's gone. He won't reach his thirtieth birthday, see his children grow up, graduate, or get married."

I take a tissue from the box on top of the coffee table, wiping the tears that fall as I speak. It's useless, the more I wipe, the more fall, and I hear myself sobbing. I'm not sure how long I cry, but once I am able to stop the waterworks, I look at my counselor who continues to watch me with concern.

"Sorry, talking about him is difficult," I whisper.

"What made you come to visit me today?"

"My kids, my . . ." I don't say Porter. But he's another reason why I decided to come. I hurt him with my behavior. Everyone is paying for the grief I'm going through. "Everyone deserves a better version of my-self—I know I do."

He nods. "Alright, so it appears we have a tentative goal. Our time for today is over, but if you're comfortable, we can schedule another appointment for next week. We can continue identifying what you need to work on and the goals you'd like to achieve through counseling."

THIRTY-FOUR

PORTER

Mac,

I heard about Finn and I imagine you're not taking the news well. There's not much I can do from here, only hope that they'll find whatever is going on with him soon. If not, we can continue searching for the right specialist. He'll talk again, I promise, babe.

Thank you for sending me pictures of them on New Year's. I had one laminated and I now carry it in my wallet.

Miss you,

Porter

I HAVEN'T FOUND a job, Molly called me because they need to do more testing on Finn and I had to send her the remaining amount I had in the bank. The doctor thinks he might be deaf. I'm no doctor, but I know he can hear. Mac must be upset and feeling alone. I wish she'd let me in. For now, I will do what I can. Like, find a way to make money. Bars are a great way to do so; they usually tip the bartender a load of money. I don't know shit about that, but maybe Reed, the owner of Silver Moon is willing to teach me. He and I go way back. I played at his joint when I was seventeen. A way to draw fans from the beginning, Chris used to say.

My excitement stops when, in place of the old bar, I find a Tudor style brick building that takes up the entire block. The sign reads Silver

Moon, but the naked silhouette lying on a crescent moon has been replaced. It's a Silver Moon, but with a violet butterfly on the side. A modern logo that gives the place a different feel. I walk around the block until I find the back door. I ring twice; the third time a man a couple of inches taller than me opens the door, his green eyes staring at me intensely.

"Can I help you?"

"I was looking for Reed, the owner."

He angles his face from left to right and frowns. "What do you need him for?"

"Reed and I go way back and, now that I've moved to Seattle, I was hoping he could hire me," I explain.

"Jax?" His frown deepens; I shake my head, *who the hell is Jax?* "Sorry, he was an old bartender who I never met. Come on in; let's talk about your qualifications."

"Butterfly, can you tell Reed to meet me by the '70s bar, please." He talks through his radio. "There's someone looking for a job that used to work here. Maybe the two of you should join too."

"He's on his way." A feminine voice responds on the other side. "We'll meet you there as soon as I'm done placing this week's order."

I whistle as we go through the corridors leading to the different rooms. I take a look at everything that they've added. "You guys have a set up for concert venues?"

He nods, swipes a door, and opens it for me. "Yes. We have vintage bars. '20s, '40s, '70s and '80s. But we also have a small venue that can be used to do acoustic recordings." He points at one of the bar stools for me to sit. "So what is it that you used to do for Reed?"

I shake my head. "No, I never said that I worked for him before. Back when this used to be smaller, I played from time to time. My qualifications are shitty. I'm finishing my college degree—business with a minor in information technology."

"Kendrick, kid!" Reed enters through the back of the bar, smiling at me. As he reaches me, he gives me a tight fatherly hug, patting my back a few times. The man in front of me steps back, as his jaw sets. "Did I hear right; you're looking for a job?" I nod at him. "Sound engineer, DJ, only music shit, because we can't have you working by the bars."

"Kendrick?" Matthew's voice comes from behind me and when I turn around I spot him, looking almost the same, holding a pink bundle and the doctor I met a couple of weeks ago is by his side. He stops, takes a deep breath and the woman, who now I think is his wife, shakes her head. "Why are you looking for a job at a bar?"

"Because I need it, and the only person I know in town that still likes me is Reed," I say honestly.

The guy who opened the door, Matthew, and his wife glance at each other. They nod, tilt their heads and I watch an entire conversation go on without one word being exchanged.

"No." The man, whose name I've yet to learn, or why he's making a decision says, "I've heard too much about you, and I can't have the liability. My fathers-in-law might believe in you, but I don't know you, and my husband doesn't trust you." I frown, looking at the three of them, while Matthew shrugs.

"I'm confused," I exclaim. "Who owns the bar, and who is your husband?" I ask the dude.

"The three of us own the bar," Matthew answers, pointing at his wife, then at the man I've yet to formally meet. "I'm his husband, her husband and Reed is the manager of Silver Moon. Tristan does the hiring. Tristan, meet Porter. Thea you can officially meet Porter, and Porter, meet Thea and Tristan. My other halves."

That introduction clears up all my questions, mostly why Tristan changed from friendly to cautious after Reed said my name. The in-laws must've warned him. Matthew marrying two people, that doesn't surprise me. That's his nature and he looks happy, but shit, can't he see that I need a place to work? What happened to the trustful Matthew I grew up with? Yes, I fucked up but I've changed.

"So I can't have a job because you don't trust me?" I confirm with Matthew.

"He doesn't trust you around alcohol," Thea clarifies, resting her head on his shoulder. Man, she's tall. "The OD episode and, Porter, the family is trying to support Chris and Gabe's decision, but we're weary about you. Try to understand our position the same way we're trying to keep an open mind. You have to earn our trust."

"How many semesters until you finish your degree?" Tristan asks.

"Four classes, it can be one or two semesters, depending on my income."

He pulls a business card from his wallet and hands it over. "Be there tomorrow by nine, tell Scott, my assistant, that we have a meeting. Bring your résumé in case I find something for you, because I'll hire you on the spot."

I read the card, then lift my gaze to find his deep green eyes studying me. "You trust me enough to hire me at Cooperson Corporation but not here?"

"It's the alcohol. But I do want to give you a chance. An opportunity to win our trust. Plus, we believe in second chances in my company." He walks to Matt, kisses his lips, and takes the pink bundle from him. "Here is different. I rather not take the chance, and my company has a program. We might be able to cover the cost of college—whatever it is that you have left."

Matt walks close to Reed and gives him a hug. "Time to go. Reed, see you in a couple of weeks. Call if you need anything, but you can also try Arthur, or my parents."

Reed walks to Thea and hugs her too. "Have fun, T, and take care of my little princess." Then he kisses the baby Tristan holds. "Don't worry about anything, boy, you four have a nice vacation."

"We will, Reed," he says, turning his attention to me. "Tomorrow, nine o'clock."

I nod, shaking his hand and looking at the sleeping baby he carries. She looks beautiful, peaceful. The way Harper and Finn look when they're asleep. Fuck, I miss them. This is harder than when I lost AJ and James. Loss never gets better, does it?

Mac,

I have a job. It's an entry-level position in the accounts payable department. Not my dream job, but it'll pay the bills. The benefits are good too. Much better than working at Big Savings. I don't smell like fuel after my shifts, or have to clean up the slushy machine every weekend. Talking isn't a requirement either. I can be silent, listening to my music for the entire eight-hour shift and there are no complaints.

Things with Gabe and Chris are fine. I've seen them a couple of times since I arrived. We've talked about my feelings, mostly. Not sure if I told you this, but Chris is a therapist. He likes to analyze people sometimes and I think he's doing that, at least until he feels like he can trust me.

How are you? I miss you and the kids. Say hi to them.

Love,

Porter

Porter,

We're fine. Harper is at a new stage. She refuses to talk to anyone but Finn. They're a pair. There is no news about Finn. The speech therapist that I found isn't accepting new patients. I'm applying for some government help, but there are no guarantees that I'll get much help.

On the bright side, I have a new job. Well, it's still at the flower shop, but I'm now working the morning and afternoon shift. It gives me plenty of time to be with the kids while I stay at home at night.

I'm happy to hear that things are working out for you. If you talk to Harper, please tell her that maybe collecting rocks is a better hobby than not speaking to her mother.

Hugs,

Mac

THIRTY-FIVE

MACKENZIE

"HOW ARE THE kids today, Mackenzie?" Dr. Welsh greets me as I enter his office.

"Doing fine," I answer with a lie. Is it wrong to lie about my children's health? It shouldn't, these sessions are about my emotional health. Well, Harper's behavior and Finn's flu are distressing me. "Sorry about the past couple of weeks, my aunt was out of town, and there's no one else who could keep an eye on the kids."

"Life happens, Mackenzie. What matters is that you're here today." He takes a seat. "Is there something special that you'd want to discuss today?"

Is there?

"Harper refuses to talk to me," I start with my precious girl. "Ever since Leo died we have trouble communicating. Our connection broke; it's as if Leo was the bond between the two of us. Porter helped, but now that he's gone, she's refusing to talk to me. Her excuse is that I'm being unreasonable."

"Porter?" The doctor asks.

"He's . . ." I pause, looking at him. Realizing that up until now I haven't mentioned Porter at all. The only other adult who knows about Porter is my aunt and, well, Virginia. During my first session I talked a little about Leo. The second session I focused on our early relationship and then his death. When Molly left for Costa Rica I couldn't visit until today. "No. I don't think it's time to discuss him."

"Alright, what do you want to discuss today?"

"Harper, she isn't talking to me, and that makes me wonder if Finn isn't talking for the same reason," I say. "I've tried everything, but he just won't talk. Porter tried to help. He'd play his guitar and Finn would sit right next to him. They'd sing 'Old McDonald' and Finn made the animal noises, but never sang the lyrics."

"Porter is no longer playing his guitar?" The doctor questions, and I shake my head. "Maybe you can find a video on the Internet, and try to copy what Porter used to do?"

"There isn't a video out there that can do what Porter did for us," I snap, then bite my lip for sounding like a bitch. "Sorry, but Porter did more than sing or play his guitar. He was patient with Finn, tried to engage with him all the time. Porter learned how to redirect Harper's angst, and my sadness."

"What happened to Porter?"

"He left. I pushed him . . . the guilt was stronger than what I felt for him."

I tell the doctor about my brief relationship with Porter. From the moment he opened the door, to the moment Virginia knocked on my door. Not all the details, and as much as I want to skip the tragic ending, I say it out loud, "While we were together I felt peace. Complete. Loved. Yet, in my head it felt wrong. Like a betrayal to my late husband."

Dr. Welsh doesn't say a word; he remains in his seat looking at me. There's no judgment, words of condemnation, or some strong advice on how to be a decent mother and wife. I didn't know what I expected him to say to all of that until now, but he doesn't blink. As usual, he waits for me to continue. To lead the session and find my way through the maze inside my head.

The silence is an invitation for me to continue. Using my time, I tell him about Virginia, expecting him to agree with her. Zero response. He remains in the same position, waiting.

"Aren't you going to tell me something?"

"Do you want to set a goal about Porter?"

"No. No. You have to tell me that what I did was wrong. Virginia is right, and I should keep myself away from—"

"Do you think Virginia is right?"

"I don't know; I need you to confirm what she said. The confusion I carry is almost as big as the pain and the grief."

"One of your goals, if I recall." He points out to his tablet. "My job here is to team up with you, help you understand your needs, and find the ways to pursue what you want in life. I'm an instrument more than a solution."

Baby steps he mentioned last time. I can take those, if at the end of the road I can find the light. Because I have to stop using everybody else's light. If I want to change, I have to find my own light.

THIRTY-SIX

CHRIS

JACOB CALLED ME with an emergency. One of the bands he's launching this month has to record a few tunes today and has a concert at Thrice Saturday night. The rhythm guitarist and the singer got into a fight and are in the hospital. The former has a broken arm and the latter a broken jaw.

"The keyboard player, the bassist, and the drummer agreed to kick them out." Jacob crosses his arms and leans against his chair, looking at me. "But we have shit already rolling that can't wait. In the meantime, I need people to cover those two positions who can mold themselves into the band's style."

"Porter," I answer his question with one logical answer.

Jacob shakes his head.

"You need a guitar player and a singer. He's both. Why not?" I lean against the wall, cross my arms and wait for the shit he's about to spit in order to avoid Porter.

"If you needed a drummer, would you call Martin Levitz to come on board?"

Martin Levitz is my former best friend and drummer for Dreadful Souls, my original band. He was a class-act asshole that put our family through a lot of shit. Too much to even remember it all.

"Martin never tried to change, Jacob." I use my fatherly voice, instead of giving him shit. "Porter fucked up; I'm not erasing the past and making him into a saint. But you can't compare the two. I'm not telling you to hire him for the band, only to have him play for them while you find two new members. Porter can cover both—guitar and vocals."

Jacob rises from his seat, walks back and forth around his office—my old office—and stops right in front of me.

"First he moves to Arthur's place, then he's working for Cooperson. What's next, Sunday dinner?" He shakes his head, combs his long strands and huffs. "As your oldest son, I want to ask you to stop before he fucks us again."

I laugh and nod my head, understanding part of his problem. It's the same issue he had the first time we introduced Porter to him and asked him to lend him some clothes until we bought him new ones. He was a threat, someone who might take away his special place. Each kid had their special place; now as adults, they still have them. Back then Porter took the spotlight when he started his career, where Jacob never could. Not because he wasn't talented, but because Jacob had a band. He's had a small competition going on with him and, on top of that, everything he's done to his sister and the family.

"Son, no matter what, he won't take your place as the oldest." I put a hand on top of his shoulder. "Or as a single act, there's no threat of him stepping in and becoming competition in any place. Aren't we a little old for that?"

Jacob shakes his head and rolls his eyes. "You think I fucking care about him taking over my spotlight? No." He growls and walks back and forth in his office again, gesturing with his hands in the air as he speaks. "Yes, that might've been the case long ago. Now I'm concerned about AJ, what if he flips and suddenly attacks her, or worse, he attacks her babies—Gracie or Seth?"

I scratch the back of my head, understanding the fear. Same fear that Mason and Arthur have expressed to me. "Porter has an agent following his every move day and night."

"Mason?" I simply answer with a nod. "Help me understand this shit, Pops. Why in the world would you want him back in our lives?"

As a brother, a son, and a friend it's hard to comprehend, but now I can talk to Jacob, the father. "Remember your plans before Gabe and Jude came into your life?" His jaw clenches the moment I mention his twin boys. "You and Pria planned on adopting. Let's say that would've been the case and suddenly that one child you adopted fucks up badly, would you abandon the kid?"

Jacob shakes his head.

"Your father and I are trying hard to balance the situation," I explain. "Give Porter the second chance he needs to stay on track and keep you guys far away because we respect your decision. Will there be a Sunday dinner with him? No, unless you three and your spouses invite him. If that never happens, I respect that.

"That doesn't mean that I won't try to give him a hand," I voice what Gabe and I have been discussing lately. "Today, I'm offering him something while I help you. If I make the call, he's here in a few. If not, it is going to take us at least a day or two to get what you want—unless you take over." Jacob shakes his head. We both know that right now he doesn't have the time. Between his family and work, he's too busy. "He's a great musician. My four children are, because I'm that fucking good. I taught the four of you, the same way I'm teaching Gracie and each one of your children. Use your head, Jacob. Push the resentment away; I'd think you know what happens when you let that take up space in your heart and mind."

"You think you're so smart, don't you?" He growls at me, but instead of snapping or doing any of that crazy shit Jacob would do, he hugs me. "I'm doing it because I trust you, and because I get why you're helping him. Make sure that Mason sends an extra agent while he's in the studio and at Thrice."

• • •

"The outside looks the same, but the inside," Porter comments, walking right next to me as we head to Pria's office. "You sure about this, Chris?"

"Can you do it?"

"Yeah, I mean it's just recording with them and then one gig," he confirms what Jacob told him earlier over the phone. Porter couldn't come right away. His work hours are from eight to four and as sweet as playing guitar sounded, he had to finish his day. "If we can tackle the recordings after work, it's doable."

"Then we're sure about it." I wiggle the handle after knocking a couple of times and open the door. "You have to sign a contract with us and then I'll walk with you to Jacob's office."

"Hey, Pops." Pria smiles at me as I enter, her dark eyes remaining cautious as Porter comes inside. "Jacob mentioned PR representation, but I don't think it's necessary. It's only one concert. What do you think?"

"Pria, let me introduce you to Porter. Porter, this is Pria Colthurst-Decker. The boss of the entire recording studio." I laugh. Because Jacob might be in charge, but Pria is the one that ends up calling the shots when it comes to the fine print. "She also owns a PR company that represents most of the artists that work for us."

"Porter Kendrick," he introduces himself extending his hand. "I'm here to play one gig; I don't think it's necessary to sign any paperwork. I play, you transfer the money you decide to pay me to an account number I give you, and I head back to my simple life." He pulls out a piece of paper and hands it to Pria.

"Mackenzie Brooke?" Pria's eyebrow shoots up and looks at him. "My adorable sisters like to say that I have orderly issues. This company has procedures and we follow them. Unless she's your agent and she's here to sign your contract, I won't send her the money." She pushes her contract and the piece of paper that he handed her. "You sign on the dotted line, I pay you when you fulfill it and what you do next is up to you." She taps on the bottom line. "Our facility is drug, alcohol, and tobacco free. No exceptions."

He signs and we leave the room after saying goodbye to her.

"How many artists did you lose with these rules?" Porter is reading the copy of the contract that she gave him.

"Lose? None, they changed the concept of the studio—Jacob and Pria. We're a hybrid label now," I explain to him. "With the bands that used to get high here, they simply refused to renew their contracts. We lease the studio to bands, other labels, and do the same with the studio down in the compound. When they sign the lease, they are aware of our policies; if they party, we kick them out and keep their money. Everyone stays clean during their sessions. Same goes during concerts." I laugh because when Pria began this movement I thought it wouldn't stick, but like everything she does, she made it happen.

"I wish you had that when I started." He shrugs. "Or that I would've let you babysit me, as you did with MJ and JC when they began."

"Me too," I address my regret. "Who hooked you?"

"Archer, from Paranoia." He lets out a loud breath. "A joint laced with cocaine. I wasn't mature enough to be by myself in an adult world."

Fuck, my chest constricts because he toured with them so early in the game. Porter started the shit way before I thought. We failed him in some ways.

THIRTY-SEVEN

PORTER

WE ARRIVED AT Chris' office, but the one sitting behind the desk is Jacob. His eyes narrow as I enter, looking at his father and then back at me.

"Play nice," Chris warns him. "I'm heading home to help Matt and Gabe with the rugrats. AJ said that we're having dinner at Matt's tonight."

"Tell my boys I'll be there as soon as I'm done," Jacob says, then his attention goes back to me. "Take a seat."

"Thank you for letting me play," I start the conversation because I know that he'd rather have me in jail, or at the bottom of the sea.

After I read the contract, I'm reminded of how sweet it is to be at the top tier of show biz. For my services as a guitarist and vocalist, I'm being paid three-hundred dollars an hour with a limit of fifty hours. That's about fifteen thousand in less than a week. There is so much Mac can do with that money, which is the only reason I agreed to do this.

"I'm doing this for my parents, not for you," he says, clearing his throat. His closed fists are ready to strike. "Camelot will get a lot of exposure by having you as a special guest. A plus for us. Personally, I'd rather send you back to where you've been for the past few years. You read the contract, you break it, and I kick you out without a penny. This is a one-time deal; don't expect another call from me."

I lift my hands shaking my head. "Since my last stint in rehab I've been clean and I assure you I work hard to stay that way every day. A part of myself doesn't want to go back on a stage. But the other . . . Music is my life, playing; composing is ingrained in my heart. A call might be appreciated because I need the money." I pull my phone out and show Jacob a picture of my boy. "His name is Finn, and he needs a lot of medical testing. I'm helping his mom with the expenses. This check is going to help, and any other gig you can throw my way would be welcome. If you can't, that's cool too."

"You have a kid?" He frowns.

I shake my head, explaining who Finn is, as well as Mac and Harper. At the end, I realized that I unloaded my love life to him. Jacob turns to look at his monitor after I'm done and then at a frame on his left and smiles.

"AJ could—" He shakes his head, but I know what he was about to suggest. AJ could help Finn. I'm aware of that, from the moment I met him. I've known that she could give me a hand, but I don't know if that's something I can ask her for. "We can always use talented fill-ins; I'll have Pria put your name on top of the guitarist and vocalist list. Email Pria your availability."

I nod, thankful that he's willing to find more gigs for me so I can help Mac.

"Porter, don't fuck up again. My parents . . . they love you like a son. Please, don't break their hearts." He rises from his seat and walks to the door. "Let's go, I want this to be ready for editing by Friday."

Mac,

Tomorrow I play live with Camelot. They're a new band who releases their first album next Tuesday. I'm their featured singer while they replace the old one who is recovering from jaw surgery and won't be able to sing for the next six months. Kids, the stupid shit you get into when you don't know better.

Harper emailed me yesterday morning telling me about Molly. I texted you about it, but I haven't heard from you. Do you need me there? I understand that it's just the flu, but you having to do everything alone worries me. Please text me or I'll be driving down tonight. How is Finn, any news?

Love,

Porter

Mac: Molly is fine, you don't have to drive and miss your concert.

Porter: Thank you for texting me.

Mac: How are things with your family?

Porter: Better than I thought they would be. It'll be a slow process to regain their trust. It's hard to see past everything I did to them and forgive me. They might not fully trust me now, but one day I hope to be a part of their family in some way.

Mac: I'm happy for you.

Porter: How are you?

Mac: Doing well, thanks. Working, taking Finn to therapy. Thank you for helping.

Porter: Is he talking yet?

Mac: No. He misses you though, every afternoon he sits on the couch and pretends to play his guitar.

Porter: I miss him too. No, I miss all three of you. Thank you for responding. It was great talking to you.

Mac: Take care.

THIRTY-EIGHT

PORTER

"LOOK, I DON'T want to fire you," Tristan lets out a loud breath. "But I have to."

That's a low blow. Fired. He was fucking paying me to go to school and his salary covered my rent and food. Now I have to worry about the essentials. I regret sending the wire transfer to Mac earlier today. Maybe I should've kept a little for myself.

"Jacob said he'd take care of you," Tristan continues. "I'm sorry, but I just can't have a line full of groupies by your desk when they're supposed to be working. Dude, one of my managers asked you to sign her boob. That's against so many HR policies within the company." He laughs, finding some humor at my expense. Does he think I enjoyed having that woman flash me for an autograph? Man, that was embarrassing. "Pria wants you to head to her office; she needs you to sign a contract."

"I don't have any money to pay for her services," I remind him I'm unemployed.

"They know what's going on, Porter. None of us thought about the aftereffects of you taking the stage."

Me either. My old music is playing again in full rotation. There are rumors about my comeback, which won't happen. Reports about what happened to me are coming out from multiple sources. There's a fucking rumor that I was exploited by the Deckers—and abused. That pissed me off. When it came out, I called Chris, who assured me that it was handled by Matt's people. I have no fucking idea who his people are and what they handle. I just hope that none of these rumors coming out touches them—Mac, and her children. Maybe moving out of Portland was a bad idea. With that in mind, I text Mason.

Kendrick: Are your men still watching my ass?

Mason: No, they're now body guarding your ass. Fuck, we forgot how you drew an audience. Are you still at Tristan's?

Kendrick: About to leave.

Mason: Take the private elevator; they're picking you two up. There's a small mob outside the building.

Kendrick: No wonder he fired me. Then what, any plans on how to get rid of them?

Mason: Then you're heading Decker Records. We're all meeting you there. Matt is spreading the rumor that you're taking a plane to L. A., the pictures are circulating right now.

Kendrick: Will this touch anyone I know?

Mason: Not sure, Kendrick. We'll meet soon and discuss further steps to prevent that.

I lift my gaze and notice Tristan is also texting. When he's done, he lets out a deep breath. "Deckers, never a dull moment. Let's go. We have a meeting."

THE MEETING ISN'T at the recording company; it's at Transcending, the movie production company, inside one of the big conference rooms. Chris, Gabe, Matthew, Jacob, Mason, and Tristan are here. Pria and Arthur Bradley are on the phone working remotely for the day.

"That's your contract with The Image Studio." Jacob pushes a paper in front of me as Pria explains. "You're hiring us as your PR company. I'll change your image if necessary and will make you look good. However, I never lie. If you have too many skeletons in your closet, please disclose them. That gives me an advantage over the press. I can bend the information to your advantage before it hits the media."

Jacob nods his head. "Trust her, she's good."

"Fill out the questionnaire that's attached to the contract, I need it today," Pria adds. "Give the papers to Jacob once you're done."

I slam my head on top of the table, covering my head with both hands. Fuck. It's been so long since I've had to deal with this media circus. Did I ever enjoy it?

"It's temporary, Porter; we're all here for you." Chris pats my back. "If I had known that putting you up there would create this kind of chaos, I wouldn't have done it."

"Did anyone listen to me?" Gabe asks. "No one asked. He was big and he was a mega-star. I'm surprised this circus isn't bigger."

"Thought you let everyone think I was a deadbeat junkie," I shout out, lifting my head, looking at Jacob. "Shouldn't they hate me?"

He laughs and shakes his head. "You think he let us really do anything to hurt you?" He points at Chris. "We spread a small rumor that you weren't welcomed back, but that's as far as we got. Other than the old OD and your man-whore ways, nothing else was released. You sold a ton of albums, the music that you played was popular. Chicks dug you. You're back and they think they can have a piece of you."

"The rumors that were spreading are slowly being replaced by other celebrities' news. Soon you'll stop trending," Matthew continues. "But, think about the place you're at. This is your chance to revive your career; we'd make a killing."

"We?" Jacob frowns at him. "I discovered him."

"No. That's not the life I want to go back to again," I interrupt them. "The late nights, the people surrounding me thinking they love me but have no fucking idea who I am. Playing is awesome; dealing with the things that come with it is rough for me."

Fuck. My hands shake and every despicable thing I've done is coming back.

"Getting a job is going to be hard," Tristan pipes up. "You're going to be looked at as the famous singer, not for your qualifications or hard work. I suggest you search for something in showbiz."

"There was a lot of fucking destructive shit that I went through when I was on top of the world. If only I could do what I love without having to set a foot on a stage. Music is what matters; I'd like to pursue it by writing or teaching. Not playing it or performing."

That might not even be a possibility, composing for other artists. Would Chris let me work at the record company? I stare at my wrists, trying to find some peace. When I look around the room, I realize everyone is looking at my wrists. Mason's red face and the vein pulsating in his neck is scaring the shit out of me.

"They're not what you think," I clarify. First lifting James. "This one is to remember James." Then I lift AJ's, "When I had it tattooed it was to remember her, now it's to remind me of the guy she once thought I was. To keep me grounded. Do I love her? Yeah, she was my first love and the first person who cared for me. She'll always have a place in my heart, but I am not *in* love with her. That's over, I swear."

Mason nods. "We're not kicking you out, but since things are working out with Chris and Gabe maybe you can go back to Portland and figure out your life there?"

I shake my head.

"No, he can't," Gabe speaks for me, "and he doesn't have to."

Chris says no, too. He knows why I had to move here and why I can't go back. "He needs family, Mase. He's our kid too."

The chaos happening doesn't feel as heavy after what Chris said. I'm their kid.

Mason's jaw clenches, but he nods in understanding. His attention turns to his buzzing phone. His features harden as he reads and taps back a reply, repeating the process several times, but he remains quiet.

"Do you have music that you can sell to JAMs'—the triplets company?" Pria asks over the speaker.

"Yeah," I answer, remembering the business that Jacob, AJ, and Matthew started back in college. They wrote and sold the music to Decker Records or different artists.

"Here's the story," Pria interrupts. "He's back at Decker's as an executive producer and composer, breaking his hiatus. He'll be teaching at the academy and working with the foundation."

Jacob and Matthew shake their heads.

"Erase the academy," Matthew opposes. "No way is he getting near the sis."

"She proposed it, Decker." Mason cracks his neck giving me a look between *I hate you* and *fuck up and I'll kill you.* "The three little sisters are weaving this plan."

Matthew looks at his phone, presses his lips together, and shows it to Tristan who smiles at what he sees.

"Yes we are. Now let's finish this before naptime is over. Your relationship with the Deckers is simple," Pria continues. "They're your foster parents and there's nothing but love and respect between the family and you. Now if you excuse us, we have five little ones who are expecting our full attention."

"Anything else we need to address?" Jacob asks. We all agreed that there's nothing else to cover. "Do we need to check on Mac or the kids?"

"I don't know," I breathe out. "Fuck, I haven't called them to check if they're okay."

"The neighbor's next door?" Mason asks and I nod.

"I'm close by," Arthur Bradley, who's been silent during the entire conversation, speaks up. "I'll survey the area and make sure everyone is alright. After I find out, I'll give you a call."

THIRTY-NINE

PORTER

"**W**ELCOME, MR. KENDRICK," my new doctor greets me. "Are you sure you're okay with me being your doctor?" Her sweet smile is an invitation to follow her inside her office. She gives off a casual vibe in her dark slacks and knitted sweater. Her violet eyes crinkle so similarly to Matt's when he smiles.

I lower myself on the couch and nod. "Yes, Chris gave me the list of counselors and, from it, you're the only one who focuses on addictions other than him, but he's like my father."

Thea Bradley-Decker nods, grabs a notepad from the top of her desk, and takes a seat in the chair across from me. "We're bound by patient-doctor confidentiality unless you become a danger to yourself or others. Nothing you say leaves the office. Now, what would you like to talk about today? We can start by getting to know each other, or you can tell me what's going on with you, the floor is yours."

I scratch my earlobe thinking about what I want to discuss with her. Every therapist has a different approach, but all of them have one thing in common: they want their patient to rehash their past. At least that's how I felt during each session I had in the past. But with her, there's something that makes me feel at ease.

Maybe she already knows most of what happened to me. She's married to the family. There's no way they didn't tell her anything. But maybe she needs my version. The other side of the story. A play-by-play of what I remember and what I lived through. What made me who I am today. I start with my parents dying and living with my grandparents; barely remembering everything in between until I met the Deckers. I don't go into detail knowing that I only have an hour to talk.

"I lived with them for four years," I shorten the version to only a few words. "Fell in love with AJ and things went from sweet to fucked up. The last time I snorted cocaine was with some dude I swore was a dealer. He ended up being part of a cartel."

"So you're over all that?" She interrupts.

I shake my head. "I never dealt with the loss of my first family," I explain to her. "Not until after the cartel almost killed me and I spent a long time in a rehab facility."

"Therapy has helped you, then?"

"Yes, for the most part," I tell her. "After I was kidnapped I had trouble sleeping. Some nights I still wake up sweating, scared that I didn't make it out of that house. That the cartel found my family and killed all of them. It's not often, and I work through it the way my last doctor taught me. It's not easy and it's not something that just goes away. Opening the door to my place always freaks me out, I fear seeing someone waiting for me." I shiver remembering what Mason did, so I tell her and she rolls her eyes the same way AJ did when she was annoyed with her brothers. Maybe I shouldn't use names to keep things separate, but instead of asking, I continue. "One of my therapists did a few hypnotherapy sessions to help me face that fear. AJ . . . I regret how I treated her so much; I'd like to do with her what I did with my foster parents. Apologize for my actions. There's not much I can fix, but someday I want to apologize to her for the shit I put her through."

Thea nods, scribbles something, and then looks up to me. "After rehab, what happened to you?"

I tell her about the ranch, how I felt I wasn't ready to face everyday life at some nine to five job. Instead, during that period, I lived in a farmhouse with other farmhands. After that, I tell her about my decision to move to Oregon. Portland to be exact.

"The compound?" She frowns.

"That's a thirty-minute drive north of Portland," I tell her, that's where I lived with my foster family for four years. She nods. "It was a familiar area, weather, and I felt safe."

Unfortunately, her clock beeps and she lets out a sigh.

"This hour went too fast and I feel as if we didn't even touch the surface," she states. "We couldn't discuss much about your goals. When do you want to come in again?"

"Whenever you have your next opening," I tell her, agreeing that it went fast and I feel as if I have to get a lot more out before it's time for me to talk to AJ. "There's a lot I want to talk through."

"Tomorrow, same time?" I nod.

"HOW ARE YOU today, Porter?" Thea greets me, as she calls me from her office. I look her up and down, as she wears a pair of jeans, a flouncy long sleeve shirt and her hair is down. "Right, sorry for the outfit, but we have a zoo to attend in about an hour." She grabs her notepad and takes a seat on her flowery chair.

"Where were we?" She clicks her pen and stares at me.

Molly. She is the next person I talked about. Thea can't help but laugh at what I tell her. The flirting is what takes several minutes to explain. Continuing with Mac. "It was this pretty woman with a lost gaze and a beautiful smile that knocked on my door. She's a widow who moved from Colorado to Oregon. Before she arrived, I used to live in the house next door; it's a two-bedroom place. But I moved out when she came."

"Why?"

"As I said, her aunt is a little off and . . ." I trail, trying not to talk distract myself again with Molly and the crazy things that come out of her mouth or the shit she does. "She had decided that Mac should sleep on the couch while the kids slept in the room. I felt as if they needed their own space. They had lost their father and their mother was going through a lot of pain. I felt sorry for the kids. Like me, they had lost a parent. I wanted them to know that they weren't alone. Life is complicated enough while you're growing up, but losing everything and moving away from what they've known was a lot to deal with. I tried to ignore Mac, stay away from them, because before them, I avoided contact with everyone, but they were impossible to ignore."

I pull my phone out and show her some pictures of them. Not sure if that's ethical or part of therapy, but sharing them feels right for me.

"Her name is Harper," I begin to tell her all about my little Harp. Her favorite color, how I taught her to ride her bike and then continue with Finn. For the next hour, I spend my time talking about the small family I had for a few months, the love I have for them and how I hoped that Mac could love me the way I did her. "I miss them."

"So why did you leave them?"

"Because we both need to find ourselves, before we can pursue something else. She's grieving and there's nothing I can do to help her unless she wants to be helped," I say. Thea nods. I look at my tatt. "I've been there. It took me time to understand that my first love will always mean something to me, but I believe in the possibilities of falling for someone again."

"You want to tell me about your tatt?" She touches her wrist. "AJ?"

I explain what it means, what I do when I'm lost, and when I finish unloading it sounds like I haven't moved on. The letters look out of place.

"Maybe I have to find out how to close the chapter." The words leave me without thinking. "Maybe, at first I was interested in Mac because she was emotionally unavailable. I was trying to hold onto AJ and James so hard I wouldn't have to open up to anyone again. But I got to know her and now . . ."

"Now?" Thea looks at me, then back at her pad.

"I want to change my life, I don't want to end up alone like my father," I admit. "That's why I moved out of Portland to confront my shit, while she confronts hers. To find myself and find a way to offer her something tangible. Real."

"As long as you're willing to walk where you think you should be, you'll get there." She closes her pad. "Tell you what, let's meet next week if that's okay with you. I have a seven o'clock opening in the morning."

"I'm meeting with AJ on Monday at eleven," I tell her.

"Well, that's great; we'd have talked by then."

"Thank you." I rise from my seat and shake her hand.

FORTY

PORTER

Mac: So you're famous? Crazy famous?

Porter: Yes, I was. Not anymore.

Mac: THE DECKERS . . .

Mac: You are related to the Decker twins, to Christian freaking Decker.

Mac: You're the foster son of Gabe Colt. We've been watching his movies and it never occurred to mention he's your dad?

Porter: Yes to all of the above, but they're simple people. My family.

Mac: Wow! You're famous. Really famous. Okay, I'm done fangirling.

Mac: Molly is wondering about the gossip that is swirling around. Is it true?

Porter: Which ones?

Mac: That your foster parents abused you.

Porter: Never. You know the true story; which I hope you keep to yourself.

Mac: Not to worry, I won't tell anyone. Not even her. She's inviting friends over to the room you slept in.

Porter: What else is she doing?

Mac: Selling your favorite cookies.

Porter: She never baked me cookies.

Mac: No one has to know the truth.

Porter: Harper and Finn?

Mac: Harper and I are having problems. She thinks you're going to come back and take her to your new house—with her own room. Can you believe her?

STARE AT the screen and erase my answer. Because yes, if Mac allowed it, I'd take them with me.

Porter: Tell her I live in a small apartment. Show her these pictures. Your house is bigger than my place. There's no backyard for her toys. Here is lonely.

Mac: Are you okay?

Porter: I'm trying to stay above water. Usually, with so many changes I lose my shit, but so far I'm sober. I began therapy again as a way to make sure that I stay clean, and I have my parent's support.

I stare at the last words. My parents. Chris and Gabe haven't rolled out a red carpet welcoming me, but they have been understanding. We talk daily over the phone, I continue telling them crap that I hid and stuff that I regret not airing out long ago. Our future is a work in progress, but I'm certain that it'll be more than just an exchange of holiday greetings.

> Mac: *That makes me happy. You'll be fine, you have people that love you and support you.*

> Porter: *It'd be better if you and the kids were here.*

I don't send the last text; instead, I get ready for my interview with Noah, from some radio station. Jacob is going to be with me. We're sitting down to put every rumor to rest. There's no feud with the Deckers; they didn't kick me out. I broke plenty of rules and had to leave. Pria's team admitted that I was in rehab for about two years. That's information I wanted to let be known. The rest isn't important. After the interview, I have another session with Thea and then . . . I have to be at the Academy to see AJ.

Fuck, this is huge. I look at my wrist and her initials are fading after the first laser treatment. The office where they're removing it said it takes between six to ten sessions for it to disappear. Sounds like a long time, but the three times I've explained out loud what it means to me, the less I like what it symbolizes. AJ is my past; she should be a memory. Not the reason why I keep going, why I do the right thing. I am my own reason. Mac, Harper, and Finn are too. My ex shouldn't take up so much space in my present, if at all. Took me damn long to realize it.

"That was easy," Jacob says, as he disconnects the phone conversation with Noah. "You seriously won't play again? Dude, I know you loved the thrill of the stage. If you ever want, there's Thrice. Matt might let you play at the Silver Moon."

I shake my head. "Maybe someday, but not now. What else do you have for me?"

He pushes a folder. "The wife found something while going through the system." I open the folder and it's a spreadsheet. "Your shit's been selling for years, but we haven't paid you the royalties in a long time." As his finger taps the bottom line, my jaw drops. Almost ten million dollars.

"That's a crazy amount of money." I read again the figure.

"You made more than that annually when you were active." He

hands me a pen. "The royalties that'll hit the bank as your music is starting to play on the radio again will be crazy. Sign the paper accepting the money and it'll be sent over to the bank account we have on file."

This is fucking crazy. That's a lot of money I have no use for right now. Mac's earlier text reminds me exactly what it could be used for. A big house. We have to talk. I have to make her understand. This shit between us has to work. It has to. After signing the dotted line, I take a picture of it to make sure I remember how much they're depositing.

"I received the songs, but you didn't sign the contract." He pushes yet another piece of paper in front of me. "You did specify that you want your music paid as royalties, which takes a long time, but since you have a nice cushion that shouldn't be an issue. Writing can be done from anywhere; your contribution to the foundation can be financial only. We're not kicking you out, but if you ever decide to move back to Oregon with your girl and the kids, that's cool too."

I nod, reading the quarterly schedule and opting to donate a percentage to the foundation. Chris and Gabe plan to sit down with me and explain what their foundation does and what I can do to help.

"Any news about Mac and the kids?"

I shake my head. "Thank you for everything, though," I say, bobbing my head. "For letting me show your parents that I've changed."

"As long as you keep yourself clean, we're cool." He extends his hand. "Good luck with everything."

After I'm done with him, I head to the academy to talk to AJ.

FORTY-ONE

PORTER

"I'LL BE OUTSIDE." Mason comes out of the office after I knock on the door. He gives me a glare and exhales. "You know better, don't you?"

"Yeah, yeah. I know better, Mason." I clear my throat and step inside her office.

AJ sits behind her desk, surrounded by blue-gray walls covered with musical pentagrams. It's a song, and as I follow their order, I realize it's one of the songs Chris wrote for her when she was a baby.

"That's sweet." I point at the wall. She shrugs, her eyes smiling as they follow the walls. I'm sure she's playing each note along with the lyrics as she reads through them. Probably with a guitar riff, as it's the way Chris would play it for her.

I did that a few times with Harper and Finn. Composed a couple of melodies just for them that I played at night before they headed to bed, or while they were playing in the backyard. Finn loved it; God, he loved anything I played. That kid could sit by me for hours and just mumble along with me. I miss my girls, but I miss him more. He was my little shadow.

"It reminds me how much my parents have always loved me," she explains, pulling me back from Portland where I left my heart. "It's fitting too, because he taught me what I know—to love music and live by it. He continues doing so with his grandchildren."

"How many children do you have?" She lifts a frame. I walk closer and take it from her. It's a picture of her holding a baby. Mason is hugging her with one arm, and a beautiful girl, who looks just like AJ, is on his lap smiling down at her baby brother. "She's a cutie, what's her name?"

"Gracie; our baby boy is Seth." She takes the frame back. "They're an amazing handful, but we love them so much." Kissing each one of her loved ones, she puts the frame back where it belongs.

"How are you, Port?" She sits back, sinking into her chair and looking at me.

"Good. I'm doing well, AJ, and you?"

"Busy with the school, home and my family," she says, looking at her children again.

"Following your dreams?" She nods. "Having your music school, planning on a big family with five to seven kids?"

"No. That's it for us, I can't have any more without risking my health," she explains. "Maybe we'll adopt, hire a surrogate, or just be happy with those two. I'm sure my brothers will fill their houses with more. Then again, people change. Life changes and they might not want to have more than they do right now. How about you? Career? Family?"

"If I hadn't fucked up you'd have James," I let it out of my chest. I place a hand right over my heart. "I'm so fucking sorry for every single thing I did to you that hurt you and for the things you never found out about. The moment I began using was the moment I began living a double life. You were what kept me grounded, but then I didn't want to be grounded and my mind just wanted one thing. Drugs. Everything I did had one purpose—feed the need to consume them."

"You were sick," she says, I nod agreeing with her.

"That doesn't make it right," I tell her. "Nothing that I did was right just because I was sick. It explains the behavior, but I should still be accountable for everything. The way I treated you when you told me about James. Fuck. I wish I could bring him back to you, that you could hold him at least once."

"It wasn't you or your reaction towards him that caused me to lose him," she sniffs, pulling the sleeve of her sweater up to clear her tears. "My body needs a lot of prenatal care before I'm able to get pregnant and carry a baby to term. Yes, your behavior was shitty and fucked up and I hated you for a long time, but one thing had nothing to do with the other."

"I was a prick and the worst boyfriend," I accept my faults. "In my head, everything made sense. What happened on the tour stayed there, therefore, I had a hall pass. Once l looked deeper into my behavior, I wanted to punch the hell out of myself. It was a lot of monkey-see, monkey-do."

"Peer pressure," she concludes, I nod. "The past doesn't matter as much as the present and the future. Apply what you learned and find the right way for you. Are you finding that way?"

I nod. "Yes, and thank you for helping me with it. Thank you for being the amazing person you are and opening the doors of your school to begin my journey.

AJ smiles that smile that she shows when she's about to learn something new. The woman in front of me looks different, but I see so many traces of the girl I met long ago. My friend. The person who held my hand and helped me discover who I was.

"What can I do to repay everything that you did for me back then?" I ask instead of sharing Mac with her. "To fix everything I fucked up."

"You're making my parents proud, that's a good start," she responds. "They love you and they want to see you succeed. Help the foundation, find a way to catch the future Porters and make sure they don't stray. Find happiness, your own little family. My parents found that grandchildren are the best; give them some more. That'll make up for a lot, Porter. It'll prove me right."

She thoroughly confused me and I cross my arms waiting for her to explain. "That you're a good person, that you're smart and a hard worker. That you're a Decker."

Oh fuck, that last part makes me cry. Shit, it shouldn't because I'm supposed to be a man and be strong but being called a Decker is fucking huge. More praise coming from AJ. Because out of anyone in this world, I have hurt her the most and still she's opening her heart and her family to me, and even if it's only to exchange holiday greetings, I can die tomorrow in peace. But I hope not, because there's a little family I'm in love with and want to spend the rest of my life with.

"Stop crying because you're going to make me cry, Port," her raspy voice claims, and when I look at her she's already crying. Fuck. "Why don't you tell me about the girl, is she nice?"

We spend some of the time discussing Mac, but I don't go in too deep. Instead, I start talking about the school and her plans for me. Of course, I can only change the conversation for so long before Mac comes back to take the front seat. Once I'm finished, AJ is frowning.

"Bring him. Bring Finn in," she says. "We can help him here."

"You know what he has?"

She shakes her head. "No, but I have people to diagnose him and therapists to help him. Maybe it's only the trauma of losing his father, but it can be something else. Early intervention is what will help him. You've done great, Porter" she praises me and smiles. "Bringing him back with music was an excellent idea." She pulls out her phone, taps it and Mason enters the room.

"You okay?"

"The family. He has a family, that's why you agreed, wasn't it?" AJ asks Mason who nodded.

"Part of the reason why, yes. The lady he lived with talked about some man who was part saint, part Channing Tatum." He laughs. "That's how she described him. But yes, Dad and I realized that maybe, maybe he had changed. I still had my doubts."

"You talked to Molly?" I question as Mason shakes his head.

"I sent people to run surveillance and a thorough background check," he says. "Sorry, but as I said, I couldn't let you near us if you posed a threat."

He makes sense and I understand his role within the family. Just like I get that Matt and his husband make sure everything works in order. Jacob and Pria do the administrative stuff. Thea and AJ, along with Chris and Gabe, do the nurturing. The family works like a well-oiled machine filled with love. I don't know if I'll be able to fit in, but I'm glad that in some way I'm a part of them.

"Well then, I know I have to start working, so do you have a schedule for me?" I want to see if I can go to Portland before I start working, but I don't want to push my luck.

"Yes, you start next Monday afternoon, but I'm hoping you'll shadow this week." AJ takes out a sheet from a folder. "Your paperwork has been filed. I outsource that part to Tristan's HR company. They have all your information already. Encrypted, I swear. No one will come and ask you for a boob-tograph?"

"A what?"

"That's what Mattie calls when a woman wants you to sign their breast, boob-tograph." I shake my head thinking about that woman that wanted her boob signed and then look at my schedule.

"I want to go back to Portland this week. Try to work shit out with Mac." I scratch my head. "Find oud if I need to lease a bigger house."

"Call us," Mason responds. "I'll hook you up with something and send a moving truck."

"Careful, I might think that you like me."

He shakes his head, "I tolerate you, maybe in a few years I might like you."

AJ raises her hand and I narrow my gaze at her because the gears inside her head are spinning fast, I can hear them. "Springing shit on Mac like *I'm buying a bigger house, live with me, etc.* might not be the best move. Romantic in a sense, but not if she isn't ready. Can I make a suggestion?"

I smirk at her. "Sounds like experience is taking over."

"Yes, there's some life experience attached to my suggestion," she agrees, and it's clear to me that she's talking about the time I picked her up from her dorm after freshman year and moved her into a big ass house without asking for her input. "Let her finish her journey, find the closure she needs. Fuck, after everything that happened to me I didn't get into any serious relationships for five years."

"That's a long time." I whistle falling deeper into the chair, then straightening up. "Your suggestion sucks."

Turning to look at Mason, I dare to ask, "Any wisdom coming from you, Mason?"

"Shut up and listen to the wife," he orders. "If you want to catch the girl, you have to join forces with the Deckers. They're devious. I've seen them work magic. How do you think I got *my* girl?"

I'm sure there's a story behind his statement and maybe someday it'll be fun to learn how Mason Bradley had to find a way to get AJ over a beer, but for now, I listen to her suggestions.

"That's all you have?" I question after hearing her plan, a plan that included a few phone calls and some crazy scheduling. "There's no magic involved."

"But it'll speed up things, trust us," AJ smiles, touching Mason's hand. "We'll be there Friday morning."

I rise from my seat, leaving the room with a lot of information to digest, but before I step out AJ calls me back, "Welcome home, Porter."

FORTY-TWO

MACKENZIE

THE HOUSE IS quiet. Finn isn't touching his guitar anymore. Harper isn't talking much these days. The three of us go through the motions, surviving day and night. Molly decided that California was a great place to visit with her friend, Rhonda. She has found out that there's more sun, less rain and a lot of activities. After only a few days out there, she's thinking about relocating to San Diego. She offered me the chance to move with her. She said it's affordable, close to the water, and I could find a better job than being a florist. The decision to move out of Portland will come with the new school year.

Harper has to finish this school year before I can drop another bomb. We're moving out and moving . . . I don't know where to go anymore to make things better for us. The morning after Porter left, she ran down the stairs looking for him. She blames me for his departure and she hates me; she hates him. Now, now we're fighting for survival again.

With Porter's departure, there's an empty spot in our hearts. Mine is missing two different men, heartbroken by two different loves and not being able to find a way to move into a place where it can beat again. With Molly out of town, I can't go to see my therapist. How am I supposed to reconnect my heart with my head again? Move on from the stage of grief and depression and learn to accept all the changes—including new friendships and happiness.

As I turn the corner, I spot the preschool. Poor Finn sits on the steps with his teacher waiting for me to pick him up. I'm late again. The last parent to drag her ass to pick her kid up. But what can I say? Getting off at one and having to pick him up at one gets complicated. I steal a few minutes from my work and just pray that I make it before one fifteen. This isn't any different from when Leo died. I'd forget to pick up Harper and receive a call from the teacher reminding me that I had slacked off again.

"Mrs. Brooke," she greets me as I reach them. "Can you try to arrive on time tomorrow? I have a class coming in fifteen minutes."

I nod because there's no use reminding her that I work until one, my aunt is out of town and maybe she can be a little more patient with me.

"We have the meeting on Friday, at noon," his teacher reminds me. Yet, another clue that maybe I should get my act together. "You have to be here."

"IF I FINISH my homework, can I email Porter?" Harper is bargaining for her computer privileges. I punished her without any electronics; she can't use my phone, the television, or the computer. After the way she behaved at school, I doubt I'm going to let her turn on the microwave. Some boy called Porter a junkie and Harper punched him in the face. I can't tell her that, in fact, Porter is—or was a junkie. That's something I'm not sure how to handle. There's no book to give you an answer for that.

So, Your Neighbor is an Ex-Junkie: How to Tell Your Children

"I'm not sure if you should email Porter, Harp." I decide to pull the plug. Maybe this long distance relationship between my kid and him is unhealthy. What if he never comes back? "He's busy with his new job."

"But he promised," she spats, throwing her notebook. "You're lying; he promised he'd have time for me. That whenever I need him he'll drop everything for me. He's not dad. He's not dead," she shouts. She shouts from the top of her lungs and starts crying.

"Harper," I whisper lost. What can I tell my kid? I don't want to break her heart; I don't want to keep the illusion that Porter is part of us. Is it an illusion? "Baby, I don't know if Porter has time for us."

"He loves us. He can be my dad. It's all your fault!" she screams, running away toward the entrance door. "I hate you. I hate you."

With that last I hate you, she takes off leaving the front door wide open. Shit. Where is she going? I grab my phone, charging after her, only to find her in the arms of the man I just told her would never be coming back here. Never. Just by looking at him hugging my frustrating, loving little girl, I'm reminded of how much I shouldn't miss him; of how much my heart shouldn't beat for him. And how this man has my stomach twisted into a knot, knot I forget is there as long as I don't think of him.

"Found someone who belongs to you close to the sidewalk." Porter approaches me with a cautious smile. Harper is clinging onto him and Finn runs out of the house and latches on to his leg like a tick. "Everything okay here?" He squats and picks up Finn with his free arm.

"Hi." I cover my mouth, holding back tears and nod. Because nothing is okay, except he's here and everything feels lighter.

"Dinner?" He questions, I look at my watch and hang my head. I've been so busy with Harper's homework and behavior that I forgot to start dinner. "Where's Molly?"

"San Diego, visiting friends with Rhonda," I respond, "Someone gifted her a round-trip ticket and she took off." I try to fake a smile, but I can't. Harper's behavior has me raging from the inside. I feel helpless.

"Sorry, I didn't think about . . ." He shrugs. "Can I make it up to you? We can go for dinner wherever you guys want to go."

As I'm about to shake my head, Harper's sob convinces me to accept. Maybe Porter is here to say goodbye, tell us that he's found the life he missed and that he's done with us. Is that what's best for us? Maybe because fighting the dreams that I'm in his arms are draining. His absence is making my heart feel numb and my soul weak. And like magic, his presence takes the anxiety away, the loneliness. The void his absence created dissipates.

The battle begins. The fucking internal battle between the lost love of my late husband and the absence of a man who . . . I don't know how to describe him. Each morning I search for Leo in bed, but I miss Porter at breakfast, during the middle of the day, dinner time, and at nights.

Playing his songs over and over on Spotify doesn't cut it. It's not the same as having him playing his guitar right next to me and singing me whatever song he'd decided to perform that night.

"Go and put on your shoes, Harper," I order her, as I look at the entire picture. She had left without her rain boots or a jacket "We'll talk about this issue later, just because we're heading for dinner doesn't mean it's forgotten."

Porter sets her down. "He came back," she fumes, stomping her bare feet. "He loves us."

"Can I ask?" I shake my head at his question. "Something I can do to help?"

"We'll talk later," I tell him without getting into any specifics. The last thing I want is for Harper to hear us talking about his presence.

"Okay," he says, walking by me and planting a kiss on my lips before turning his attention to Finn. "Let's get you ready, buddy. I'm taking you guys to celebrate."

Fuck, I missed him.

"ARE YOU OKAY?"

"I . . ." I shake my head. "No. Not tonight. Maybe we can talk about it another day. But thank you for dinner. They had fun."

"My pleasure," he smiles at me, extending his hand, and taking mine. "And you?"

"I enjoyed it too," I say, biting back the rest of the words I want to say, like I missed you. Because maybe, maybe he's here to say goodbye. Or maybe that's what I want him to do. Finish what we never started, because my heart couldn't take another loss. Once again, I'm confused as hell. "I missed you."

He hugs me with his strong arms, whispering in my ear, "I missed you too, babe. Can you tell me what's going on?"

Pressing myself closer to him, I shake my head. Talking about Harper will bring up my own thoughts and maybe his new life. Tonight I only want to enjoy a little piece of heaven. A little piece of him. "I'd rather not."

"No worries, it doesn't matter right now." He releases me and grabs his jacket while looking around the house. "I came to spend some time with you guys and give you a heads up about tomorrow. Chris, one of my foster dads, is coming over along with AJ and Thea. They want to help with Finn, but only if you allow it."

Walking closer, I study him, allowing myself to actually look at him for the first time since he arrived. His hair is longer, his eyes softer, and he's thinner. Did he lose weight? I find his eyes. My heart flutters as his soft brown eyes radiate that tenderness that makes me feel safe. "What's bothering you, Mac?"

"I have a meeting tomorrow with the school about my punctuality and Finn's behavior. Virginia threatened to come next week to check on the kids."

"Oh, baby. You're supposed to call me when things like that happen." His hand reaches for mine, as he chews on his lip for a second. "We'll be here tomorrow morning. Thea and Chris are counselors. AJ studied early childhood and speech pathology. I can't remember all her degrees, but she knows her shit. They're family and Finn will be in great hands—loving hands. Once we have a plan, we can go to the meeting and show them what a kick-ass mother you are. As for Virginia—she can't touch you, Mac. I have the money to hire the best attorney, but I hope it doesn't come to that."

I raise my eyebrows, staring at him with admiration.

He smiles, kisses my hand and then my cheek. "Everything will work out, but I need you to have faith. About Harper's little issue, I'm sorry. Maybe Thea can help me think of a way to explain my past to the kids in a positive way." My breath hitches when his hand caresses my face.

"It's time for me to go, but I'll see you soon."

FORTY-THREE

CHRISTIAN

"TOO FUCKING EARLY," I grumble closing my eyes. "Thank fuck we flew and thank you for this coffee. That crap your dad prepared me earlier was decaf. Shit, that's what I drank. This is why you're my favorite. I love you, sweetheart."

"You're welcome, Papi. Just don't tell Dad," AJ responds. "He'll have a conniption. Do you think you'll be ready to face the children?"

"Have I ever had trouble facing my grandchildren?" I open my eyes and give her a stern look, feigning insult. "No. I'm a professional when it comes to handling kids. Your children adore me—they like me more than they like Arthur."

She laughs, shaking her head.

"We agreed that there wouldn't be any sort of competition, Christian," Thea calls out from the front seat. "Everyone get ready. Remember first impressions matter. We don't high five the seven-year-old girl for punching a boy's face, Chris."

I laugh for the last time, before I have to gather my shit and be a responsible adult. AJ smirks at me. We both are proud of Harper for standing up for Porter. "Yes, Doc, I'll behave like a responsible adult. Now let's meet my new grandchildren."

"Please don't scare her, Pops," Porter warns me. "Mac isn't there just yet, so don't introduce yourself as their grandfather."

I pat his back. "Don't worry, kid. I have this."

Calling me Pops is one of the big steps between us. He's working hard to show how much he has changed. I've seen my sons tempt him with beers, but he doesn't even look at them. Porter fights daily against his demons and he has no problem calling Gabe or me in the middle of the night if he's having a bad dream. Not like when he first moved in with us, when he tried to show that he was strong and could do everything by himself. Maybe if we had looked into it closer, shit wouldn't have happened.

But the past is there for us to learn from. He is working hard not only to show the family that he has changed, but also that he wants to be one of us. Gabe and Porter are working on their relationship too. My boys are watchful, but they changed their attitude the moment AJ welcomed Porter into the family. Our family is almost complete; he just has to find his happy ending.

"Porter!" a small girl flies out of the house in front of us, jumping into his arms. "You came back. Are we going back with you? Do you have a big house where all my dollies can live?"

"Harp, meet part of my family." He moves closer to us. "This is Pops, one of my fathers—"

"Harper Elise Brooke, come back here or I swear you'll be in time-out for the rest of your natural life."

"She's at it again," Harper sighs, resting her head on Porter's shoulder as she hugs his neck tightly.

"What happened, Harp?"

"Mom called the school to tell them that Finn wouldn't be there today. Then, the principal of my school phoned her about . . . she told her that I called a boy names. They claim I'm terrorizing the school."

Thea shakes her head, biting her lip. AJ drops her eyes and shakes in laughter but she's silent enough not to drag attention to herself. Harper is adorable and funny.

"Great, I'll have to schedule your death sentence for later, as we have company." My attention is drawn to the front door again, where a woman who looks a lot like Harper appears, wearing a frown. "Put her down, Porter Kendrick, or you'll be the next one." She fights the smirk back when their eyes connect. "She's in so much trouble."

"Chris Decker." I extend my hand. "You must be the lovely

Mackenzie. I've heard a lot about you."

"AJ Decker-Bradley," AJ introduces herself, waving at the little boy peeking out from the door. "This is my sister-in-law. Thea."

"Sorry, I thought you'd be here later." Her voice softens and she tries to fix her hair with both hands. "Please come inside, sorry for the mess. It's been a chaotic morning."

"Chaos?" I laugh because she hasn't been by my house when there are four babies and a toddler. That's pandemonium, which I love. The little boy with amber eyes hides behind the couch, holding a small guitar and glancing at everyone. "He's your boy?"

"Yes, that's Finn," she confirms.

"Good morning, Finn," Porter calls out to him and the little boy runs toward him. With ease, he scoops up both kids, who are squeezing him hard. "I missed you too, sport."

Thea tilts her head slightly toward Mackenzie, who stares at the picture perfect family in front of her. She pulls on her sweatshirt sleeve and bites on it. We discussed Mackenzie during the week, as we searched for a family counselor around the area for her and the children. Porter is weary about taking this step, because I explained to him maybe once she's past the emotional vacuum, she might not want to be with him. I hope that's not the case, because I can see and feel the love he has for them.

"Well there's nothing like the present, let's get started." Porter sits the children down. "Finn, I'm going to introduce you to my friends. They're here to play with us, would you like that?" Finn nods.

FORTY-FOUR

MACKENZIE

FROM THE COUCH, I watch Thea and AJ playing with Finn. They've been doing that for the past couple of hours. From puzzles, to board games and flash cards they've been keeping him busy while asking him questions and directing some to me. Porter and Chris have been spending time teaching Harper music.

"There aren't any delays," AJ informs me, sitting next to me. "If you can forward the hearing study, I can combine that with what I have for today. Would you agree to come to Seattle for a few days?"

"Seattle?"

"I run an academy," she explains. "I also have a therapy consult. My entire team can work with him for a couple of days and come up with a plan to find his voice. Thea believes that it can be a combination of several factors. Grief, change, loss. Did you guys visit a counselor after your husband died?"

I shake my head. "Once, but the doctor wanted me to talk and I . . . I've met with one a couple of times after Christmas. But without my aunt in town it's been hard to keep up with the appointments. I guess I have handled everything the wrong way?"

Is there a wrong or right way to handle loss?

She pats my hand. "Understandable. Losing a loved one sucks. Some stuff happened to me and I handled it by behaving bat-shit crazy, or that's how my brothers described it." I try not to laugh, but when she does, I join in. "We can suggest many things for you and your family, but we're not here to impose anything."

"Why are you doing this?"

"Because that's what we do for our family," she answers, looking up at Porter who is setting Harper's fingers on the chords. "Porter cares for you; he loves your kids and worries about Finn."

Porter stands up, setting the guitar on the pedestal and walking to where I sit. "Mac, will you be okay if I take the kids to the park with Pops?"

"Harper is grounded."

"Just a few minutes, so she can burn off some of that energy inside her," Chris adds. "I promise not to let her have too much fun."

"Yes, that's fine."

It takes me longer to say the sentence than for them to get ready and leave the house.

"Have you ever gone to a grief counselor?" Thea asks from where she sits, piling the toys and putting them on the boxes they brought.

I let out a big breath. "I've gone a couple of times, but with my aunt of town, and the cost," I repeat what I told AJ, adding the second problem I have with the therapies. Fitting the fee into the budget is hard.

Thea stands from the chair she's been sitting on and hands me a folder. "There's a list of counselors who will work pro bono. Call them; find the right fit for each one of you." She takes a seat next to me. "I think you're doing great, but there's nothing wrong with asking or accepting help from others. My card is inside the folder, next to AJ's. Pria, our other sister would love to meet you and help. No matter what you decide, we're a phone call away."

"Even if I choose not to be with Porter?"

"Even if," AJ confirms. "But don't close yourself off to the possibilities."

I STARE AT the list that Thea gave me last week. Calling a couple of those therapists was easy. Unfortunately, the hours they had available are during the mid-morning. Their times after lunch are full and there's a waiting list for when they open. But I need to find someone to help all of us. Things are getting worse, like today. Harper is having a terrible breakdown. She arrived home from school with a flyer. Father-daughter dance. There's a fucking father-daughter dance next month and Leo can't be here to go with her.

"I want my dad back," she starts crying and my heart breaks for her.

When will the intensity of the pain of his loss diminish a little? At least enough for us to have some kind of happy-normal life. "I'm going to look for Porter. He might want to come with me." Harper goes to her room and comes back with a backpack and boots. "I'll talk to Porter. He said he loved me, why can't he love me enough to be with us?"

"Harp, I know this is hard for you," I console my kid, hugging her tight. I don't know what to tell her about Porter, I'm at a loss. "How about if we prepare some dinner and find a solution? This is hard for the three of us, baby. But I believe that someday it won't feel as painful."

Harper and I hold onto each other as a second wave of tears hits us, but they wind down by the time I have to serve dinner. Harper falls asleep and I leave her on the couch. Finn stays by the coffee table playing with his blocks. Today feels like one of those take-out kind of days. A day to hide under the blanket and forget the outside world. Instead, I go to the kitchen to cook. Some grilled cheese sandwiches, asparagus soup, and fruit should cheer her up; it's her favorite meal.

I set the table with the fancy napkins that Porter used to own, then use the formal silverware and china to go with it. I feel like a thief keeping his furniture, but having it here makes me feel safe. Fuck, I sound stupid. Half an hour later, I'm done preparing dinner, dessert, and setting a fancy table.

"Time for dinner," I whisper in Harper's ear.

"I don't want food," she cleans her eyes.

"I have chocolate chip cookies." I brush away the hair that got into her face. "Your favorite."

Mom's right, everything is better with cookies. No matter what kind, they always make you forget your sorrows.

"Finn," call for him, but he's not playing by the table. "Finn, baby, time for dinner."

I still hold out hope that he'll answer, but he doesn't. So I head to search for him. He's not in the bathroom or his room. I check in the kitchen and then my bedroom and the bathroom inside it. Nothing.

"Harper, have you seen Finn?" I call after her. "He's nowhere in the house."

We search up and down, but he's not turning up. Harper comes down the stairs frowning and shaking her head. "His cow and his guitar are gone."

"Don't panic," I tell her, but I'm speaking to myself. "He's in the house. There's no way he can get out without us noticing."

I walk to the door and notice it's slightly opened. Opening it all the way, I only see the street and cars passing through. He's not on the step waiting for anyone the way he used to do in the old house. Shit.

My heart drops as I pull out my phone to call for help.

"Mac?"

"I can't find Finn."

FORTY-FIVE

PORTER

"WHAT DOES THAT mean?" I bark as I look around the room. I have four teenagers holding their guitars expecting me to continue their lesson. "When was the last time you saw him?"

"I don't know," Mac sobs on the other side of the line. "Half an hour ago, maybe more because we've been looking for him."

Fuck. "Call 9–1-1," I order her. "I should be there soon. Don't move from there; make sure Harp stays with you. Do you hear me?"

"Yes."

I tap the phone, praying that Jacob is still across the street working. "Yeah?"

"Where are you?"

"Home, with the wife and kids. Why?"

"I need to head down to Portland, but I'm teaching a class," I explain. "Know someone who can cover me?"

"Why the sudden emergency?"

"Mac can't find Finn."

"Shit, call Mason. He can help you find him faster," he orders. "I'll have someone cover for you soon."

I call Mason Bradley, who asks me a bunch of questions and leaves me on hold for a long time, or at least that's how it feels. A few minutes later, the substitute music teacher Jacob sent arrives. As I'm heading out of the school, one of the agents who used to watch me intercepts me. He's driving me to a building nearby per Mason's orders.

As we arrive at the building, I find Gabe, AJ, Mason Thea, Matt, and Jacob waiting for me. The other part of the clan stayed behind with the kids. The flight isn't long and as we're heading south, Mason explains to me that he already has people combing the area. The police have been called and there's someone with Mac and Harper.

The helicopter lands by the park close to Mac's house. There's a truck already waiting for us to take us to my old place.

"Any news?" Mason asks the man outside the door, and he shakes his head.

"It's going to be okay," Gabe says, placing his hand on top of my shoulder. "We're going to find him."

We step inside the house. Mac sits on the corner of the couch holding onto Harper, who is crying. It takes me only a couple of strides to reach them; I take my little girl into my arms and hug her tightly. Then sit beside Mac and hold her against me.

"Any ideas of where he could've gone?" Mason starts asking questions to Mac. "Favorite places? I say we head out to search for him, Porter. You know him, you know the area, and he trusts you."

He's right, and I try to get Harper to sit with her mom again, but she's clawed onto my body. So far, she hasn't said a word to me, but she can't seem to be able to let me go.

"Hi, sweetheart." Thea squats right in front of me. Gabe sits down right next to me. "Remember me?"

Harper huffs and turns around, holding me tighter.

Thea tilts her head. "Do you remember the last time I was here? You promised to show me your dolls. Why don't you do that? Porter has to go in search of Finn?"

Harper jumps out of my lap and takes Thea's hand in hers. I'm glad that Thea knows so much about my girl that she's able to distract her. Once she's gone, I hold Mac closer to me. "I'll bring Finn back in a few; keep your faith." Mac holds on to me tightly for a few seconds before she lets me go.

"Don't worry, I'll take care of her," Gabe promises.

I didn't understand why everyone joined the search until I step outside the house. AJ and Gabe are with Mac. Thea is with Harper and Matthew, Jacob, and Mason are with me. They wanted to make sure everyone was taken care of. We walk around the neighborhood. Visit the ice cream shop, the convenience store, and finally arrive at the park.

"Porter, they already combed the park," Mason informs me. "I need you to think of another place. Where did you go with him often?"

Often? We visited the park regularly. The days I had afternoons off we'd come to the park to practice on his bike, or just play on the playground. Sometimes we played hide and seek, but he was the only one hiding, until I'd find him in . . ."The tree house," I whisper, rushing through the trails toward the house. The place where he always hid and I'd always find him. Reaching the handle, I swing it open and find him squatting in the corner hugging his legs.

"Hey, sport," I call after him.

Finn lifts his head; his eyes brighten when he finds me. "Porter," he says, standing up and extending his arms towards me.

Fuck. My entire world comes undone and comes back together in an instant. One word, that's all I needed to know that this boy is *mine*.

Holding onto him tight, we march back to the house to check on Mac and give her the good news. As she sees us, she rushes towards us with her eyes filled with tears and a gratifying smile lighting up her face.

"You found him!" Her voice wavers, "Thank you."

"Anytime," I whisper, trying to hand Finn to her, but he tightens his grasp on my neck.

"Porter," he repeats, and doesn't let me go.

Mac gasps, staring at both of us. "He said your name. That's a miracle!"

"I know." I pull her into a hug and rub her back as she cries. The emotions, after such a big night, must be running too high for her to keep it together. "He's going to be okay, everything will be okay."

FORTY-SIX

MACKENZIE

PORTER'S FAMILY IS a force to be reckoned with. One moment they storm into my house and the next, they're dragging me out with my stuff and taking me to some secret house in Malibu. When we arrived, the house was silent. Thea showed me to my room. The kids are sharing a room, but Harper doesn't mind because there's a pool in the house. Porter's parents treated me like their daughter from the moment I stepped in here. Everyone has been wonderful to us, as if we are part of the family. After settling down, and Porter telling me he'd take care of the bedtime story, I decided to walk down to the beach.

"How are you feeling?" AJ sits on the sand next to me.

"Better," I respond, staring at the ocean. "Maybe I should've stayed at home, instead of coming here to relax."

She shakes her head. "This is much better than murky Oregon. Don't get me wrong, I love where I grew up and where I live. But coming here to enjoy the sun, the sand, and the sea helps a lot."

I nod because I do enjoy the ocean. The two times I've visited my parents, going to the beach is one of the things I did first. "Thank you, for opening your home and helping me."

"The house is Thea's, and we're happy to help," she responds. "I heard Finn. He said Porter's name several times. That's a huge step. I'd love to introduce you to my team; I think they can do a lot of great things to help your kiddo."

"Thank you," I tell her, not wanting to discuss the subject. At least not after the day I had.

"Found them," I hear a voice, looking over my shoulder I see Thea walking toward us with another woman. "Mac, how are you feeling?"

"Better, still shaky. Finn's disappearance is the scariest moment of my life by far."

"I'm glad you're better." She gives my shoulder a slight squeeze. "Mac, this is Pria Decker, our other sister. Jacob's wife. Pria, meet Mac. She has a couple of adorable kids."

"Hi, Pria." I shake her hand. "It's nice to meet you."

"Nice to meet you, Mackenzie." She takes a seat and looks around. "Finally some peace."

"Where's everyone," AJ asks.

"Let see, Mason is taking care of your kids. Jacob is with his twins. Though Gabe and Chris are helping him. Piper is asleep." Thea lifts the baby monitor in her hand. "Matt and Tristan went to check on a couple of our bars." Thea releases a laugh. "Tristan has a thing for having sex at his bars. They invited me but I'm exhausted."

I look around, making sure I'm not the only one hearing that she's talking about her husband Matt planning to have sex with another man

"TMI, Thea," AJ complains. "Matt is my brother. Knowing when, how and where he's having sex is disgusting."

"I'll remind you of the same the next time you mention sex with *my* brother."

By now, I'm so confused I have to ask them to stop. "Is your brother Tristan or Mason?" I ask Thea.

"Mason is my brother, Tristan is my husband," she explains. And then adds to it. "Tristan and Matt . . . and I together. A couple—triad."

My mind goes into shock. The behavior of the other guy, Tristan, now makes sense. He held onto Matthew and Thea when they arrived. Then the three of them disappeared for a little while.

"But that's impossible," I say out loud. "You can't love two men at the same time."

She smiles at me and bobs her head. "Yes, I can and I do. Just as they love each other. It's beautiful to see them together. The two of them love me so much I feel cherished every second of my life. It's all about love, not rules."

I shake my head wondering if that's true. Could something like that apply to someone like me?

"I don't think I could love anyone other than Leo," I spit, but the words don't feel accurate. "We made promises, plans. How can I move on? I'm not sure if it's fair for him. Or if I can be whole again."

"Losing your loved one isn't something you get over with," Pria says. "More like you learn to live with their absence and move into a place where you can find happiness. It's a process; finding the new place is difficult. But once you reach it, you find you survived. There are cuts and a few bruises, but you made it—undefeated."

I'm not sure if I've learned to live without him, but I have survived. So far I'm still standing. Maybe she's right. Things might not be as bad as I think they are. Certainly they aren't as bad as they were when Leo died.

"It's getting late," Pria says, squeezing my hand. "Tomorrow is a long day, try to get some rest."

"Mackenzie, you're not alone," Thea reassures me. "You have this family to give you a hand. We're noisy and nosy, but loving."

"One call and we'll come to the rescue," AJ adds.

"Our house is always open, and we can do so much for you in Seattle," Pria concludes. The three nod, while smiling. "Are you coming with us?"

"I'd like to stay a little longer." I touch my temple. "Thank you, for everything."

They make their way away from the beach, leaving me alone with my thoughts once again.

"HEY," I HEAR his voice before he sits next to me.

"Are they asleep?"

"Yes, they finally settled down," Porter confirms. Earlier, Harper begged him to help her with her nightly routine. Finn didn't ask for much. However, he wouldn't let go of Porter at all. "Harper mentioned a father-daughter dance."

"What did you tell her?"

"Nothing," Porter responds. "There's not much I can say until you and I can move forward, Mac. I want to offer so many things, but not until you're ready. I wish I could offer you more than my patience and love. I have this dream where you let me into your life and we build one of our own. I love you and your children and you mean everything to me."

I gulp, because as he speaks, I can imagine his dream. "Part of my dream died years ago. Replacing him sounds wrong; the guilt stops me from enjoying life." I tilt my head and our eyes connect. "It's hard, but. . . ." *I want to work on it.* The words don't make it out, because even when my heart feels them, I don't feel they are strong enough to voice them out—yet.

"I understand, and I'm not asking you to replace him," he adds. "I love the three of you so much. And there's no way I'll love you the way Leo did. But I'll love you the best way I can if you give us a chance. You have a big heart and I know there's enough space for me."

"I've missed you," I say, looking at the ocean. "Thank you for coming so fast, for finding Finn."

"There's nothing to thank me for. I love Finn. As I searched for him, I kept thinking about James, I never met him, yet I still love him. That love I have for him is similar to the one I have for Finn and Harp. Even though I know they have their own father, I'd work hard to be a father figure to them. Not to replace him, but more like make sure they grow up with someone who loves them."

"Porter," I sigh because tonight he's saying the right things, but I'm not ready to say much back.

"I love you, Mac, and you can't change that," he explains. "Your smile that comes out so naturally no matter how shitty the circumstances. Your inquisitive mind, the love you have for your children. You don't give yourself enough credit for all you do." He sighs touching my hand. "I wish you'd give yourself a chance to feel again, to live instead of guarding your heart. Will I leave you?" He shrugs. "I can't promise that I won't, because I don't know how long I'll live, but no one has a crystal ball and knows what's going to happen tomorrow, or in five minutes. I'm asking you to give me those five minutes."

FORTY-SEVEN

MACKENZIE

HOW MANY TIMES can a person hit the restart button? Is there a limit?

I don't know, but after the almost week I spent with the Decker family, I want to do that. Give myself another chance. Find a happy place; make sure my children feel like we're a family. Not just three people sharing a last name with the only goal of survival. Families share everything, the good, the bad, the happy, and the sad.

Moving to Seattle offers more than a team of therapists for Finn. It includes friends. Friends, who in a week, taught me that life is better when you have someone to lean on. That if I let myself share some of the weight I carry, it's easier to manage. My children fell in love with the entire family. By the end of our time together, they were calling the grandparents by their nicknames. Even Thea's father welcomed them both and let them call him Papa Arthur.

For those many reasons and more that I may not have thought about yet, I want to try living in Seattle. This won't be an easy move, but it'll be worth it. I've been weighing the pros and cons for the past month. Harper worries me, as she'll have to start a new school. She's going to be the new girl again, but we can face that together. We'll find a good support for the two of us. My goal is to find some common ground and find a way for us to relate. When I ran my idea by her, she was ecstatic. Seeing Papa Gabe and Chris was her second thought, her first was Porter. She'd be closer to him. We'll be closer to him. Only I have no idea what the best area is to search for an apartment in Seattle. Schools . . . taking a nice sip of coffee and a deep breath, I decide to call AJ. She lives there and has an academy too.

Asking for a little help is a good way to start.

"Hi, you reached the voicemail of AJ Bradley-Decker. You know what to do."

"AJ, this is Mackenzie Brooke," I say after the beep. "Call me whenever you have time. I made a decision, and I need your help to find an apartment in Seattle. I have a few questions about the area. I've been thinking about the kids' future, your offer to help with Finn. Starting another chapter might be the last push I need to find our new normal. Anyway . . . Please, call me when you have time, thank you."

After hanging up the phone, I look at my list one more time.

1. Find a job.
2. Find an apartment.
3. Find schools for the kids.
4. Send the transcripts from the old school to the new one.
5. Get boxes.
6. Pack.

Am I doing them in the right order? I hope so. My phone rings, AJ's name appears.

"AJ, thank you for calling back," I answer.

"Mac, how are you? Are the kids alright?"

"Yes, we're fine. Better," I say looking at the written list and reading possibilities in between the lines, not chores, or extra work. Possibilities.

"I heard your message, Pops, my brothers, and I are puzzled. When do you plan to move?"

Hmm, I wanted this to remain between the two of us until I was ready to move and my life made sense. Does it matter that they know? No. Maybe between all of them we can find a place faster. "It's a slow process. But I'm actively searching for a job."

"You've been doing some admin stuff for the flower shop and you can handle the office, right?"

"Yeah?" Her question doesn't make sense and all I hear are muffled voices in the background and I wonder if I made a mistake by calling her.

"Let's figure out housing . . . No, Mattie, my other house is occupied and Porter is living at Arthur's."

"Tell her that we'll call her in a few hours, baby girl. Let's finish this track and then organize the move."

"Pops says—"

"No worries, I heard. Thank you, but, I don't want to burden you guys."

"You *are* part of our family, and if you could, you'd do this for us too. Wouldn't you?"

"Yes, of course."

"Then it's settled, we'll see you in a few days."

A few days?

NEW LIFE, TAKE two.

"Welcome home." AJ opens the door, Harper zooms by without saying hello. Finn follows right behind. "How was the trip?"

"Exhausting," Chris answers, walking right behind me. "I'm no longer in shape to move my children around."

"I said we should split the move into two days," Gabe complains, climbing up the stairs. "You chose not to wait for the weekend so the boys could help and to do everything in one day."

"My mistake," Chris grumbles, following his husband. "Ainsley Janine, take them to your house for an hour. We have to decompress."

She shakes her head and we all leave the house through the backyard.

"I wish my old house had been available for you. Though we'll love having you here," she comments, as we walk through a stone trail. She suddenly stops and points at the house in front of us. "The house next to my parents is mine, the next one is Jacob's, the small cottage is where my grandparents live, and at the end is Matt's. We all have room for you guys, but my parents wanted to have you with them." We stop in the middle, where there's a small, fenced in play area. Harper and Finn go inside and we sit on a bench that's outside.

"Thank you for answering my call and helping me settle in." I study

the area. There are trees, a pool, a greenhouse, a pond, and a lake surrounding most of the property. "You guys didn't have to go through all
this trouble, but I appreciate the hospitality."

After spending a couple of days with Porter and his family in
California, I kept thinking about my life. They were offering me a
chance to start a new chapter. Guidance to navigate the next stage.
Finn needs more help than I can give him. AJ offered me a job, and as
an employee I get free classes for my children. That means Finn's preschool fees, therapies, and music lessons for Harper will be taken care
of. Looking for a place to stay was out of the question, seeing as how
their homes are big enough to accommodate us. Chris called to offer his
house, saying that it'd be an honor for him and Gabe to have us.

"I still think you should've told Porter."

"Soon. I'm planning to talk to him before we bump into each other
at work. Right after we settle in."

We have to unpack and meet the new counselors. Thea sent me
a list of therapists in the area who are also pro bono. We all are going
to go to grief counseling. Seattle might be our final destination. If everything works out for us, I might use the money I have in the bank
for a down payment on a house. Aunt Molly was sad to see me go, but
relieved because she found a great place in San Diego to settle down.
My parents are supportive about this step, but I didn't mention Porter
because I am not sure if I'm ready to deal with that part yet.

Mac: *I'm making a few changes.*

Porter: *I'm happy to hear that.*

I stare at the screen, wishing I could see more than the picture I
have of him with the kids.

Mac: *You already did a lot, but I might need moral support. Today I
start a new job. I began therapy yesterday.*

Porter: *The kids?*

Mac: Harper is starting a new program, Finn a new preschool and therapies. Plus, both began grief counseling too.

Porter: Sounds like a great start to a new life.

Mac: I hope so . . .

Mac: I'm not sure how you'll fit into our lives, but I hope we find a place for you.

Porter: Me too, Mac. Me too.

Mac: How about if we start slow?

Porter: How slow?

Mac: Lunch?

Porter: I can't today. I'll drive to Portland next weekend and take you out for a nice dinner—no kids.

Mac: Do you know of any place where I can have lunch that is close to Decker's Art Academy?

Porter: Many, but where are you?

Mac: The reception desk, covering Sonny's lunch. She comes back in ten minutes.

Porter: I'll be there in nine.

PORTER RUSHES THROUGH the sliding doors. "How?" His large frame hovers over the reception desk. His features soften as he gazes down at me.

"I took a small leap, for the kids—for me," I offer, not sure why suddenly I'm feeling shy.

"Where are the kids?"

I grab my purse when Sonny arrives back from lunch, wave at her and join Porter on the other side where he gives me a quick hug.

"Finn is here. AJ opened up a space for him in the preschool program," I explain, walking out of the academy and wishing our hug had lasted longer than it did. "He'll be going to therapy right after. Harper is with Chris at the library—I'm unsure about sending her to school. Maybe they'll help me homeschool her."

"Fuck. I can't believe you're here." He runs a hand through his hair. "Let's go around the corner, you're going to like this place."

We arrive at a bistro within minutes. Porter opens the door for me, asking the hostess for a table for two. Several women turn to look at him while we walk to the booth, but his eyes are focused on me. I scoot down to the end of the booth and he slides next to me. As I look around, it hits me. This is the first time we're out without the kids. Just the two of us. It feels different, intimate. All his attention is on me, but of course not having the kids doesn't mean that we don't talk about them. He listens to every word I say about my decision to move, Harper's joy finding out that she can use AJ's pool every day, and Finn's love for AJ's cat, Toby.

"Harper wants a pet and twin sisters." He chokes with the chicken soup. "Or at least, another brother or sister."

"What did you tell her?"

"I ignored her because anything I say will be used against me," I remind him of my darling girl.

"I miss them."

"Porter . . ." I shrink, wanting to disappear under the table. "My therapist thinks that until I know what I'm doing, I should keep them stable. What if things between us don't work?"

Changing the subject he asks, "Tell me what you do at the Academy."

We talk about the admin stuff I do on a daily basis, also the project that AJ has been planning. *Grow a garden*, while the kids are learning. He shares his newest project with me. Along with Matthew and Jacob, they're opening auditions to discover the next big band. Matt might make it a reality show, but he's working on the details. When his phone buzzes, I realize that somehow we've been talking for a little more than an hour and we barely touched our food.

"We have to go back, Mac." He signals the waiter. "Let's plan on doing this tomorrow, but only for an hour."

I shake my head because that's not giving me space. He places a finger on top of my lips. "You have to eat; I have to eat. Unless you bring food that we can share to my office, I'll take you out to lunch."

"Only for tomorrow," I agree, but he grins, and I can feel the battle about lunch just beginning.

FORTY-EIGHT

MACKENZIE

AFTER EIGHT WEEKS, life has settled for the kids and for me. A couple of weeks after we arrived, we moved into a cute three-bedroom apartment. We live close to the Academy and within the city. Counseling has been beneficial for the three of us. Harper and I have learned to cope with the loss and start building a new relationship without her father being the center of it. We love Leo and understand that he's no longer among us. His ashes are inside a black box and his soul is in heaven. As long as we carry his memories with us, he'll be in our hearts.

Finn is making progress. He says the basic words and asks for Porter more often than I'd like to hear from him. Not because I have a problem with Porter, but because we all want him to express himself further. Porter misses the kids, and though he's seen them while they are at the academy, he has kept himself away from them. My lunch during the week is a trip to the record company with food that one of us prepares the night before.

"You outdid yourself today, Mr. Kendrick," I close the container of food and set it on top of his desk. "I'm thinking that tomorrow should be your turn again."

"Fell for that once already, Mackenzie Brooke." He opens his drawer and takes out a Snickers bar. "Catch. We'll have to call this dessert, the weather is too shitty to go for ice cream, and I have a recording session soon."

"So are the rumors about your return to the music biz true?" My heart drops, because of the uncertainty. Porter the singer wasn't a great person back in the day. I fear how it'll affect him.

He shakes his head. "We're releasing an album in a couple of weeks," he explains, setting his arms on his desk and leaning forward. "It'll benefit the foundation. The Decker girls are planning some big summer camp and it should offset the cost."

A slight knock on the door makes me jolt. Porter walks to open it.

"Five minutes," a woman dressed in a pair of skinny jeans and a see-through camisole announces. She stares at me and then moves her attention back to Porter. "That's your lunch date?" She turns around, leaving a bad taste inside my mouth.

"You're singing with her?" I rise from my seat.

"No, she's an intern," he explains, going to his desk and shutting his laptop. His eyes travel up and down my body and he smiles. "Careful, with that attitude I might think you're jealous." He winks at me, taking my hand.

"No, I . . ." His brow arches, his dark eyes stare at me and I huff. "Maybe a little."

"You shouldn't. I'll walk you across the street." Not waiting for me to say anything, he pulls me toward him, putting his arm around me. "So about Saturday—"

"Porter!" I hear the squeak, before we're tackled by a four-foot tall tornado.

Porter releases me, bends down to Harper's height, and hugs her tightly. "How are you, beautiful?"

"Chris, I didn't know you were here," I greet him.

"I have a song to record and she insisted on coming along with me," he explains.

"Mom, can I go to California for date night?" I narrow my gaze looking at both Porter and Chris, then stare at Harper who is expecting an answer. Who the hell told her about that? "Please, pretty please. It's going to be fun."

"Who told her?" I lift my palms shake my head and leave. "Never mind, I have to go back to work." Stepping closer to her, I kiss her cheek.

"Love you, baby. I'll see you at home."

"Hey wait," Porter calls behind. "Harp, I'll be right back. Pops, tell them I'll be there in a few. Mac, wait."

"I can't go to Malibu for date night." I turn around to look at him. "Can we just keep things the way they are?"

"One date?" He takes me in his arms, kissing my forehead.

"Porter . . ." I rest my head on his chest.

EACH NIGHT, I go to bed with a heavy heart and a lot of conflict inside of it. Would Leo accept that I have another man in my life? Porter wants us to move forward and I want the same. The next obvious step is a date. For the past week, he's been asking me to go out with him on a simple date. Then, he invited me to California along with the entire Decker family. He doesn't understand that I'm not there yet. Or am I?

The transition from the woman I was after Leo died, to the woman I am today is impressive. I no longer have trouble opening my eyes, facing the day, or making my own decisions. I've registered for online classes to earn my teaching degree. Between this one and my other degree, I can become a science teacher at a high school and still do what I want. Finding my passion is one of my goals.

Harper didn't mention the trip to California with the Decker family. But I know she's disappointed about tomorrow. Should I go? The manual of widow-mothers has nothing on when, how, and what to do when you're falling for an amazing guy. Am I betraying someone? All the questions I have sound stupid. Mom insists that I start to date.

My phone rings, and hoping it's Porter, I run toward my purse. Unfortunately, the caller ID reads Virginia Brooke. We haven't spoken since last December when she accused me of being unfaithful to my late husband. My thumb hovers over the bar that reads *slide to answer.* I didn't inform her that I moved to Seattle, unlike the last time when I moved from Colorado to Oregon.

"Virginia?"

"Mackenzie, how are you?"

"Fine," I respond, clearing my throat. "Great. The kids are also doing well. How about yourself?"

"Better, I—I'm calling because things between us ended up ugly the last time I visited you," she speaks with a soft voice. "You were trying to move on with your life. That's something I can't do, Mackenzie. Find a new or different life. In this new life you're creating, I no longer have an active role. It crushed me and the sadness became anger. In my mind, telling you those hideous things would keep you close to me, but it didn't. Did it?"

My heart hurts for her because I understand her fears. Her child died and no one or anything can replace a kid. That's the biggest loss someone can endure. We all lost an important piece of our lives when Leo died and we dealt with it in different ways.

"No," I respond. "It only made me want to stay away from you. Look, Virginia, I want my children to know their grandmother. I love you because you're a part of Leo. If I ever decide to start a relationship with someone, that'll never change. Unless you continue to treat me the way you did that day."

"I'm sorry," she says softly. "For everything I said. It was hard to see the picture in front of me. You had a family. A handsome man who adores you and the children love him. I had become an outsider."

"You only assumed, Virginia. Porter's a friend. Nothing happened between us." *Before that night.* The memory of that horrible night makes me shiver. Porter trying to make everything better, while I treated him like he meant nothing to me. "He's a friend."

"My biggest fear is losing you and the kids. You're finding a new way to live. I know it because I've known you since you were young, Mackenzie. You're the one who pushed my son to find the perfect college where he could study his career of choice. He ignored my pleas to stay in North Carolina. You're always moving forward, looking for the next big thing, making things work for both of you."

Virginia goes from how we moved out of Charlotte, to Leo's childhood. She talks about his love for physics, cars, and computers. Stories that I never knew. Him breaking an arm at the age of seven trying to use a remote control car to power his skateboard. She wants to give my kids his spelling bee trophies and some of his old toys.

"Maybe over the summer," I propose, clearing the tears caused from talking about Leo, and his life. "We can try to visit you over the summer and then I can drive to Florida to see my parents, too."

"Will you bring your boyfriend?"

"He's only . . . I don't know," I stutter trying to explain that Porter isn't anything more than a friend, but having trouble, because lately, I want him to be my everything.

"I hope you do. I'd like to erase the bad impression I made on him."

"Thank you for calling, Virginia." I swallow the tears because the little trip through Leo's childhood and my doubts about Porter are about to make me wallow. "Maybe next time I'll call you while the children are awake, so they can say hello."

"Looking forward to it, Mackenzie."

The conversation with Virginia exhausts me. I haven't cried this much about the good moments in a long time. Everything has been related to Leo's loss, but I've never celebrated his life. He had a short, but happy life. After letting the tears wash away from the conversation with Virginia, I decide to finally shut my eyes in hopes that I can rest. But in a blink of an eye it's day and when I open my eyes he's there, sitting down by my side observing me, smiling down at me.

"You're back?" He shakes his head. "But you're here."

He taps my temple gently. "I'm here." Then he touches my heart. "And here. No matter where you think I'm at, I will always be in your heart."

"It's hard, Leo," I complain. "Nothing has been easy since you left. We promised to confront every obstacle we've faced together."

"Now you know that you're strong enough to face them without waiting for me or anyone," He says it with conviction, believing in me, even when I have failed so much in the past years. "But life is easier if you share it with someone. That guy, Porter, isn't half-bad and the kids love him. What's stopping you from falling for him?"

"You," I say simply.

He laughs. A rich laugh reminding me of Leo the prankster. It's been so long that I forgot how much I enjoyed it and how it filled my entire body with happiness.

"I'm not expecting you to forget me, I hope that you'll always remember me and the good times we shared, baby," he whispers, laying down next to me. "I expect you to find a new happy that brings back your smile. He does it—Porter. He brings back the smile, but in a different way from how I used to do it."

His hand caresses my cheek, our eyes meet, and they shine with a light that's almost blinding. "I've seen you cry too many tears since I left. Remember me with joy; hold on to those happy moments we shared. When it's time to celebrate, know that I'm right beside you celebrating. Don't be sad because you don't see me; be happy because the life you gave me was perfect. What we shared no one will take it away. I'm in a good place, enjoying a different kind of life filled with our memories. Be happy; let the light back inside your heart. Give yourself the chance to believe in love again."

As he leaves my side, the heaviness is gone with him. The moments that we shared together swirl inside my head. Our science labs, our first kiss, our first time, our first home, and so many more that bring tears to my eyes, but they're happy tears. Tears of pure joy. It's time for me to come to terms and accept that my life will never be the same without him, but I can find a new way to live. It's been three years since he left and I've been holding onto his memory so tightly that I've suffocated my children and myself to the point of almost dying of sadness.

"It's time," I say out loud.

"MAC?"

"How are you?" I ask trying to sound casual but it doesn't work, not one bit. One o'clock in the morning is a little late for house calls, but I can't help it. I have to do this now. "Where are you?"

"Working, can this wait until later?"

"Yes, no . . ." I sigh.

"Give me five," I hear him say, and as I'm about to hang up he speaks again. "I'm all ears, are you okay?"

I bite my lip and nod, but then remember he can't see me and that I have to talk. "Can we spend the next two days together, but without going to California? Gabe and Chris agreed to take Harp and Finn with them. There's so much I want us to talk about. To decide. Like where to bury Leo's ashes, your father's too."

"Can I call you after my session?" he asks. "My father's ashes can wait a couple of more hours. But I swear to get them out of your hair soon. Any particular reason why you're calling this late at night with these crazy requests?"

"A few months back I had a dream, where you were part of our family. Part of me. And I was part of you," I confess. "Tonight it was so real. Maybe it is time to allow myself to reach for it, to allow myself things I thought . . ."

"You're talking about an 'us?'" Porter says, pausing way too long. "Mackenzie, be clear about it because you're killing me here."

"Yes, it seems that even when I didn't want to make any room for you, you had already made your way into my heart," I answer. "Porter, I do love you and every day our love grows."

There's laughter on the other end of the phone, a hysterical laugh, nervous laugh that is contagious because I find myself doing the same.

"I love you," he whispers. "I'll be there tomorrow morning."

"I'll be here, waiting for you."

FORTY-NINE

PORTER

I PARK IN front of the building where Mac lives, which is only a couple of blocks from my place. My stomach is in knots. The adrenaline flowing through my veins has kept me on a high since the moment she called me. After the late recording session, I went back home, but instead of going to bed, I went for a run. Afterward, I showered, picked up some coffee, and came to look for her. I learned from Chris that Harper and Finn were thrilled about going to California with the family. The kids fit perfectly with the Deckers and knowing that the children are accepted by them is important.

Climbing out of the truck, I spot her shutting the main door of the building.

"New truck?" Mac asks as I open the passenger door for her and help her climb inside.

"You're already out." I touch the bags under her eyes.

"I haven't been able to sleep all night. Well, not after . . ."

"The dream?" I finish; she nods. I shut the door, walk around to the driver's side, and get in. "Want to tell me about it?" She bites her lip, and before she says a word, she looks around. "I bought a new SUV a few weeks ago as I heard Jacob and Matthew talking about all of the security features their wives' cars had to prevent accidents. Fancy shit for the kid's car seats."

"Why don't we talk about the dream? No. Fast-forward and repeat those three words you said to me over the phone."

Her looking around comes to a halt and she redirects her eyes toward me. "We should talk?" I growl, shaking my head. She laughs. "I had a dream?"

"No. Those are four." I cup her chin with both hands. "Something about liking me, caring about me . . . loving me?"

She scrunches her nose and I'm starting to lose my bravado. The courage is leaving along with the excitement of her call. "Don't leave me hanging here. I'm in fucking love with you. And every day I fall more and more for you. It's the smile on that beautiful face, your beautiful eyes, your bravery, everything. I adore you. So do you . . . love me?"

"I do." She gives me a peck. "I love you, Porter Kendrick. Because of the way you care for others, the music in your heart, your honesty, the way you love my kids, your ability to listen, and the way you make me feel safe."

Leaning closer, my hands move to the side of her neck. Our mouths are centimeters apart. I brush her lips once. "This." I do it one more time. "Is official." I give her a peck, but pull apart far enough to meet her lustful eyes. "Our first." I kiss her softly, my teeth toying with her lower lip. "Kiss." Her breath hitches as my mouth crashes against hers. My hands drift down her back. My lips taste hers before they part and my tongue pushes into her mouth.

Her arms are now around my neck, letting herself go. This kiss is different from all the others. Everything about this moment is different. There's no hesitation. The crazy internal fight she carried is gone. She's mine. Each breath, each touch, each heartbeat. They belong to me. Most of all, I am hers. I move my lips down her neck, wanting to kiss her all over. But I stop because we have the weekend and hopefully a lifetime. Today is about giving her a proper date and helping her make those decisions that woke her up in the middle of the night.

I sigh and kiss her forehead, using all my strength to separate my body from hers. "Fuck, I never thought I'd say this, but we have to talk."

"About?" Her eyes glisten and I'm close to forgetting about my plans and trying the reclining feature of the passenger seat.

"You mentioned the ashes," I say, opening the glove compartment and handing her the letter that Steven left me.

Dear Porter,

If you're reading this letter, it means I left this world. That you found a way to change the life you had created for yourself. Hopefully, you forgave me for all the wrongs I did. The few lines I now write you are to wish you happiness, hoping that you're ready to start a family of your own. When you are, keep it safe, guard it with your life, and enjoy every laugh, every tear, and every fight because they are what makes life worth living.

Love,

Steven Kendrick.

P. S. If you haven't, spread my ashes around some green pastures, let them be part of the circle of life.

"I don't want to do that with Leo." She straightens her back. "The kids might want to visit him. He'll always be a part of me—of us."

I brush the hair around her face, kissing her flushed cheeks. "Of course, he will always be a part of you, Mac. I wouldn't expect it to be any other way. He's Harp and Finn's father. I love them and I'll take care of them as if I am their father, but I know that I'm not. It'll be different for the twins." I add to lighten the mood, her eyes widen and the wrinkle on her forehead appears. "You mentioned Harper wanted twin sisters."

She gasps, shaking her head.

"We'll talk about that later, don't worry," I offer, smoothing her forehead and nibbling on her chin. Reaching for her seatbelt, I help settle her in the car and we leave for the next destination. Finding a place to bury Leo's ashes. Steven's will have to wait until I find a place to call home.

A month ago, I went to pick up Steven's letter. It wasn't much what he had written, but it means a lot that he wished me happiness. I wish him peace; I hope he found it once he made it to his final destination, wherever it might be. Maybe with my mother and my siblings. I don't know much about the afterlife, but I want to believe that our loved ones can listen to us. That every night when I say goodnight to James, he's listening and wishing me a goodnight too. That mom has been caring for him since the moment he made it to heaven and that maybe he's with our family.

As I drive along I-5, I take Mac's hand, kissing it a couple of times. She's been battling a load of grief for the past three years. I want to promise her many things, but for today, I will be by her side, being the emotional support she needs to finish this journey.

MACKENZIE

I READ STEVEN'S letter, and even when Porter and I agreed to follow his request, where we'll do it is yet to be decided. It became part of the "to be discussed" list. The list includes our future and when we're telling the kids that we're together. The decisions we made yesterday included our residence in Seattle is permanent. The kids have taken so well to the city and they love being a part of a big family. I'm going back to school and will continue working at the Academy. Porter, well, he wants to continue doing what he's doing. Teaching music, producing music and writing it.

The most important decision that we made was about Leo's ashes. For Harper and Finn's sake, we found a place to deposit them here in Seattle. The same place where Pria's parents were buried a few years back. As we already had a funeral for Leo, we decided that today it was only Porter and I. The kids remain in California with Gabe and Chris. They won't be back until tomorrow. I notified Virginia and extended an invitation to join us. Porter offered to pay for her plane ticket, but she chose not to be present. Maybe in a few weeks she'll come by to visit her grandchildren and Leo.

Doing this alone is fitting. Well, not alone. Porter is next to me, supporting me. The same way he has done since the moment we met. Today I'm finally letting go of a part of Leo that I had been holding onto for too long. The anger that he left me, along with the wanting to join him and stop living. Today is the first day of the rest of my life, however long that is. Lucky me, I have two beautiful children by my side and a man who loves me and has been patient with me since the day he met me.

I kiss my fingers, touching the temporary stone. "I'm ready," I whisper. "Thank you for everything, for every moment, every smile, and every second you shared with me."

Being prepared doesn't make this any easier, or less painful. Tears stream down my cheeks, as I'm closing the chapter. Porter hugs me tightly, taking away the pain. His arms always soothe the hurt, replacing it with love. I think that's what I love most about him. Porter Kendrick makes me feel safe, and when he's close, I'm strong enough to face the world. Because I know that if I fall, he'll be there to soothe me and help me get back up again.

FIFTY

MACKENZIE

WE HAD LUNCH at the bistro around the corner from Deck-er's Records. Afterward, we went to the studio where Porter played the song he recorded a couple of days ago. Matthew and Jacob are trying to convince him to do a concert. It'd be at Thrice and the tickets will be sold at an outrageous price. The ticket and alcohol sales for that function will benefit the foundation.

"Why wouldn't you do it?"

"Are you sure you want to hear this?" I nod.

"I wanted to be famous because I thought it'd be the only way to care for AJ when we grew up." I raise an eyebrow and signal for him to elaborate. He lets out a loud breath, running a hand through his hair. "She was the first person who loved me and I believed that it was my destiny to care for her. But once I was living the life of a rock star, I wanted to go back to my family. Instead of agreeing with Chris and Gabe, that I wasn't ready for showbiz, that I should've waited, I pushed myself to continue with my career. Then I discovered women, drugs, and alcohol. All of them helped me forget the shit I hated. I didn't have to deal with any emotions. Each time I wanted more, needed more. Looking back, I think I never enjoyed the spotlight."

"How about now?" I ask, walking closer to him, caressing his jaw. "You're sober and most importantly, you're a great musician."

"Music is a part of me, of who I am. It doesn't mean that I have to be up on a stage for everyone to enjoy what I create. I can share it in ways that I'm comfortable with," he explains with a soft voice that makes my heart skip a beat. He takes my hands, his eyes smiling at me, letting another loud breath. "Alcoholism and drug addiction are illnesses that have to be treated for life. I've learned to control the urge, to reach out for help when my brain is craving shit. I fight the need every day. For me and for my family. Until I feel that I'm emotionally ready to step onto a stage, I won't do it."

"I understand now. Thank you, for sharing." I hug him tightly, stretching my neck, meeting his lips. I can't find the words to express how much it means that he keeps sharing himself with me.

He releases me, kissing my nose. "Enough about me. It's time to take you home, we have a date tonight."

IT'S BEEN YEARS since the last time I went out on a date. Porter didn't give me a hint about his plans. For a change, I went to the mall and bought a couple of new things to wear. A flowery top that hugs my torso to go with my black, short skirt, and a pair of black heeled booties. When I looked in the mirror, it said, fun and sexy. A change from the everyday jeans and tops I wear to work. Dinner was at his place. A candlelight dinner for the two of us. He prepared shrimp scampi with pasta. Chocolate cake for dessert.

By the time we were done with dinner my alarm rang, it was time to call Gabe so I could say goodnight to Harper and Finn via FaceTime. They were happy, tired, and ready to sleep. Tomorrow they'll arrive at noon. Once I put the phone down, I look up at Porter's handsome face. His eyes are sparkling with happiness.

"Penny for your thoughts?" I offer, reaching over the table and placing a hand on top of his.

Porter lifts his gaze from the candle and looks at me. "Just thinking about how much you've changed my life," he says, with a hint of nostalgia. "A year ago I had no idea how to turn my life around. That day when you knocked at my door, something clicked. I found myself doing more than just working a mindless-dead-end job. Meeting you and the kids made me realize that there was more to life than what I was doing.

You three are the spark that ignited the flame and became my reason to become a better person."

He sighs and looks at me again.

"In this short period I fell in love, found my way back to my family, and now we're planning on a future. Our future."

He turns his hand over and places his other hand on top of mine. We remain silent for a few seconds, our gazes locked. I see it. The reflection of my soul within his. We're kindred spirits. Two broken people who found each other. He helped me find the broken pieces of my soul and stayed by my side while I put them back together.

"If I try to kiss you tonight?" He breaks the silence. "Would you let me?"

I bob my head in slow motion, wondering how far I'd let him go.

"If I try to touch you?" My heart drops into the pit of my stomach at the lustful look in his eyes. "Because I want to, Mac, but I don't want to push you if you're not ready."

Regret from the last time flashes in front of me. I squeeze my eyes shut trying to erase that night from my mind. As ugly as it was, he moved something inside of me that made me push myself further into finding a new me.

"My only regret from that night is the way I treated you," I say, opening my eyes. He's looking at me cautiously. His hand squeezing me gently, lovingly. "It wouldn't be fair to you, Leo, or to myself to explain what I felt or needed that night. But know that I am sorry for hurting you."

I take a drink of water, rise from my seat and walk to where he sits. Pulling him out of his chair, we find each other toe-to-toe. I wrap my arms around his neck, stretching myself enough to reach to his lips, kissing them.

"Tonight I want to be in your arms, to become an extension of your soul." I smile at him moving my hands along his neck, holding his square jaw. "So to answer your question—if you try to touch me, I'll let you."

My hands slide down his neck, traveling to his arms, and touching his chest. "But I'm ready for more. More than just a kiss, or a caress. I'm ready for us to become one."

Porter's hands reach the hem of my top. His calloused fingers touch my bare skin. He dips his face, kissing my neck. "You're full of surprises, Mackenzie Brooke. Amazing, sweet, surprises." His lips meet mine as our kiss begins slow and sweet, but as our heartbeats increase, so does the speed.

"My room," he gasps, breaking the kiss and leading me to the second door down the hall.

"Fuck, you're gorgeous," he says, as he pulls the top off me.

I unbutton his shirt, leaving it open. My eyes move to his sculpted-inked chest. My hands trace the lines of the dragon tattoo. Helping shrug off his shirt, I continue to trace his back and the rest of the design.

"You're perfect." I plant small kisses on his back.

"Mac," he whispers as I reach for the top of his slacks and I unbuckle the belt.

One hand captures my waist, while the other tangles through my hair, clutching my neck. He leans closer to me, capturing my lips. He groans, sliding his hands across my torso, finding the clasp of my bra and undoing it. Pushing my skirt down over my hips, he walks me backwards until my legs hit the bed.

"You undo me, babe," he says in a low, gruff voice. His hooded eyes gazing at me. "On the bed," he orders, and with a light push, he sits me on the edge.

Stepping backwards, he licks his lips. His hands move to the front of his slacks, and with a couple of movements, he's sliding them down. The muscles in his stomach contract as he bends, his biceps flexing with every move. The sight of him is beautiful. When he joins me in bed, he moves me to the middle, laying me on my back.

Kneeling between my legs, he gazes at me. "I've never seen something more beautiful in my life."

And I believe him, because I've never felt as beautiful or as loved, as I'm feeling right now. It's the way he looks at me; the way he touches me. Lowering his body down, his mouth moves to my breasts. He glides his tongue over my nipple, then closes his mouth over it, sucking it into his mouth. Then, he repeats the process with the other nipple. I grasp the bed covers as my body ignites.

His tongue traces a trail that begins on my chest and stops right at my pelvis. Then, he continues kissing his way down lower. I inhale sharply the moment his mouth closes over my clit. His tongue lashes against it and then he pushes two fingers inside me. My back arches at the same time I cry out his name. "Porter!" He devours me sending me higher and higher. I'm tugging his hair, rocking my hips against him until a powerful orgasm rips through my body.

"Mac," He whispers. I pull him closer; he comes to me without protest. His eyes looking into mine. Not sure what he's searching for but I feel completely exposed. "I don't want anything between us. I'm clean, but do I need a condom?"

I shake my head, with my hands around his neck I pull him down for a kiss. As our mouths touch, he pushes himself forward, filling me completely.

"This feels so fucking good," he says, breaking the kiss, withdrawing just a bit. Our eyes connect again. "Don't close your eyes."

His thrusts are slow, deep. He pulls out the same way, then pushes himself back in even deeper, his pelvis grinding against my tight bud. Every time he slides back in, I shudder with pleasure. As my body heats, our bodies move faster. My hips meet his with each thrust, my body aching for the release. My inner muscles begin to clench and with one last hard thrust from Porter, I come undone.

"I love you," I murmur.

Porter shakes on top of me, letting out a big groan. Our eyes never losing the connection. "I love you too, Mac."

He lowers his body, hugging me tightly, and I can hear it. His heart beating along with mine. Porter's ear is on my chest, "Listen. It's like our hearts have become one."

FIFTY-ONE

PORTER

I COULDN'T SLEEP all night. The first hour I watched Mac sleep in my arms. The next hour I wondered when I'd wake up from the best dream I've ever had in my entire life. That's when she woke up and we made love a second time, convincing me that she was real and that she's mine. As she fell back to sleep, I stayed up thinking about our future. Wondering when I can ask her to marry me, discuss our family, and how soon can we move in together?

"Morning," I greet her when she opens her eyes.

She smiles. "So this is what it's like to wake up next to Porter Kendrick." I give her a confused look. "Every morning since I met you, I've wondered what it would be like to wake up next to you nestled in those strong arms."

"Is it everything you imagined?" I kiss the top of her head. "Because waking up with you in my arms happens to be a dream of mine and it exceeds every fantasy I had."

"Better than I imagined. I could do this forever; in fact, I don't know how I'll survive without them after today."

"You don't have to live without them," I hint and in return, I only get a frown. "You just need to wish for it."

"It's not that simple. There's a world of difference between what I desire, and reality. But we can find ways to do this often."

Her words are like music to my heart, the answer to what I've been wondering all night. Because after the earth-shattering night we experienced, I can't imagine not having her in my bed, in my arms, and next to my heart every night.

"Marry me," I blurt out, hugging her tight. Then climbing out of the bed, I look for the engagement ring I picked up from the jeweler last week. Going down on one knee, I take the leap. "Mackenzie Brooke, would you please do me the honor of becoming my beloved wife? The woman who would walk by my side supporting me, as I support you. Be my companion, my lover, my friend, and the person I seek when I need to share the good news and the bad news and everything in between. Let me share your joy and take away the sadness. Be my wife because I can't imagine my life without you by my side."

Her eyes open wide, looking at the ring. She's silent, as tears start peeking out of her beautiful eyes.

My heart drops to the floor. "We don't have to . . . please, don't cry. I never meant to hurt you, overstep, or . . . forget—"

She gets out of bed, going down on both knees and taking my hands. "Your words didn't hurt me, Porter. These are tears of joy. You've always been gentle, understanding, and loving with me, and my kids. And after everything I've put you through, you still love me. Not only that, you want to marry me. The answer is yes. I want to be your wife, share everything with you. The good, the messy—all of it, because at the end of the day we'll make it better, together."

I pull her to me kissing her like I've never kissed anyone before, loving her like I'll only love her. Trying to share with her my every thought, my every heartbeat, my entire soul.

"I'm forever yours, Mackenzie."

AFTER A MORNING of celebrations, house hunting, and a long discussion about how to handle the kids, Mac and I went to pick up Harper and Finn from Chris and Gabe's place. Afterwards, we drove about an hour outside of downtown Seattle.

We found the perfect house.

Our dream home.

Once we drive by the open gate, where the big sign reads Evergreen

Farms, Harper begins to ask questions, "Where are we going? Are we getting a new tree, a horse?"

There's a for sale sign and the only thing we can see are pine trees, a small lake, and green land. Harper quiets down and I spot her from the rear view mirror looking out the window.

The moment I spot an alpaca, I hear Finn. "Porter, moo."

"No, Finn, that's an alpaca" I correct him. "What sound do alpacas make?"

"I think they make some sort of humming noise," Mac answers. "I need to find out more about them if we're planning on owning them."

I park in front of a beautiful two-story house and turn my attention toward Mac. "Ready?"

She nods and we climb out of the truck. I don't have to give any specifics to the kids. I'm sure they don't care about the size of the property, or that it's a Christmas tree farm. Those are details Mac found important, as important as the greenhouse and the seven bedrooms in the main house that was built only five years ago.

"Why are we here?" Harper asks again, walking closer to Mac. Finn stretches his arms out and I pick him up right away.

"To look at the house," Mac announces. I grab her delicate hand and the four of us walk inside the empty house. "Maybe talk about the possibilities of moving here."

Harper frowns, the same way her mother does when she's in deep thought. "I like where we live. It's close to your work, Mom. There's a park nearby, and the academy where I take my dance lessons. I don't want to move ever again."

"Someone once taught me that never and ever should be used with caution. They are words that mean forever." She gasps as we climb up the stairs. We stop right on top of the stairs; I point to the left where the row of bedrooms starts. "If we stay where you live, I won't be able to fit my things." Her eyes narrow and her lips twist to the side.

"We couldn't have a pet," Mac adds. "There's plenty of room here to have more than one."

"How about a little sister?" Harper asks, looking from Mac to me. "If we move, can I have one?"

"There's a possibility of adding one or two siblings, but I can't guarantee if they'll be girls," Mac says.

Inhaling, I set Finn on the floor next to Harper and kneel in front of them to be at eye level. "Harper, Finn, I love you two very much. As much as I love your mom. The three of you mean everything to me. And, if you let me, I'd like to be part of your family. If you do, I promise to always love you, protect you, be a father figure, a friend, and always support you no matter what happens in life."

"You want to be my dad?" Harper's bottom lip trembles, her eyes shine as they fill with moisture. I nod. "Are you staying with us forever?"

"I'll try my best, Harp. For you three, I promise to take care of myself and be by your side for a long, long time."

Harper's arms hug my neck tightly. "I love you," she murmurs between sobs.

As Finns arms wrap around me too, I can't help but let the tears flow. After all the loss I've experienced since I was a kid, I finally found my place in this world.

EPILOGUE

PORTER

Three years later

TODAY WAS A busy day at the recording company, having to produce an entire record within a week takes a lot of my energy. It was good, though, we're ready to release it, and this new band will be playing at Thrice on Saturday night. This is the third project Jacob and I finished from the reality show that Matthew created a couple of years back. Today is one of those days I'm grateful for my life. I have a great job and a loving family. As I enter the house, the sweet smell of cookies hits me. Sugar cookies, my favorite.

"Daddy," I hear before Finn, my seven-year son, reaches me. I hug him tightly, happy to see him and thankful that I had another day to enjoy him. Each day I'm thankful for that, because things change so fast.

"Where's Emmerson?" I ask Finn who shrugs.

Usually, my two-year-old follows her brother everywhere.

"Dad," Harper greets me with that new cool voice she's experimenting with. "You're a few minutes early."

"Or you forgot to set the table?"

"That too." She marches to me and hugs me. "How was work?"

"I thought I heard the door. Welcome home, handsome." Before I answer Harper, Mac appears with Emmerson in her arms and her beautiful round belly showing with our other little bundle of joy. A boy,

Oliver. Em extends her chubby arms toward me and I pull her tightly to my chest, kissing my wife.

As the entire family gathers in one room, I look at them and remind myself how lucky I am. Thankful that I was able to find my way into the light and that Mac and I crossed paths. It's been a hard journey. We met when she was grieving the loss of her husband and when I was still closed off to the world. Our two broken souls found each other in the dark and began to heal each other's wounds.

That doesn't mean that we're completely healed. I struggled with my demons, but I work hard to keep them at bay. With the help of my counselor, I remain clean and focused on my goals. Mac is my rock. The woman believes in me and sees who I really am and who I want to be. She's my companion and now thrives as a mother and a botanist. She grows different crops and sells it to a local organic grocery store.

We created a dream together and we work to make it a reality every day.

UNEXPECTED EPILOGUE

CHRISTIAN

LIFE IS FRAGILE. One moment we're enjoying a nice dinner with friends, the next week one of us is dead. Well, I'm not. But Peter, the bassist of my old band, Dreadful Souls, died yesterday night. Really fucked up, as we had lunch only days ago in California. Today I receive a message from his daughter announcing that he passed away last night from a heart attack.

"Are you okay, babe?" Gabe hugs me from the back, his hands resting on my chest. "I should have kept all the electronics away. At least for today."

"My band is dead," I blurt, wanting to laugh and cry. We were four friends with nothing. Stupid kids who gambled with our music and hit the jackpot. In only months, we climbed the billboard charts. Our first single was on top for weeks and we became famous. Things ended on a shitty note between us, but we shared a lot for several years. It makes me sad and makes me think about my own mortality. How much time do I have left? "Literally. I'm the last man standing."

"Because you were the only one who grew up, babe," he says, kissing my neck. "You found a different passion and you've always said it: you're a Decker. Deckers can take almost anything."

"You became my passion." I turn around to kiss him.

"AJ called, she wants some help with the grandkids."

I laugh. "We both know why they want me over. I'm going to walk into the house and everyone is going to scream 'surprise' give me some credit, college boy."

His smile stretches, shaking his head. "Can you pretend to be surprised?" He kisses my forehead and I can't believe we remain together after all these years. He might have a few wrinkles, but he's still the same pretty, college boy I fell in love with. "They're trying to make your birthday special."

"Yes, I can act surprised," I agree, walking to the backyard through my office's back door. "Though, since they came into our life, they've been making it special every day. Is it only the kids, or did they invite friends?"

"Only my parents, our four children, and their families. Yesterday was the big bash with friends and family."

Last night the boys organized a concert at Thrice. Decker's band played a few songs. Porter joined us for the first time on stage. A few of my musician friends played some of my old songs to pay tribute to me and celebrate my big day. It was a cool night. A nice birthday present from my family. The only downside is that none of my little ones could be there. My grandchildren had to stay behind. The oldest is ten and the youngest is only three weeks old. I guess today is when I get to enjoy them.

"Surprise!" everyone shouts when I slide the patio door open. As they sing happy birthday, AJ, Jacob, and Matt stand in front of everyone, holding a cake that says Happy Birthday Papa Chris.

My arm goes around Gabe's waist; my head rests on his shoulder. He gave me this, my own family—our family. Which grows every year. There's always a new addition to the Decker clan.

AJ and Mason have three adorable children. Gracie, Seth and the little surprise baby, Nathan who was only born a few weeks ago. The pregnancy wasn't planned and the weeks that followed after we learned that AJ was pregnant were fucking scary. They barely made it, but both fought hard and they're on their way to recovery.

Jacob and Pria have three adorable boys. Jude and Gabe are the terrible twins, but there's never a dull moment with them. Sterling is only one, but he will soon follow their steps.

Matt, Thea, and Tristan have their precious baby girl, Piper; Grayson is a year old and there's a new baby on the way.

Porter and Mac have four little ones. My oldest granddaughter, Harper is the leader of the next generation. Finn, her brother is her second in command. Little Emmerson is adorable, just like her mom. And Oliver is only three weeks old and as precious as every other member of this family.

"Thank you, college boy," I whisper when they finish singing. "Without you, I wouldn't have my family. I love you."

"Happy Birthday, rock star." He kisses my cheek. "Thank you for sticking by my side through the good times and the bad times. For your patience, for accepting me. Most of all, thank you for loving me after all these years."

"We worked hard to transcend, babe."

"I love you, babe," he murmurs, hugging me tight. "Stick around, there's so much more to come."

The End

ABOUT THE AUTHOR

C LAUDIA GREW UP with a childhood that resembled a caffeine-injected soap opera. She lives in Colorado, managing her household filled with three confused dogs, a techy-nerd husband, two daughters wrought with fandoms and a son who thinks he's the boss of the house. To survive she works continually to find purpose for the voices flitting through her head, plus she consumes high quantities of chocolate to keep the last threads of sanity intact.

TO FIND MORE ABOUT CLAUDIA:
www.claudiayburgoa.com

OR STALK HER:
www.facebook.com/groups/ClaudiasBookaliciousBabes
www.goodreads.com/group/show/176276-claudia-burgoa-reader-group
https://twitter.com/Author_ClaudiaB
www.facebook.com/ClaudiaYBurgoa
www.pinterest.com/yuribeans
http://www.amazon.com/Claudia-Burgoa/e/B00EADAOLI
http://instagram.com/claudia_b30/
https://www.tsu.co/ClaudiaBurgoa
https://plus.google.com/u/0/+ClaudiaBurgoa
SHOOT AN EMAIL . . .
claudiayburgoa@gmail.com

ALSO BY CLAUDIA BURGOA

Made in the USA
Columbia, SC
14 March 2020